CODE of the NIGHTBIRD

CODE of the NIGHTBIRD

Mike Pratt

CODE ^{of} the NIGHTBIRD

This book is a work of fiction. Names, characters, places, and incidents are the product of the author's imagination or are used fictitiously. Any resemblance to actual events, locales, or persons, living or dead, is coincidental.

Formatting: Enchanted Ink Publishing
Logo Design: Danny Haffel | Haffel Design
Cover design: Erika Dillon

WWW.MIKEPRATTAUTHOR.COM

@THEMIKEPRATT

ISBN (E-book): 978-1-7372287-2-1
ISBN (Paperback): 978-1-7372287-0-7
ISBN (Hardcover): 978-1-7372287-1-4

Library of Congress Control Number: 2021909721

Thank you for your support of the author's rights.

To Jon,

Kasey,

Mom,

Dad,

and Grammy,

Who have written the story of my life.

"Art can be morally good, lifting men to higher levels. This has been done thru good music, great painting, authentic fiction, poetry, drama. Art can be morally evil in its effects. This has been the case clearly enough with unclean art, indecent books, suggestive drama. The effect on the lives of men and women is obvious."

- Motion Picture Production
Code note on the value of art

"In the case of impure love, the love which society has always regarded as wrong and which has been banned by divine law, the following are important:

1. It must not be the subject of comedy or farce or treated as the material for laughter;

2. It must not be presented as attractive and beautiful;

3. It must not be presented in such a way as to arouse passion or morbid curiosity on the part of the audience;

4. It must not be made to seem right and permissible;

5. In general, it must not be detailed in method or manner.

- Motion Picture Production Code
note on same-sex 'sex perversion'

CHAPTER 1

The story goes that a fisherman, once long lost at sea, came upon a seaport far from where he had set sail. He walked across long stretches of sand looking for someone, anyone, to tell him where he was. After some time, the fisherman feared he'd landed in a ghost town, a place wiped clean by some mysterious illness or perhaps the site of a mass exodus. After all, any number of things can travel a great distance just to cause some trouble.

Across the way, the fisherman noticed a man drawing up a large basket who, when asked, was more than happy to supply an answer to the lost fisherman's question.

"Why, you're in Galilee," the man said, raising a welcoming hand to the fisherman.

"And what's beyond the sand?" the fisherman replied.

The man set his catch down and stood up, pressing his hands firmly into his back as he rose. He worked a good deal, and the aches came daily. With some effort and the sun shining in his eyes, he finally answered.

"Jerusalem, I suppose," he said with a wry smile.

Of course, neither the fisherman nor the man who claimed the land to be Galilee were actually in the biblical fishing town, but rather a small seaport on the tail of Rhode Island; smack dab in the middle of clam chowder and anchor button-up territory; a hop, skip, and a jump away from the rolling hills which, in a century's time, would raise great mansions of marble into the air. Rosecliff. The Breakers.

Despite the lack of truth in its origin story, the name has nevertheless stuck to the area like a barnacle with restaurants and taverns alike proudly displaying "Galilee" in bent neon, the name repeating like a whisper written into the salty nighttime breeze.

It's not the worst place to associate yourself with, I'll admit that. There's something quite romantic about the idea of bringing a bit of the past into the present, and "Galilee" carries with it a promise of endless bounty. So endless in fact that in Galilee no one need worry where their next meal will come from. The laundry list of people who fished in the ancient Sea of Galilee reads more like a Who's Who of the Bible than anything else. (And what fish wouldn't just *throw* itself into the net for a chance at being slain by an apostle?) The water held within the sea also feeds the Jordan River, and people *love* the thought of their dinner having swam in the same water that baptized Jesus. And now, because of a name and a folktale, that water has found its way to southern New England. Zero degrees of separation.

When the sun hits the sand just right—when the clouds begin to thin out, about midday—the waves of the new Galilee appear to crash on beaches of glittering ash, interrupted only by pink umbrellas and teal beach towels topped with tanning bodies. Combined with the quaint charm of the town's many shelled walkways, you'd believe any name given to a place like this.

For me, though, Galilee has come to mean something else. Something far more sinister. Water can indeed change a great deal as it moves toward its destination, but not even a pretty name can undo an ugliness that lurks just below the surface.

In addition to those restaurants and taverns, a church not unlike any around it also took the name Galilee. This Galilee came into my life from so far out of left field that I might as well have been that fisherman in the fabled origin story. Within the course of a single week, I went from sitting on the plastic-covered recliner of a dentist's office, barely awake as an infection was drilled from my mouth, to standing before a receptionist as she told me I had no choice but to willingly hand over my body for further drilling, this time of a different sort.

My Galilee was not a place marked by friendly natives, and the water there didn't bear fish. Beneath the spire and chipped white paint, my Galilee sought to change me.

And change I did.

CHAPTER 2

I've always hated the dentist.

I don't think I've ever walked into a dentist's office confident that I'll walk out. As soon as I set foot in the door, I can feel my throat sink down into my stomach and settle like cut potatoes into a sickly stew of fear and dread; dryness of mouth and the inexplicable taste of iron is just par for the course at this point—the celery and onions of the stew, if you will.

Of course, it didn't help that my dentist at the time worked out of an old Victorian house that looked from the outside to be the perfect setting for a murder mystery. There were certainly more rooms available than were being used for dentistry, and laughing gas inspires a uniquely macabre kind of creativity. The same kind that creeps in at night when a sweaty leg breaks free from the safety of blankets. It's not under normal circumstances that you fear the monster under the bed. It's possible to cohabitate comfortably with it, actually, when the day is bright and new. You only fear the monster when darkness closes in on your world, making it small and vulnerable. For me, going to the dentist creates this feeling just as well as any demon monster hiding under the bed could ever hope to.

If you ever take a trip to New England, you'll quickly find out that every so often one of those Victorian houses will just pop up, turrets and all, seemingly out of thin air. One moment you're driving past a Dunkin' Donuts, with its line inching out into the street, then an in-progress apartment complex with orange-mesh fencing and a sign declaring "A New Kind of Luxury," then *bam*, a great big Victorian-style mansion is staring you right in the face. Maybe your wipers will sweep away enough rain to catch a glimpse of it, or maybe a dutiful backseat driver will point it out. Either way, someone is bound to "ooh" and someone is bound to "ahh."

I, personally, have always thought they were creepy, possessing about as much charm as the Bates' residence in *Psycho*. I can almost imagine the architects of the houses sitting around a table dotted with steaming cups of coffee wondering how else they could bring an element of sentience to their creation. These houses sit patiently on corner lots for years, watching cars and clothes change with every passing generation, while they go on relatively unchanged, whether by historical reverence or local fascination. Regardless, I can feel their eyes lingering long after I drive away. *I swear someone just moved behind that curtain!* Even more bizarre is the fact that no one seems to live in them anymore. Dentist offices and hair salons have found their way into most of them, settling into the shells and breathing new life into their gothic hosts. My fear, I guess, of visiting the dentist lives in the possibility of becoming its Marion Crane, of ending up face down on the cold tile waiting to be swallowed up by the perpetual, clockwise swirl of time. *Whoosh!*

The particular mansion my dentist occupied was well tended. It was painted regularly, a nougat-y gold color, and adorned with three large painted signs: Community Dental Associates, Parking in Rear, and No Loitering. Miniature white picket fences ran the length of a barren pathway to two large front doors, each decorated with a stained glass flower: a lily on the left door, a sunflower on the right. Old, chewed-up pieces of gum were stuck to the ground like pimples on the pavement. People anxious about being caught with their toothbrushes down, I guess.

Opening the flowered doors didn't reveal some grand foyer like you'd expect, but rather a small, rectangular room that served as the dentist's check-in. Dirt tracked in from shoes and wind had wedged itself into frayed patches of carpeting made light from years of passing sun and vacuum cleaners. In another life, this must have been the mudroom because it was so small. Three people in line made the room feel cramped, and four meant someone was standing outside. In short, it was not a space meant to comfortably hold people for long periods of time. So, naturally, that's exactly what its purpose became.

Beside the check-in was an even smaller waiting room with a couple of low-sitting chairs lined up against the wall and a magazine rack nestled in the corner. Even in a room that small, trying to hear the radio meant engaging in a losing battle with your sanity. You'd think any volume whatsoever would have wisped across the room with ease, but it never did. Intense focus was required to catch, at best, one word, but if you listened too closely, you'd start to hear the sounds of the drills. *Zzzz.* The air conditioner was louder than any music in the office; it was old and cranky, but always chugging along.

On that particular day, I feared my nerves might actually get the best of me because I wasn't going in for a routine check-up or anything like that. I remember everything about that day, not only because of what happened afterward, but because that was the day of my much-dreaded root canal. I had put it off as long as humanly possible by the time I finally caved and made the appointment. (The woman who scheduled it made sure to remind me of the $25 no-show fee.) It was a valiant effort, the avoiding. And one that took considerable planning and diligence on my end to pull off. I was careful to ignore any calls with a 508-area code, for instance, and drove to the opposite side of town to shop for groceries because I ran the risk of running into my dentist at the one closest to me. It had happened once before—an awkwardly polite conversation in the self-checkout line that I was under no circumstances going to have again.

After a while, though, the extra trips to the gas station weren't the anxiety remedy they once had been. A part of me was sick of being scared, too. It's one thing to be scared of the dentist, but it's another to go out of your way to create stress where there wasn't any in the pursuit of lessening the stress that *was* there. All in all, I think we broke even with that one. Anticipation, for me at least, works in mysterious ways. Sometimes it's butterflies that rage over the outlines and curves of a boy in tight pants walking by, and sometimes it's sweaty palms and fear of dental drills. How different are they really? It's all about where in the body the anticipation lives.

I must have spent a good forty-five minutes in the parking lot just working up the courage to meet the glass flowers face to face. By no means an easy task either. Despite it not yet being June, summer had decided to pay an early visit to Massachusetts. Heat rang in the air and clung tight to the body. This was the kind of day you would hear people all over town describe as "too hot."

Massachusetts residents are some of the most fickle people in the world when it comes to the weather. We spend all winter swearing up and down we're moving to Florida if as much as one more snowflake falls, then turn around and spend all summer complaining about the heat. It's something to talk about that proves native status, I guess. A badge of honor worn—and discussed—proudly. You'll hear the same song in winter too; only then people will compete to see who lived through the worst nor'easter.

"Nemo was nothin', Gary. I lived through the blizzahd ah '78."

I can hear them now.

To anyone walking by, I must have looked certifiable— talking to myself at the steering wheel of a hot, parked car, still white-knuckling it. If only I had a southern drawl, my panic would have read like a scene ripped straight from the pages of a Tennessee Williams play.

It's been said of me for as long as I can remember that I take far too long to get out of a car once it has arrived somewhere, even under normal circumstances. As soon as an opening is found between faded white lines, all car doors will open in unison. Except, of course, mine. Truly, I never noticed this until it was aggressively brought to my attention when I was younger. My mother's patience must have run a little thin one day at the supermarket because I distinctly remember her popping her head into my window to curse me out.

"I swear to God, Julien, if you don't get your ass out of

that seat by the time I count to five," she said, veins raging across her face and neck, "I'm gonna fuckin' lose it."

Swearing never seemed to fit her, not even with the practice she put into it. Right before the words would come, her face would tense up, like the words were stuck in a mental filter. She'd form a claw with her hand, which she'd twitch near her mouth for a moment, and *then* she'd swear. It was always a performance, but for who? Your guess is as good as mine.

My parents were the type that always wanted to get in and out as fast as possible because they had a long list of places to get in and out of. Supermarket trips were tiring and constant and, therefore, the perfect setting for an outburst. I don't blame them for nagging me. In hindsight, they worked enough to know that every passing minute has a value attached to it. They rushed me into grocery stores to save time for later. Now, I'm very much aware of my tendency to stall and selfishly embrace those final few moments before my feet hit the pavement. In my defense, I like walking into whatever situations lie beyond car doors knowing not only what to expect, but what will be expected of me. Another thing I learned from my parents early on is that uncertainty doesn't favor the poor. Time and energy went into everything with us, even what food we bought. We chewed on thought when food was scarce and ate sparsely when it was available. Within my mother's crossed-out shopping lists, I read the importance of having some sort of plan thrown together. She was a proud woman and imparted that pride onto us. This was tougher to hold on to during those moments when I saw her lose her cool. Behind the facade was a real struggle. There was plenty to be proud of, that I never questioned, but not in the financial sector. The only pride in poverty is getting out of it. She was never mad at me, I don't think, not really; she was mad at what she couldn't do for me.

I swear though, if baby eyes had digital recall, I would forever loop the footage of my mother frantically altering grocery lists in Stop and Shop parking lots whenever rapping knuckles fell on the passenger-side window. Time is money, but like money, it can be wasted if poorly invested.

By the time I had worked up the nerve to get out of the car, I was running late. On that particular day, tardiness worked in my favor, as it meant less time in the waiting room listening to a drill interrupt Carole King singing something from *Tapestry*.

Looking back, I don't actually remember much of the root canal itself aside from the initial fear. What I do remember, however, is feeling my consciousness slip away as the laughing gas kicked in. The dental assistant, an anxious-looking graduate intern, tried out a few different masks before finding one that fit me. The first one had a petite little nose cavity I knew wasn't going to fit, but I kept my mouth shut for fear of her turning off the machine halfway through the procedure. Marion Crane, remember? To her credit, the intern definitely tried to make it work. She'd lightly push the mask down and then furrow her brow when she realized it wouldn't work.

"Well, that's not right," she'd say under her breath.

Then she tried out one that looked more like an athletic cup than a laughing-gas mask. I offered her an enthusiastic smile anyway and waited for her to realize it was too big.

"That's not right either!" she said. Eventually, she found one that fit and exclaimed in total seriousness, "Not too big and not too small. This one's juuuuust right!"

Shortly afterward, she had me count backward from one hundred. I made it to about eighty-five when, all at once, I became acutely aware of the radio. Music flooded the room, but it sounded warped and slow by the time it reached me. I was drowning below the words.

Ten minutes later and I was completely deaf to the conversation around me. The words of the dentist and her assistant converged with the music from the radio and hovered in the air like cars idling in traffic. Every so often, I'd catch a few words, maybe "coffee" or "It's a scorcher out there," before sinking deeper into the chair. At one point, I looked down at my body only to find that it had separated from the tension I had carried in with me. I don't remember relaxing, at least not willingly, but there was no denying that I had.

I have come to realize only recently that what has always scared me about the dentist isn't so much the pain. Anyone with eyes can see the fear on my face the moment I walk in, and knee-deep in my twenties, I still get laughing gas. I know they aren't there to cause me pain. What I'm really afraid of is losing control over myself, of forgetting there is pain.

When the root canal was over and I began to come to my senses, a second dental assistant instructed me to stay in the chair until I felt the weight of my body return. He was a younger guy, probably here on his clinical rotation like the others running around the practice He was short and lean, with orange bed-head hair. I acknowledged what he said with a slight smile, but the numbness only allowed the corners of my lips to rise. He smiled politely, concealing a giggle, and walked away.

With no one left in the room, I started to feel like I was overstaying my welcome. I tried to find the most interesting thing in the room to occupy the time until I started feeling normal again, but somehow that ended in me staring at my feet. I could look outside if I wanted, at the passing cars and swaying tree branches, but I could also do that from the safety of my car. It was too bright anyway, and my head was starting to pound. The dentist had taken some X-rays earlier, too, so my phone was in the other room. The orange-haired assistant had sat me up in the chair, but I was still leaning at an angle, something I was starting to become more aware of. I sat up as straight as I could and went back to staring at my feet.

To my left was a large counter with some plaster impressions intended to show patients what braces could do for them. Above the counter was a set of cabinets my dentist had gone through earlier to fill a small bag with floss and a toothbrush.

"Soft," she'd said, since I brush too hard.

To my right was a rolling tray with a few instruments strewn about. All in all, not much to look at. Not wanting to spend another moment in the room, I got up before I was ready and had to brace myself against the wall the whole walk back to the tiny check-in. I became intimately familiar with the wallpaper on my return journey, at times resting my forehead on it, but I still didn't have my bearings about me enough to catch that there was a rip in the paper until it ripped me back. I stopped for a second time to feel the cut grow wet with blood and spent a moment propped up by my shoulder, using my free hand to stop the flow. The full weight of my body returned in a cold rush. I looked down at the red spots and looked away quickly, but it was no use. The spots reappeared wherever I looked, as if I had stared into a flashlight. It was becoming less likely that I would make it back to the old mudroom on my own.

Wasn't there a bathroom somewhere around here? Yes! The door was only a few yards away from me, on the other side of the hallway, and I began to wobble toward it. I straddled my legs for balance as I moved into the middle of the hallway, bobbing back and forth like a surfer until I could finally press myself against the other wall. Right as my fingers reached the bathroom door, it swung open. I put my hands up in anticipation, leaving behind a small fingerprint of blood as the door pulled away from me.

"I'm so sorry, Mr. Grant, I didn't see you there." It was the dentist, and she was clearly startled.

We laughed for a moment before she took my arm and led me back to the waiting room. Droplets of water followed her hand as it found its hold on me.

"You're not planning on driving home, are you? You're gonna have to wait a minute if you are," she said.

I told her I was indeed driving myself home, but I was more than happy to stay in the waiting room for a while and color one of the pages laid out on the table until I recovered fully. Again, she laughed. My dentist was the type of person who began and ended everything she said with a loud, booming belly laugh that never seemed to connect to the conversation. Sometimes she would slap her thigh or fuss with her jewelry when she really wanted to make a statement.

"You're a funny guy, Julien. Girls must be just banging down your door," she said, tacking on a bracelet twist at the end of the laugh for good measure.

With that, I felt my stomach drop. *Girls.* Her hand landed on my knee and jokingly pushed it away as she said it, her laughter growing louder. People are always asking me about girls, sometimes without even saying it explicitly. Compliments on my hair from the lips of a smirking someone always hide the suggestion that it's coiffed for some lady-in-waiting. Every time I see someone lean in closely, I've trained myself to brace for impact. If they're right and there is a lady-in-waiting somewhere, I hope she's not holding her breath. Heterosexuality sits pretty behind every seemingly casual word thrown my way. *Date. Love. Marriage.* It never sticks, but the words themselves do. Hands on my body, chests pressed together, a life of love. Of course, I want that, too.

"Well," I began, "up until a month ago I made *one* boy laugh, but things are pretty quiet these days." I tried to produce a laugh like hers to punctuate the story, but it fell flat.

When the words left my mouth, I could see her smile fade, turning slowly into something she had to force. Her eyes began moving around the room for something to excuse herself from me. Phantom patients must have passed in front of her several times. *Scan left, scan right.* For whatever reason, coming out usually signals the end of a conversation for me. I keep them waiting for the conversation about girls, and they deny me the conversation about boys. It's a lose-lose every time.

"Well, it was nice to see you again," she said, this time with more formality in her voice than before. This was the voice I assume she would use when telling someone they have a cavity. There was no accompanying laugh this time either.

"You as well," I replied.

I'm used to this kind of encounter by now, but there's still a twang of pain that washes over me when the person walks away. I don't know if I'll ever get used to the image of people walking away. I couldn't help but feel a little bit naked with what I had said lingering in the room like a half-deflated balloon that people are batting around, never letting it land. As I looked around the room, I could see that people were peering over magazines at me. Their eyes said it all, but one person, without breaking eye contact, readjusted his newspaper just to make sure the message was clearly received. I have friends who will oblige people in their suggestions of heterosexuality solely to avoid these stares. They'll forego holding their boyfriends' hand so as not to invite the attention I was now getting.

It seemed like hours had passed, but I was called up to the desk only a few minutes after the dentist walked away. The receptionist sat low behind a wall of glass with files stacked on either side of her. Each one had a colored tab protruding out of it, and I craned my neck to see if my name was scratched across one of them.

"I know today was a tougher day for you, Mr. Grant," she said, breaking my focus away from the files, "but I'm afraid you're going to have to come back in a week for part two." The receptionist wasn't a short woman, but still, I had to look down to meet her glance.

"What do you mean?" I asked.

She explained to me that, even though my tooth needed both roots worked on, they only had time for one today. I was going to have to face the chair again in a week.

"Fine," I said, collecting my things with the same gruffness as the man who had flurried his newspaper at me.

As bad as it was to think of having my teeth drilled again, it was even worse to consider that the drill would be sitting between the fingers of the woman who had just reacted so awkwardly to a topic as innocent as dating. One she brought up in the first place! *She corners me, walks away, and leaves me to lick my wounds.* I could feel my face turning red.

It's nothing new, though: the stares, the fading smiles,

even the subtext of both those things. I've learned a lot in the time I've spent licking different wounds. For instance, I've learned that being gay isn't something you do. It's something used to scare you away from doing.

"No weak wrists."

"Don't dress like that or people will think you're gay."

"Don't run like a fairy."

The accusation alone signals ultimate devastation.

"No homo. I ain't no faggot."

When gay *is* something you do, it's because someone along the way failed in keeping you from it. A father was missing, or perhaps, he was too close. A mother was over-bearing, or maybe, she was too freewheeling. When gay is something you do, what you've really done is failed. Then people walk away.

At least that's what I've learned.

And so, the day ended—as it so often does—where it had begun, with me sitting in a hot car somehow unable to put myself into motion.

CHAPTER 3

I'm somewhat obsessed with things that are outside my time here on Earth.

I find great comfort in things that have existed long before I was born but, through some miracle, continue to find ways to connect me in the present time. Another word for these things, and one people will frequently say to me when letting me know that my interests are, in their minds at least, less than cool, is "old." That, I have learned to say in return, is way too simple. Yes, some things are just plain old, and now they sit collecting dust while life goes on around them. But life carries the messages of those few special things in the whirlwind that inevitably knocks us all down. And guess what, in the end, those things will still be around! In that way, they're timeless—unbound by corporeal restraints.

This fascination with "old" things all started when my family moved for the first and only time in my life when

I was ten years old. Being ten years old, I was devastated by the changes that accompanied the new zip code. The biggest of these changes was the new school, which I cried about for weeks. The thought of going to class and sitting among a sea of new faces was enough to make ten-year-old me seriously consider running away to join the circus. If I remember correctly, the only thing that prevented me from actually following through on that particular threat was the fear that I wasn't flexible enough.

I went with my parents and my sister on a tour of the school a few days before classes started, and the moment we walked through the front doors, I was just completely overwhelmed. There was a smell in the air that I didn't recognize, and these great big staircases that led up to long hallways marked up by unseen kids carelessly running in sneakers. A kindly, if a little overexcited, balding man greeted us at the door before the tour and introduced himself as Mr. R., the vice principal. My mom looked at me with an expression that told me I should be impressed, but I couldn't focus on anything past my nose and that mysterious smell—something like ink and rubber mixed together. The tour was short: a quick trip to an empty classroom, the gym, the cafeteria, and then back to the lobby. The school colors were green and gray, and the walls were painted accordingly. I remember thinking it looked very much like a dungeon. Mr. R. shook my hand and said he was excited to see me on Monday. I lied and said I was excited to see him too.

I protested the school the moment we got into the car and all the way home, really leaning into the smell as a reason to move back to our real home. My mom was unusually quiet for the duration of the ride, but my father held her hand over the center console and kissed her cheek at red lights. We had moved because her office had, and I resented that fact. I even refused to visit her at work the whole time I was in middle school because I blamed her for the smell that I couldn't seem to get out of my nose. In hindsight, I can't imagine how bad she must have felt listening to me complain, bringing to light her worst fear about moving— that her family would be unhappy. It wasn't fair, but I was ten and didn't care.

When we got back home from the school that first time, I ran up to my room to sulk. My bed was set up with a new comforter we had bought before the move, but other than that, all of my stuff—my old stuff from the house I wanted to go back to so badly—was in boxes that took up most of the room. I looked over at them from my bed and vowed to never open them up, thinking that I'd feel better if at least my stuff didn't have to know the new house, even if I did.

My mother knocked on the door a little while into my sulking and placed a box down on my bed that had a bunch of books in it, which pretty much everyone had forgotten we owned; some that looked like they had never even been opened. She told me they were some of the books she had brought with her when she and my father had moved into the house I grew up in.

"I know how you feel because I felt the same way," she said. "I didn't want to throw anything away or leave anything behind because it just felt wrong. To be honest though, Jules, I don't think I ever looked at them even after I had adjusted to my new life. I thought maybe you would get some use out of them. Either that or I'm throwing them away for real this time."

She brushed my hair gently, as mothers do, and waited for me to stir. I was still mad at the whole situation, so I didn't say anything, but when she left, I looked through the box and grabbed a world record book that had a bright teal cover with huge lettering on it. It was the only thing that really grabbed my attention. The first page I opened up to was a page about best-selling albums. There were pictures all over it showing the different ways people have listened to music through the years. One picture showed someone listening to a record player, while another person was running with a Walkman strapped to his arm. It was a timeline of listening that went all the way up to cordless headphones. I looked at the pictures and the different albums that were, as the page had promised, the best-selling albums of all time up to that point and felt a strange comfort in the fact that all the people in those pictures could have been listening to the same music. All different lives and circumstances but with this one common thing among them—the music. No matter what separated them, there was music to bring them back together.

I thought about that idea for a while and eventually determined that I would try to survive my new middle school or, at the very least, avoid telling my mother every day on the way to school that she had ruined my life. If for no other reason than I had found proof that my life didn't need to start over; it just needed a quick jump-start to feel normal again. Same music, different way of listening. In the next few months, I also developed an obsession with a few things—mostly music and movies—that were the points of connection among disparate lives. I wanted to know how it was that they could exist now as easily as they had way back when.

The search for an answer to that unanswerable question reached near meltdown territory when I was placed in gym class during my freshman year. First of all, I want to say that I'd be willing to testify to Congress as to why gym class should be a criminal punishment and not a high school requirement, but that's for another day. My high school's locker room, much like the school itself, was old (the bad kind of old), which meant it was a mostly open space with only a few low benches here and there. In the middle of the room was a communal shower, used almost exclusively by the football team. There were even some carvings in the metal in the shape of the dates when big championship games had been won.

I knew I was gay well before high school, but I hadn't told anyone yet. It wasn't so much that I was afraid—not that I would have admitted that at the time either—instead, I was waiting for the very moment when the stars would align and the angels would sing. When that happened, I'd know it was time. Most people suspected it—and made that suspicion *very* clear—but every time someone would accuse me of being gay, I'd lie and say I wasn't. I thought that no one was allowed to say anything about it until I came out, but I quickly found out that wasn't the case.

I was changing for gym one day in that large, open locker room when several boys from the class walked over and stood in front of the bench my clothes were laying on. I think back to that moment now and all the things I wish I had said; but in that kind of moment, realistically, nothing ever comes. They were all quiet at first, but one by one, they began asking me if I was gay. Asking and laughing as though this was something they had planned out and it was all going very well for them. I didn't know what to say, so I just said nothing and continued changing as though nothing out of the ordinary was happening in front of me.

One of the boys in the group moved forward and grabbed my shirt as it was coming up off my head and, on the downswing, grabbed my change of clothes, leaving me in just my underwear. I asked for my clothes back, but he only asked why I needed them. Another said if I admitted I was gay, he'd give me my clothes back.

I've never liked having my shirt off in any situation and tried to cover myself as best I could while continuing to ask for my clothes back. As the exchange went on, I could feel my face growing hot. I looked down to see my body was paler than I remembered it being, but I could tell my face was beet red.

"Come on, dude, we all know you're gay. Just admit it and we'll give you your shit back," the leader among them said. As if he were doing me a favor.

Again, *now* I think back on all the things I could have said, but in the moment, I could only think of one thing: that I wanted my clothes back. The only thing keeping them from me, too, was technically a lie. What I still don't understand is why that information about someone they didn't even know was so critically important to them in that moment.

"I am," I said quietly, my voice directed at my feet.

"Am what?" the leader asked pointedly.

"I'm gay."

That was the first time I came out to anyone. In the middle of the locker room and almost naked.

Keeping his promise, the leader threw my clothes back at me and looked around at the group gathered on either side of him before throwing a nod over both shoulders. In unison, the group of boys began undressing and throwing their clothes at me until I couldn't find mine.

The assembled group stood in front of me in their underwear grabbing their bulges and thrusting toward me while asking if I liked what I saw as their laughter grew and grew. I didn't like what I saw. In fact, I was horrified by it. Eventually, the laughter caught the attention of the gym teacher, who swept in and asked them to behave themselves. They agreed, grabbed their clothes, and left me alone to finish changing.

I had no intention of telling my parents what had happened in gym class, but they caught on to the fact that something was wrong; and the pressure to keep lying was too much, so I told them. I couldn't tell if the shame I felt in the moments immediately after I told my parents was because of the circumstances of my coming out to them or because I had to do it in the first place. They were both quiet for some time afterward, and I swear they looked at me differently; but even if that were the case, they were sure to remind me that they loved me.

I felt more alone after that day in gym class than I had felt since the move years before. Like I was different in a way that no one else could possibly understand. As I thought about it more, though, I came to find a hidden superpower in the differences I held within me. I was still *me*, after all. And that *me* couldn't be distilled down to something as simple as who I had a crush on, no matter how hard people might try to do it. I had an epiphany in the weeks following the incident in the locker room, which was that I was forever going to be one of those people from my mom's world record book who was listening to the same music as everyone else, but doing it in a different way. I would always have a Walkman on my arm for all to see, but it would become more bearable as I got older.

The problem for me soon became that the world around me was growing more and more wary of the amount of Walkmans they were seeing. There was a period of time when pride parades were populated with as many rainbow-covered bodies as the streets could hold, but as the floats traversed progressive city blocks, a countermovement was quietly forming underground. A collection of voices began to rise in unison, projecting a voice that claimed to be crying out from under the boot heels of a changing world. As empowered as I felt by the differences within me, the gap between myself and the rest of the world was beginning to form something of a gaping hole, and I found myself at risk of falling into something that I couldn't get out of. There were the blood drives in college I wasn't allowed to participate in and the increasingly hostile line of questioning that became commonplace when adjusting to any new social group.

"Can we count on you to donate this weekend?" someone once asked me from behind a colorful trifold in the dining hall one day.

"Oh, no, I can't," I responded. And it was true, I couldn't. The ban that keeps the memory of AIDS alive was the content of the lettering at the bottom of the trifold.

"Why?"

"I'm anemic."

She obviously didn't believe me, but it provided enough time to safely slink away and avoid any further questions.

When I came home from college for summer break one year, I was greeted by a large, billowing flag on the front porch of a neighbor's house that read: Social Preservation Society. It was navy blue with a golden shield encircled in white on the front. Neither one of my parents mentioned it—I think they hoped I hadn't seen it—but I caught them staring at it whenever we went outside.

The Social Preservation Society (called The Society for short) was, at the time, a growing conservative movement with chapters all over the country. One almost started on campus, but their constitution was deemed "prejudice" by the administration. So, they weren't allowed to gather formally in any public buildings or event spaces; they gathered quietly in dorms instead, emboldened by their inability to use any other space. Any rejection they faced just seemed to make them stronger. The Society had been created to advocate for social reform, and their excitable and significant online following soon gave them enough of a platform to be taken seriously. They then started showing up at major press events and lobbied outside of every possible government-affiliated building they could find. They knocked on doors until someone was willing to give them an audience, and then, even the politicians referenced their work in glowing political prose. The Society seemed to grow by the day, and it became more and more common for their flag to fly outside the homes of people we thought we knew pretty well. None of those who flew the flag would have admitted to being prejudice, which they were often accused of, let alone listen to anyone refer to The Society as a "hate group." Their gut response, as if it had been vetted and rehearsed, was to call any dissenters crazy liberals and tout the idea that it was us who politicized everything, not them.

The greatest success The Society had was in securing local political seats. A few prominent members—the figureheads, if you will—tried running gubernatorial races, but they quickly found that widespread support was more of a long-term goal than a short-term one. The larger branches chose individuals from all the local chapters and funded their campaigns for things like counselor at-large or parks and recreation. Turnout was low, and they won in landslides all around the country. Me and all the other politically in-active citizens would have woken up one day not even re-alizing anything had happened, but it absolutely had. Once in the town, The Society started planting seeds through increasingly larger and more spectacular fundraisers and events. They dazzled the local townspeople with expensive guest speakers from big cities and fancy tablecloths until they were seen as more or less integral to the community. Only then did they press on with their agenda. It was all carefully planned. For all their faults, and there were many, no one could accuse them of being unorganized.

These local successes also granted them access to wan-ing social and religious institutions. In most Society-occu-pied towns, there were at least a handful of churches whose owners were fearful about the state of their congregations. In my hometown, it wasn't at all uncommon for people to work two, maybe three, jobs in order to support themselves. If your kid's teacher waited on you at dinner on Saturday night, you wouldn't politely pretend not to know them, you'd tip 25% and hope they'd do the same if and when the situation were reversed. Sunday meant time-and-a-half for most people, and the little time they had off wasn't going to be spent thinking about their mortal sins. The Society found a particular groove with these churches because they could schmooze potential attendees through partnerships at community events that essentially indebted the churches to them without anyone batting an eye. They're less wolves in sheep's clothing and more kindly shepherds with a hid-den pistol.

Every generation likes to think they're better than the one that came before them. Certainly, where technology or medicine is concerned, but also when it comes to morality. The generations prior are only used as a dead statistic to compare to the now. In the end, though, it's all the same. The same old song transmitted in a new, shiny way for the masses to hear. All they've ever really needed is someone to listen.

CHAPTER 4

Stick-on floor tiles.

That's what occupied my mind during the time spent waiting for appointment number two. Real tile was out of the budget and, therefore, out of the question, so stick-on it was. Two years ago, right as the keys to the apartment were handed over to me, I realized how awful my kitchen floor was. Anticipation, again, got me to sign without considering much beyond this being a place of my own, and one badly needed. Communal living in college took the glamor out of roommates, and I didn't have a boyfriend to split the rent, so a bad kitchen floor was the price I paid for independence.

Haley, my sister, came over the day I bought the box of tiles and spent the whole day slapping them across the floor with me. She arrived in ragged overalls, a box of donut holes in one hand, the other hand knocking furiously on the front door. She knew I was feeling some type of way about the floor as soon as we started. We stepped back at the end to admire our work only to realize that the tiles were supposed to create a repeating geometric pattern. The one Haley and I had managed looked more like a *Shining*-style labyrinth. Now it makes me laugh when I look at it, but it definitely took some time to get to that point. You're supposed to be proud of your home, but for the longest time, the mismatched floor was a constant reminder that I couldn't seem to handle adult things too successfully on my own.

Step. Step. Pivot left. Step. Step. Pivot right. A collection of dust and debris gathered on the soles of my feet as I walked across the mismatched floor carefully avoiding the cracks. Partly superstition, partly safety. Two years of dragging my feet lifted up some of the tile corners to the point where the whole square rotated if you caught it just right. The literal tackiness was almost gone. The metaphorical tackiness, on the other hand, was still going strong.

I didn't really listen to music or watch any TV the week leading up to the second appointment. Anything I tried to get into just made me feel worse. Instead, I circled the kitchen table like a quiet vulture scavenging for something to occupy my time. The table in question was nothing special: a thrift store find my mom tried with total sincerity to convince me was better than it really was.

"No, Jules, I'm serious. This is really a nice one!"

In reality, it was all I could afford. The plan was always to buy a new one when I got the money, maybe even a fancy one from Cardi's, but I never seemed to be able to save up much of anything. Something always happened that required me to shell out the little I did manage to save: car trouble, apartment trouble, boy trouble. Some kind of trouble.

Whether it was real or imagined, I began to feel a pain deep within my jaw that worsened as the days wore on. As much as I didn't want to go back, I found myself wishing the second appointment was the next day just to get it over with. I couldn't take the anticipation any longer. In what can only be described by the bittersweet-ness of the moment, I finally woke up to a calendar square bearing the scribbled words: "Dentist 11:30."

The office was a good thirty-minute drive from my apartment; but the roads were lined with trees, so I didn't mind very much. I've always loved New England roads anyway. They vibrate with a life that shifts with the seasons: blushing pastel summers on the Cape; pumpkin-patch falls; long, gray winters; and tulip-ed springs. People crossing, people moving, people coming, people going. The sidewalks— sometimes bricked or cobblestoned—move the pedestrians past storefronts and stacked houses. "Trippledeckahs," rather. New England roads paved the way for a modern life now lived on colonial grounds, hallowed by revolutionaries and Ivy Leaguers, by witches and Damons.

On either side of the road, the leaves were bright green. Eager to soak up the almost summer sun, they had opened themselves up as wide as possible. The ones that had extended to the point of being almost transparent held the sunlight best, giving off a golden-green glow. The few visible branches flashed with color as robins passed by them, flying high above the Canadian geese families en route on foot to one of the many ponds dotting the backroads of southeastern Massachusetts.

I must have watched it all too closely that day because I was, once again, late for my appointment. This time I didn't have the luxury of waiting in the parking lot to center myself and hopped out of the car carrying my anxiety with me.

"Hi, I have an appointment at 11:30 with Dr. Sears . . . I'm sorry I'm late, I hit some traffic on the way in . . . hopefully she's not on to the next person."

In response, the receptionist pointed a knobby finger in the direction of the waiting room without looking up from her computer. *Point taken.* With a defeated smile, I took the sunglasses off my head, letting the hair fall down onto my forehead, and spent the walk to the waiting room fussing with it. *It's a long couple of steps, so best look busy.* As I was about to take my seat, my eye caught the gaze of a young girl, maybe five or six years old. She was wearing a pink, Disney-princess shirt adorned with Cinderella, Belle, and Ariel, and she was crying hard.

I tried for a moment to ignore her sniffles by picking up a magazine that sat on the table next to me and reading the first article I found. It was a thick, glossy magazine about finances—probably what they thought dads were interested in reading while their kids got their teeth pulled. The article I landed on was about conquering interview fears and how to "get that green!" Before long, the crying became more interesting.

"Are you afraid of the dentist?" I asked the girl, leaning over on my elbow, the magazine flopping to a close. As kids often do when older people talk to them, and to her I was a full-blown adult, the little girl ran to her mother and hid behind her knees. "Can I tell you something? I'm afraid of the dentist too," I whispered.

This piqued her attention.

"You are?" she asked, moving out from behind her mother.

"I am, but *you* seem like a brave girl! It's okay to be scared sometimes though, even princesses get scared."

With that, she wiped her nose along her sleeve and walked over to me. As she got closer, I noticed several patches on her shirt where the pink fabric was darkened with tears. She told me she was waiting to get a loose tooth pulled and threw her mouth open to show me just where it was.

"See! It's all wiggly! And Mommy told me we can take my tooth home . . . and . . . and . . . while I'm sleeping, the tooth fairy will take my tooth away and leave me money!" Her mom nodded happily in my direction as she talked. I considered for a moment if maybe the girl had read the finance magazine.

She was on a roll, telling me about the tooth fairy like it was a secret only she knew about. Words fell out of her mouth like teeth in a nightmare, scattering on the floor in all directions. When she finally finished talking and stopped to breathe, her inhale caught in her throat several times, and she held a look in her eyes as if she had just told me something very special and *very* secret. I caught the mother covering her smile with a shy hand. I was in the middle of telling Sara, or S-A-R-A as she had spelled it out for me, some insider tooth fairy tips that I had learned from my mother (the tooth fairy is more generous if you put everyone's plates in the sink) when the receptionist walked in and gestured to me with a quick jerk of the head. She wore a beaded lanyard, weighed down to her stomach with a name tag: "Dawn, Serving Smiles Since 2017." She remained stoic as I walked over to her, directing her full attention toward a hidden room behind the check-in desk.

"Is everything okay?" I asked.

"Not quite," she said, still avoiding eye contact.

With an outstretched arm, Dawn motioned me into a small office lined with bright red wallpaper. A huge desk sat in front of an equally huge window in the middle of the room. With the desk there, there was hardly enough space in the office for anything else. I didn't even think Dawn could fit by it to sit in the chair on the other side until I saw her do it myself. Someone must have had a strong attachment to the desk to justify the space it took up. Sun-lit spider plants hung all over the red room, their limbs dragging in messy knots on the ground. Some of the longer ones had been crushed by careless feet. When Dawn sat down, I could hardly see her face. She was silhouetted in the bright light from the window behind her, which hung around her face, illuminating the outline like Gloria Swanson in *Sunset Boulevard*. After she took a minute to fuss with the curtains, I could see her face more clearly. She moved her hands idly over some pencils for a moment before finally looking up at me.

"Mr. Grant, we value our patients' time here so I'm going to keep this brief," she began. "Unfortunately, we're not going to be able to complete your scheduled root canal procedure at this time—"

"Why not?" I interrupted.

Irritated that I had spoken up, she continued. "As I'm sure you're aware, this is a Christian institution"—

I am aware.

"and this is a Christian country . . ."

Where is this going?

"and we have decided that we are no longer able to keep you on as a patient due to your lifestyle choices, and wish you the best in your search for a new provider."

She followed that up with palpable silence.

"I'm confused, what do you mean by my 'lifestyle choices?'"

She looked at me as though she wished I hadn't asked.

"Dr. Sears mentioned to the staff that during your last visit you referenced your being a homosexual, is that correct?"

"Yeah . . . that's correct. And what does that have to do with my root canal?" Now I was getting mad.

She went on to tell me that my healthcare plan had recently changed, and the office now reserved the right to refuse medical care to individuals whose "lifestyle choices" went against the practice's religious beliefs. This was, of course, so long as they provided alternative options for the newly rejected patient.

"That's bullshit! I pay like everyone else! I have *never* given this office any trouble . . . I might come in late sometimes, but I'm never an issue."

Dawn didn't move at all during my counter and, when I was done, said only, "Well homosexuality is an issue for us, Mr. Grant." Her mouth barely moved as she spoke.

It might be worth it to mention that, at this point, the national opinion on queer people had only just begun to take a turn for the worse due in no small part to the dutiful work of The Society. However, not to the point where a statement like that could come out of confident lips. We still had the right to marry, after all. Oh boy, did we ever *still* have the right to marry. The problem was that, before anyone knew it, marriage was about the only right we had. That decision put into a lot of people's minds that the path to freedom was finally complete. As things began to change— as more people were found dead in the streets and people started protesting it—someone would smugly remind them that they still had the right to get married. With her statement, Dawn was testing the waters like everyone else.

Loose lips might sink ships, but tight lips pave a clean road to hell.

"So what, I'm supposed to just not get the root canal and suffer the consequences? That's the price of being gay now?"

"Mr. Grant, this has nothing to do with your being a homosexual."

God, I hate that word. *Homosexual.* It sounds so clinical. It's a word thrown out before some kind of cultural diagnosis, a word used to the same effect as a slur but polite enough for use in classroom or talk-show discussions.

"This has everything to do with the values of this office and who it chooses to service. We'll happily serve a homosexual patient who is quiet about their lifestyle."

She paused again. I thought maybe her voice was about to give out on her, that maybe she realized there was venom in what she was saying. I thought her pause was an attempt to dilute it through small, swallowed breaths. Instead, she rose slowly and moved over to the curtain, opening it slightly. Light poured in and washed over the desk, sending a warmth over my body and a sting to my eyes. Within seconds, the light was gone. While I was talking, Dawn must have noticed that a portion of the curtain's fabric was caught on one of the plants, causing its leaves to bend down at a particularly sharp angle. She moved the plant and carefully smoothed out the curtain before turning her gaze back to me. But not before taking a moment to enjoy the fact that I was now frantic while she had maintained an icy calm.

"You know, Mr. Grant, if I'm being quite honest, you people wonder why things are changing . . . well, maybe if you didn't try to shove things down our throats so much, maybe we'd be more accepting."

The silence I had mistaken for a sign of hope transformed into something altogether different in the speaking of those words. I'm used to stares and hushed voices, and I often find myself wondering what is held within them. But there's something in the brazenness of those kind of statements that confirms the thoughts that keep me up at night and unleashes the monsters under the bed. No longer are the monsters abstract, the dangers associated with them as difficult to make clear as the whispers surrounding two men holding hands, rather, they're suddenly evident and very much alive.

"I'm not having this conversation with you right now." It was the only thing I could think of to say at that moment. "Just tell me what my options are."

As it turns out, I had two. The first was to take my pride—and unfinished root—home with me to find a dentist who would take on a *homosexual* patient in need of immediate dental attention. The caveat of option one was that very few of those dentists existed, and the ones who did exist were currently overwhelmed with new client requests. Others had seen the writing on the wall and changed dentists way before they, too, were taken to the little red room behind the check-in desk. I—obviously—was not one of them.

At that point in my life, political grounds were never ones I felt comfortable navigating. In all honesty, when the conversation would turn political, I used to feel a shiver run up my spine, especially during debates over gay rights. It was me they were talking about, and me whose body was at the other end of their propositions. Instead, I lived and breathed the arts, film in particular. Flickering pictures and glamorous actresses told me everything I needed to know about the world around me. I first understood things were changing when the Motion Picture Production Code had been reinstated a few years back. For weeks leading up to the decision, The Social Preservation Society had taken out ads that detailed why the current state of film was a threat to the proper social order. The most popular ad boasted the headline "Deviant Films Make A Deviant Nation." One day, the newly approved code arrived on the doorsteps of all the major movie studios and dictated things that could no longer be shown on film because they had been deemed too dangerous to the fabric of America. Over the course of a single day, showing any level of queerness in movies was completely banned.

On the one hand, it's a great idea. Film regulations have wide-reaching consequences, especially given the myriad of ways you can watch movies now, but the apparatus itself, the thing responsible for the consequences, is practically invisible. No one will ever notice! How could they? Then you just have to let the seed sprout roots and tend to it carefully with some more overt changes over time, but never anything big enough to turn heads—the plant needs to be watered, not drowned. Only after enough time has passed can you start denying medical interventions, or as some of the smaller newspapers reported, allow them to turn up dead on the side of the road in the middle of the night.

A similar code had come around nearly a century before, just after the war ended and the effects of the Great

Depression had started to soften. After WWI, the Catholic church took one look around and decided beyond a doubt that America was on the decline. The Depression stripped jobs away from men and, to the church, made women of them. Newspapers declared that American men had become too feminized, an identity that now subjugated them to the doomed life of a woman. Stuck at home, I guess they had nothing else to do but go to the movies. What a shock it must have been for them to see bare breasts and men dancing; what a mockery to their state it must have been. And it had to be; nothing so cruel could have come from anything but the logic of a scorned toddler in the body of a grown adult. Even feminized, these men had absolute power and no reason to wield it. No reason not to either. Under the original Production Code, Mae West became Hitler and gays were comparable to Nazis. Marlene Dietrich's same-sex kiss in *Morocco*, the gentle gay sensuality of *The Dickson Experimental Sound Film*, all of it was now as antithetical to America as anything could possibly be. This victory for The Social Preservation Society made it a darling to the growing conservative movement, which saw the new Production Code as a sign of hope for the future of their movement.

I remember studying those films in college and finding them nearly impossible to get through even once. When the Production Code was reinstated, I wanted nothing more than to watch them over and over again. To watch the men in *The Dickson Experimental Sound Film* hold each other and rock to the silent violin until the end of time. Were they in love? Probably not. Did I believe they were? I still do. Queerness in those early films might have been played for laughs, but still, there it was, captured forever in celluloid. But that was then and this was now.

The second order of the new Production Code, of course, was the banning of all "deviant films," both old and new. No more *Morocco*; no more *Philadelphia*; no more *Love, Simon*. And that was just the gay films. Movies with interracial relationships or ones that critiqued any part of The Social Preservation Society's mission, were also snuffed out. I've always found it suspicious that in times of change it's the powerful deviants who get to determine what is truly deviant behavior. The burning of the celluloid closet was nevertheless intended to seal it shut forever.

After the new Production Code tore through film, its next target was literature. Now, to give them credit, not even they were stupid enough to jump right to burning books. That's far too cliché. That would have caused some roots to wither and die. With books, it moved slowly—how an owl moves on a night-blind rat before swooping in and snapping its neck. As I made my way through college, I found it harder and harder to find copies of certain textbooks. The name Judith Butler was often spat back at me with venom as I was told, "Sorry, we don't carry that anymore." Red flag number two.

The original Production Code lasted until the late 1960s, but that's just what's on the books. Gay bodies were represented; and then they weren't; and then they were again. The underlying message has always been the same, though: queer bodies are never to be seen as being cut from the same cloth as everyone else's. Movies were popular, and so they became a political ground on which a culture war could rage. The spectacle of gay suffering has captivated audiences for what seems like eons, and that's because it has always served a purpose. AIDS, beatings, and buried gays have each altered the lens through which these bodies are manipulated, but it's always the same thing. *Manipulation.*

A reminder of how we were meant to be seen. In between the lines for popcorn and blockbusters, bodies fell neatly into spaces where light didn't reach, until they disappeared, codified away into nothingness. What remained was their silent screams, heard from outside the frame, flicked away by tossed hair, camera pans, and extreme close-ups. What's old becomes new again, and this time old became new so slowly that it seemed warmly familiar. The feeling of not being asked at fancy dinner parties how long you and your partner have been together or who said I love you first; the feeling of everyone assuming you met on a hookup app and that your life of love and monogamy is some cosmic fluke; the talk you have with your partner through pursed lips right before taking their hand in public. There's always been a code; that much isn't new. Now there was just a clear punishment for failing to abide by it.

Dawn also told me that my dentist wanted me to know the chances of my tooth abscessing before a new dentist would take me on were high. Should my tooth abscess, I ran the risk of bone damage and needing additional surgeries later. Switching insurances would produce the same result.

Option two, in contrast, was presented to me with a smile and without a scary "but" from the dentist. Clearly, this was the option they wanted me to choose.

Option two was to attend an insurance-approved Christian retreat and come back to the office with a certificate indicating my completion of a two-month-long conversion therapy session. Then, my insurance wouldn't be flagged, and the office would green-light the second half of my root canal.

It didn't sound real. I had known conversion therapy camps existed, of course, and I knew they were growing in numbers. But I had never thought it would get to that point. Politicians get elected; people declare the beginning of the end; and then the end doesn't come. My problem was not looking closer. The end hadn't come for me, but it had come for so many others; and that laid the foundation for the end now laid out to me in two options, each one threatening and immediate.

"How am I supposed to choose one of those?"

Nothing.

"I really can't afford another dentist, and my mom found me this . . . this is my *whole* family's dentist, and now you just . . . fine." I had made up my mind.

I'll go to the camp. I'll lie and pretend to be a good little breeder for them, and then I'll sashay myself back here and lay the paper down with the limpest wrist I can possibly muster. I'll do what so many of us do when we walk through doors bearing certain symbols. I'll do what some do to make a paycheck or walk down the street unharmed. I'll pretend.

Dawn reached into the drawer beside her and pulled out several brightly colored papers. She tapped the sides of them so they fell in line and stuck them in a manila folder that she handed over to me.

There was no going back now.

CHAPTER 5

I didn't think it was real even when I left the office with proof inked on paper.

There was some part of me still holding out hope for someone to swoop in and make everything right, or for the receptionist to burst into laughter and point me to a camera hidden among the tangled limbs of the spider plants; but that never happened. It wasn't until I was home that it all hit me, and it hit me hard. I half expected to walk into an apartment torn to shreds, but that didn't happen either. Everything was just as I had left it.

I made my way into the kitchen but couldn't get any farther before the tears came. My whole life now felt temporary, the future lived and behind me now. All the knick-knacks and boxes of food that were scattered around the room would be in the same place two months from now. They wouldn't stir in my absence. My apartment had become a museum exhibit soon to go off display. It wasn't even so much the months ahead that were making me feel this way, but the undeniable proof that my world and the world outside of it were no longer compatible. I wasn't scared of the now, I was scared of the next. And the *next* next.

As I always do when I find myself in trouble, I called my mom to figure out what I should do next. I've always found it amusing that no matter how old you get, or how *adult* you think you are, you still believe wholeheartedly that your parents can solve any problems that come your way. Admittedly, I was nervous to talk to her about this particular problem because it invoked sexuality more directly than I was used to. She was game to meet the people I dated, but she definitely appreciated the heads up to mentally prepare for the handshake at the door. At least I think she did; I never asked. She answered my call, her happy voice mindlessly starting to recount a story about her day when I interrupted through a voice crack.

"What's up, Jules?"

I thought of how I wanted to begin the conversation, hoping not to scare her too badly, but it seemed impossible to strike the right tone.

"Mom, I need your help I . . ."

"What happened?"

"You know how I had to go to the dentist to . . ."

"Yeah . . ."

"To get the root canal thing?"

"Right," she said, starting to understand where this was going.

"They can't do the full thing because the insurance is . . . um . . . it's not gonna let them approve it. They're telling me I have to go to this program first. Is that true?"

"Oh, honey," she said with deep sympathy. "You know,

I got this packet of stuff from the insurance people a little while ago, but I didn't want to scare you. I didn't think they'd ever do anything with it to be honest. I'm sure if you call them, they'll be able to figure something out. That's just ridiculous."

We kept talking for a while, but after she mentioned calling the insurance company, I couldn't think of anything else. Nothing she said after that really registered in my mind. Most of the call consisted of me offering a few enthusiastic grunts to let her know I was still interested in the story she was telling. Something about someone she ran into at the grocery store who she used to work with before I was born. I remember her asking me if I remembered meeting them, which I didn't. When she finished her story, she laughed to herself and waited for me to offer something up that would keep the conversation going. I don't think she wanted the call to end because she was anxious about the whole insurance thing. As long as the call was going, we could put off the scary things on the to-do list a little while longer. I was nervous, too, although I dreaded calling the insurance company less after talking to my mom. She didn't break down or give any real sign that I should be too worried.

"Thanks, Mom."

"Good luck, Jules."

When I called the insurance company to double-check their policies, I was directed to an automated message that confirmed what the receptionist had told me. Even though I knew there wasn't going to be a loophole for me to access, the recording sent a warm prickle over my body. I really was cornered. Sitting at the table, tracing splits in the wood with my finger, I researched the insurance change until the sun had moved enough to shine directly through the kitchen window. It wasn't even as if the information was hidden. That would have at least given me some solace, but it was all out there for me to notice. I just never had. There were clickbait videos on YouTube from early morning talk shows where sharp-dressed men and pretty women took turns shivering and shuddering whenever anything even remotely gay was mentioned; there were the news stories about gay men having public sex in parks, intercut with testimony from reliable and frightened straight couples; there were signs for local elections demanding trans people be jailed for using public restrooms. There was everything you could think of. I had finally found the key, but the building was on fire.

The comments under the videos were plentiful and mostly from people dead set against queer people and dead set on voting to express that. Hostility, the great motivator.

The first Production Code was the end of gay people in film. The very few that did make it through the cracks were the villains or the sad, tragic figures who paid the ultimate price for their gayness. Then, people got used to them being gone and got hostile when they popped up in real life. There was no longer an image for people to point to, good or bad. Absence created monsters of us—ones that lurked in nonexistent shadows, waiting for an unsuspecting child in the bathroom or for any opportunity to dismantle the sanctity of marriage. Cleverness and innuendo were avenues to challenge the code, but very few in the mainstream understood the references. Like with westerns. After the Code was law, westerns started including scenes of sweat-slicked men comparing their guns. If you knew, you knew. But guns were guns, and two men comparing their guns was nothing more than that to most.

My eyes glazed over while watching one of the videos—a somber think piece from a late-night talk show—until a thought popped into my head. Faint at first, then screaming toward the front of my mind. *Work!* I was going to have to call out of work for two months and at the last minute. Somehow that call seemed scarier than the one with Mom and the insurance company combined. There was no way they were going to accept the request, and there was no way I was going to explain to them why I was making it. One Google search away was another piece of information regarding changing business practices, and I wasn't protected under them either.

My mind and body were now engaged in a desperate battle to escape each other. I wanted to crawl out of my skin or to transform into something so small that no one would be able to find me. On my phone screen, the number to the office stared back at me for quite some time.

My parents always said school was the only way to make a better future for myself. In their eyes, first came school, then came a job, then came stability.

Somewhere in my parents' house is a box containing every school project I completed before going to college. The paper is torn and stained, and the box is probably ripped and spilling its contents now, but it's proof of what they did for me. Something we made out of nothing. We would sit up for hours putting together dioramas, then study guides as I got older, and eventually term papers. College wasn't an option for them, but they would have died before letting it slip out of the realm of possibility for me.

I was always excited about the idea of college—until I had to decide which college to attend and what to study while I was there. Then suddenly it was much less fun. Distance played a large role in the glamor of college for me. I slugged along happily through elementary, middle, and high school, doing this and that to make myself more marketable to the academic towers on the horizon line. At a safe distance, they illuminated the night. I was Dorothy clipping along down the yellow brick road toward an emerald city that was about to reveal itself to be less illuminating and more blinding. Even still, my parents were satisfied when I told them I'd be studying marketing.

"A valuable skill," they said.

My parents were proud of me to a fault. I could do no wrong in their eyes.

Eventually, I settled on a school that probably pops up when you google "New England liberal arts colleges." Red brick buildings and rolling fields of green grass included for four easy payments of $60,000! My senior year, I scored a fairly prestigious internship with a marketing firm in Boston. It had all the markers of success I was supposed to be looking for, from the personality-lacking co-workers to the pristine office spaces, but I knew immediately that it wasn't for me. What *was* for me, on the other hand, was a question I didn't dare ask myself, but whatever it was, forty years in a cubicle wasn't it.

My first week at the firm wasn't filled with coffee run after coffee run as I had expected, but with a series of collaborative projects. I was selected for the internship to do brand writing and was surprised every time they asked my opinion on drafts for major projects—things people would see on billboards or their phones.

"What do you think, Julien?" someone would ask during a meeting.

I'd sit at the other end of the boardroom, contribute

something small, and wonder how anything I could say would prove beneficial to people who already work for the company. Regardless of what I thought, the firm seemed to think highly of me and my little contributions. When added up, they gave me the reputation of being the quiet, thoughtful one.

My supervisor took an interest in me and, like my parents, worked with me to refine my skills. Her name was Rae, and she prided herself on the fact that she started her career as a hairdresser before going back to school and working her way up the corporate ladder to her current position. She wasn't shy about this and told virtually everyone upon meeting them, myself included. At first, I thought she was bragging, but after getting to know her a bit, I realized she fashioned herself a bit of a role model. She got me to talk more in meetings, which I appreciate in hindsight, and even though I didn't feel any more confident, I learned how to convey confidence to other people. Like my parents, though, I didn't have the heart to tell her how I was really feeling about the internship. Instead, I tried to make it work.

I was decent enough at marketing but lacked the drive to develop my ideas into anything seriously worth pitching. For my whole run at the firm, I stuck to contributing to other peoples' ideas during workshopping sessions. Pitching original ideas, which Rae would force me to do on occasion, meant hours of actively ignoring everyone else and picking apart my fingers while convincing myself that whatever I had brought to the table would inevitably fail. Alone in my dorm room, the ideas sounded great, but in the mouths of other people, they became unbearable. It was like hearing a recording of your own voice; it's undeniably you, but it feels like someone else. I didn't like the some-body else I was. I was powerless to stop him, though.

Back at school, things started falling apart rapidly as graduation approached. I still wasn't sure about what I wanted to do, but I applied for marketing jobs anyway, figuring I could at least get a killer recommendation letter from Rae. Every job I applied for was quick to respond with a thanks-but-no-thanks email, and the thought of graduat-ing without a job was enough to make me physically sick. With no emerald city on the horizon this time, I began skipping classes and sleeping in later and later. I had be-come so used to opportunities slipping by me that I didn't consider that the internship could potentially lead to a job. I was just grateful to have the internship at all after class fell off my radar. I had no lurking desire to manifest destiny my way into a full-time position by any means possible. When Rae offered me a job at the end of the semester, I was gen-uinely surprised.

Recollection is a funny thing because you become someone else when viewed in hindsight—like when you hear your voice on a recording. The false objectivity of it all makes it possible to put yourself put through an endless choose-your-own-adventure story because of the very na-ture of being removed from the situation. You did this, but what would have happened if you had done *that*? Where would *that* have led you? I couldn't help but put my recol-lected self through the hypothetical choose-your-own ad-venture situation in which Rae found out I'm gay. Would nothing have changed, or would it all be different? There was no way of telling for sure.

I pressed call.

Ring.

It was too much. I hung up.

CHAPTER 6

A thought: How much of a story are we entitled to? Are we entitled to Cinderella's happy ending? Or Harry Potter's defeat over Voldemort? Could the prince have found his princess without the fanfare? I doubt it. Then our minds wander. We always want to know what happens next.

"You mean all this time we could have been friends?"

Well, what happens next? Do they become friends? Magic. Mice. Pumpkin. Shoe. Happily ever after. The bones of the story are as important as the meat, but they're left in lonely piles after the vultures come. I wonder now how much of my story others are entitled to.

Some people, in hindsight, have said that we were taken, but for me that wasn't the case. Others have said that no force whatsoever was employed against us, but that isn't entirely true either. Reality is split here, as it often is, between creators. I had no choice but to choose.

The idea is, incorrectly assumed, but believed none-theless, that histories can be broken down into specific, black-and white-entries. One day all is normal and then the next—this will be the date in bold at the bottom of the timeline—there is a new normal. Maybe it's a good new normal, maybe not—even that's subjective. With a time-stamped dog-eared page in the history book of time, we can delineate between pre and post, before and after. We can muse about what else happened on October 29th, 1929, for example, but all that makes the timeline is that big other thing. Years later, we step back and retrace our steps one war at a time. Conversion therapy didn't just become the new normal overnight, nor do I don't think it will warrant a timestamp of its own, not in the long run at least. That des-ignation will be assigned to a swing in political leanings, the specifics of which will be lost in the footnotes. Maybe a photo of The Social Preservation Society's flag will make an appearance to encapsulate everything else, but on the whole, the stories will die with the ones who lived them.

The days leading up to my session are blurred and enigmatic now. Few details remain, only the most relevant ones that I've had to repeat to reporters, lawyers, and his-torians; all people who actively wield an entitlement over the stories of others as some kind of prerequisite in their profession. What I do remember is that a list of facilities was express-mailed and officially delivered to me in an or-ange envelope, the shade of which is usually reserved for parking tickets and court summonses. Also included in the envelope was a step-by-step guide on how to schedule your session.

"Step One: Locate your insurance provider and select the facility of your liking from the list provided in section

2.A. Please note, only facilities listed under your designated insurance plan can be selected.

Step Two: Complete the application provided in the "More Info" section of the facility profile.

Step Three: A copy of your application will be emailed to you, please review and resend the email to confirm your session.

Step Four: Attend the session!"

The exclamation point threw me. I racked my brain as to what part of this whole ordeal warranted an exclamation point, or if they really thought one excitable punctuation mark would smooth over the feelings gurgling inside me. "Attend the session!" Looking at it, it was hard to be convinced. You can't just throw out exclamation points all willy-nilly. You have to consider what comes before them. "Attend the session!" has all the excitement of "Grandma's funeral!" But in both cases, no one's really that excited about it. Regardless, you still have to go to "Grandma's funeral!" at the end of the day, so you might as well suck it up and embrace the exclamation point. There was no confusing what was going on; I was sending myself away. How could I, then, be mad at the form for trying to soften that blow?

The step-by-step guide was printed on extra-long legal paper with some infographics and cartoons scattered about its folds, serving the same purpose as the exclamation point. Self-admission was the preferred method of capture as the insurance companies wanted a clearly mappable paper trail. Just in case tides changed again. That way, if anyone complained or used the "forced against their will" argument, they could be kindly redirected to their own signature. If the companies found themselves on the wrong side of history way down the line, then it would be easy enough to write a short piece of marginalia about the whole situation and move along. If history sided with them, then huge volumes could be written not only about the great things that came out of the era, but how, even when confronted with something as troubling as us gays, they showed enough respect to keep a record of our brave participation. It was all very methodical.

New England had fewer facility options available than most other parts of the country. Whether or not that was a good thing is a complicated discussion. Each of the facilities were described with only vague identifying details. There were no specific names in the pamphlet either, only the names of towns and cities printed in bold, black ink—the facilities themselves were housed in operating churches, YMCAs, and Boy Scout lodges after all. Conversion therapy outed the participant, but it protected the faces of those running it at all costs.

Most of the bolded names in Massachusetts and Rhode Island were familiar to me; they were all places I had once visited comfortably and without fear. Seeing those names in a new context seemed wrong—impossible even. Dots on a New England map no longer represented the places of my childhood, but places I had, naively, thought I belonged. Choosing a town meant forever switching my association with it to "that place where I went to conversion therapy."

My finger eventually landed near the end of the list in a section of beach towns, and I lazily drew imaginary loops around them. Dartmouth. Onset. Narragansett. I imagined what a conversion therapy camp might look like on the beach. The trails of sand that would breeze through open doors and the wafting scent of frying seafood. Would it still have the red, blue, and white color palette with shells and seagulls dry-brushed on bookshelves and lamps? Would the instructors wear boat shoes and Vineyard Vines, and put their cigarettes out in turned over clamshells? Maybe I'd even be able to go to the beach somehow? I pictured the ocean before me: its waves lapping at my feet and collecting foam around my ankles as my fingers buried themselves deeper into the sand—perhaps to look for something to grab. If nothing else, that image was manageable. In the end, I chose Narragansett as I had the fewest prior attachments to it.

We weren't allowed to drive ourselves to the locations, mostly because there wasn't adequate parking, or so I was told when I scheduled my pickup. A breathy, nervous voice on the other end of the phone then added it was preferred that our license plates not be seen on campus anyway. For our protection, of course. The inflection in the voice performed some impressive gymnastics as it continued. "A win-win really."

I had woken up early to pack my bags that morning, even though I hadn't slept much during the night to begin with. A deep-blue afternoon sky turned into a cotton candy sunset and then went black as night descended—I watched it all happen in real time from my bedroom window. People say a watched pot doesn't boil, but that's probably because the heat isn't high enough. I couldn't bring myself to fall asleep, but there wasn't much to do in another room besides what I was doing in bed. *Waiting.* Not a good enough reason to move past stirring restlessly under the covers. Somewhere in the early hours of the morning, I moved myself, and my suitcases, to the couch in the living room.

At 8:00 a.m. sharp, the lights of a huge Escalade rolled

across my front window as it pulled into the driveway and idled, waiting for me to make my way outside. Several times during the whole Galilee experience, small gifts were given in order to ease me into submission. This was one of them. As the Escalade continued to idle in my yard for a bit, I took a deep breath and grabbed my keys. My hands unexpectedly began to shake, half ignoring the vehicle waiting for me. When my hands were steady enough, I texted the Galilee address to my mom and powered down my phone, which I wasn't allowed to bring with me anyway. I tossed the phone onto the couch, but the impact caused it to bounce onto the floor, creating a considerable thud when it hit. After checking to make sure the screen wasn't cracked, I set the phone down gently and stared at it for a few seconds, trying to divine some kind of strength from the sad situation I had found myself in. Sans phone, I grab my keys and opened the door, breaking the shield between myself and everything that was about to happen.

Do I even bother locking the door? Yeah, I guess I should. In case someone comes looking for more evidence to hide, or worse, not hide. Tufts of grass peeked out of nearly every crack in the driveway all the way to the car. *Why hadn't I done something about those before? Too late now.* The apartment door clicked sharply behind me, indicating that it was locked, and I stuffed the bundle of keys down into my pocket.

The Escalade was now producing a noticeable rumble. The driver, whoever it was, had probably turned on the AC. As I made my way over to the back of the car, the keys I had pocketed began digging into my thigh. My nerves were making me sweat, and the sweat was making my pants feel tighter than they were. I quickly de-ringed all the keys, keeping only the house key I would need when I was done, ran back to my apartment, and tossed the others through the door before locking it a final time. Now convinced I had packed too much, I tried to mentally run through my inventory, but time wasn't on my side. What was left on my side, as it happens, seemed minimal at best.

There was no denying the threat of summer that day. The sun was high, and the grass danced lightly in the breeze. Before long, the sidewalks around my apartment would fill with joggers, iPhones brandished to their biceps, a dog or baby stroller in hand. There was an older couple who walked past my door every day while I was getting ready for work, too. They walked slowly, always holding hands, and allowed joggers to pass them as they shouted: "On your left." They'd be out soon, too.

It became readily apparent that the driver was not getting out of the car to help me anytime soon, but I stood outside the car anyway in an act of defiance. I wasn't sure how many opportunities for defiance I would have at Galilee, so I didn't shrink when the anxiety hit in my stomach. The driver was obscured by a tinted window, but I stared directly at where I figured a pair of eyes would be, no doubt protected by another layer of glass. It didn't seem fair to me that I couldn't see the driver. I knew they were looking at me, and I wanted nothing more than to look back, to match their stare. If I wasn't getting direction, I at least wanted acknowledgment.

The trunk of the Escalade creeped open with a prolonged groan to reveal the empty space my suitcases, which were ready to burst, would soon fill. I had packed and unpacked them several times over, going back and forth wondering how strict the guidelines could actually be. From the looks of it, I had decided they didn't warrant too much concern. I had to clothe myself for most of the summer, after all.

Taking my second deep breath of the day, I lifted my foot up onto the landing that ran the length of the bottom of the car. Before I shut the door, I noticed the driver had pulled up onto my lawn and crushed a patch of dandelions that had just recently sprouted. I've heard you can eat them or make tea from the heads, but I've yet to try it. Something about it seems too desperate, feral even. After hoisting myself up into the car, I snapped the door shut with a loud bang. A gust of summer breeze filled the backseat, and I immediately felt overheated.

The inside of the car was spotless and provided more room than I needed. The black leather seats made my bag look dirty, so I moved it back and forth from my lap to the seat until I decided that it didn't matter. They already thought I was dirty; that's why the driver wasn't looking at me. Before the car rolled backward, I heard the driver move the gear shift, clear his throat, and open the window to spit.

I spent much of the ride to Galilee looking out the window. Green road signs popped out of greener trees, their branches cut away strategically to reveal town names in bold, white lettering. The sun threw a golden shine on top of the leaves. Everything looked like it was glowing. A day like that was either mocking me or giving me something to hold on to, like a sort of parting gift. That particular highway was one I had driven many times before. It had carried me to the mall, to college, to the Cape, and beyond. I knew the turns well and could remember which ones had crosses stuck in the ground around them. They were remnants turned to relics turned again to reminders. I remember my mom, her arm outstretched as she pointed at the crosses, saying, "That's why you don't text and drive." Every once in a while, the trees gave way to humungous rocks, monolithic beasts which had long ago been cut to allow for the road to be paved. Nearly every flat section had something written on it: usually, two names contained inside a lopsided heart but, sometimes, profanity. To this day, I don't know how those messages get there, or who is so motivated that they would scale what is basically a small mountain in the middle of the night to write "Fuck Ronnie" or "You My Baby Forever, Britney." Just tell them in person and save yourself the risk. It's just going to be power-washed anyway.

Once we had traveled a good distance, the driver began talking—but not to me. Regardless, I sat bolt upright when his voice started. It was higher than I had imagined, with a nasal quality to it that was reminiscent of a child mocking their teacher. The voice took me by surprise. Not because it was contrary to what I had expected, but because of how quiet the ride had been to that point. The front of the car was made up very much like a police cruiser, with a sheet of opaque glass separating the driver from the passengers seated in the back. I was, apparently, not the only passenger either. The radio, which was tuned to some God-awful station, grew louder as they continued speaking, but I was able to catch enough of the conversation to realize that the other passenger was an agent from my insurance company. *What was he doing here?* Before I had a chance to gather more clues, the car veered off into a rest area. Traffic swished by us—some people honked at us as they went—but soon the sounds outside grew muffled as I rested my head against the window. Instinctively, I grabbed my bag and opened the door once we bobbled to a stop.

Long trails of smoke puffed out from all around the

hood of the car, clouds of black thinning out to gray and then disappearing without a trace. I remembered my mother telling me once to put as much distance between myself and the car should I ever find myself in that scenario, so I took off running toward the Jersey barriers lining the highway. I could hear the driver swear to himself and start running after me, the change in his pockets rattling the whole way. He was a heavier guy and running nearly winded him. I was leaning up against the barrier when he finally made it over to me, hustling at the very end to make up for resting earlier.

"*Shit*. I thought you were gonna fuckin' run," he said, although more to himself than to me. Winded, his voice sounded lower.

The cars on the highway continued on their routes, apparently not at all taken aback by the smoke or the running. The driver moved in front of me after gathering himself, making sure I was covered on both sides. Standing in front of me, I was finally able to get a good look at him. He was dressed in a navy-blue polo shirt with black dress pants that had grease stains around the pockets. As he heaved, his belly revealed, and then covered, a brown leather belt with a shiny metal buckle. Judging by his hair, which was graying on the sides, I guessed he was maybe in his early fifties. He had a round, rosy face, which looked like the ones on the labels of marinara-sauce bottles.

"I didn't think that was an option," I replied while taking stock of the situation. I didn't either. I hadn't even considered it. I ran because I didn't want to blow up with the car.

Watching relief and surprise take turns moving his face around, I was reminded of a story I saw on the news when I was younger about a barn fire. Some old man had fallen asleep with a cigarette in his mouth, and before he knew it, everything had caught fire: his house, the barn, everything. Even though it put him in danger, the old man's first thought was to save his animals, so he unlatched the stall doors and pulled the horses out by their halters. Only they didn't want to leave. He begged them, whipped them even, but they wouldn't budge. They just ran right back into the flames, and he couldn't get them out.

"Just . . . don't move, please. There's another car comin', you're just gonna have to finish the rest of the trip in that, sorry," he said, turning himself around to face the smoking Escalade. *Sorry.* He sounded disappointed when he said it. Like the Escalade was taking me to prom or something. He walked away with his hands clasped behind his head. I think he really thought it was going to explode. Through the smoke, however, I was able to make out the silhouette of the other man, who was still planted firmly in the passenger seat. He was typing furiously on the screen of his phone. Clearly, the insurance agent didn't think the car was going to explode.

The second car was nice on the outside, but the interior revealed its age. It wasn't the kind of age that raises market value or throws straight guys into midlife crises, but the kind of old that means dirty cloth seats and windows you have to roll down. There was hardened gum on the seat next to me and probably on mine, too. Strands of hair whipped around my face as the car pulled back out onto the highway.

I felt more comfortable in this car. I looked like I belonged in it.

After driving for another hour or so, the car again veered off the highway. I rolled up the window as soon as we took the exit because I didn't want to miss anything the driver and insurance rep were saying to each other. Again, the music rose and drowned out their words. This time it was Sam Cooke's "Summertime." Cooke's voice rolled along, smooth as a still sea, while piercing high notes, the sound like birds down a marble hallway, settled into an all-consuming sense of peaceful unease. Rambling melancholia.

Out of the sky, a large spire could be seen far before we reached the property line. As more of the church became visible, reality started coming into focus as well. The familiar sound of rock under rubber signaled the beginning of the church grounds.

My first impression of Galilee was that it looked like a village set up for tourists in the way the different buildings sat atop perfectly manicured hills encased by perfect cobblestone fences, not a single rock out of place. There were hints of imperfection, though, and like ants at a picnic, they grew in number once you found the first one. There were several knobby trees on the front lawn, some with neglected swings hanging like sour fruit. Stone benches rose out of long tufts of grass where lawnmowers couldn't reach. There were patches of grass that had been burnt by the sun, revealing the cracked earth underneath. I noted each imperfection as we followed a stone pathway until it turned to dirt on the other side of the main church building. As we rounded the corner, a quick flash of black took my attention away from the trees.

Galilee staff members were stationed all around the property. They were dressed in shadowy uniforms and were watching the car carefully. I would get to know the uniform well. A black shirt tucked into black pants, the legs of which ran down toward black shoes. The pants secured at the hip by, you guessed it, a black belt. Each of the men in black had a clear plastic coil protruding from behind their left ear and connected to something tucked into their collars. From time to time, they'd turn and whisper into it. There was something ominous about their presence that first day, but the longer I was there, the easier it was to forget them. They became a part of the landscape as much as the trees were, whispering secrets into the air in much the same way. One moment they were there, and the next they were gone. That first day, one of them, a particularly large, bearded man, directed my driver toward a section of the backyard that had been roped off to create a temporary parking lot. I reached over across the backseat to grab my bag and hurried it to my lap. Double-checking the inventory wasn't necessary, but it was something to do to occupy my mind for the few moments leading up to my formal introduction.

We weren't allowed phones, computers, or cameras, which lightened the load quite a bit. They didn't want any documentation of any kind. Nothing for us to take away and bring back to haunt them. Sharp objects of any kind were also strictly prohibited, so I had left razors at home. The contents of my bag were reduced to earplugs to help me sleep and some soon-to-be stale snacks. I heard the trunk of the car open as another Galilee staff member took away my suitcases to be searched and returned to me at a later date. I doubted I'd ever see them again, but it turned out the driver wasn't lying. I was reunited with my clothes just as the ones I arrived started to turn ripe.

I watched from behind the glass as more cars entered the makeshift parking lot, each throwing dust into the air until it became difficult to see. Tan-colored clouds swirled across the glossy exteriors of the cars, scraping them as they pulled in and parked. The dust cloud was thick enough to amble for a while, floating like a stage curtain, rising slowly to reveal the set behind it. When the final car arrived, all the engines turned off in unison. What followed was a deafening silence as the Galilee staff made their way through the cloud of dust—the men in black were getting into places for action.

By the time the dust settled, doors began to open. I think I counted twenty or so Escalades, and my beat-up car of course, but I can't say for sure. Out of each one came hesitant feet. One foot would pop out, stop, then eventually, be met by the other foot. *One small step for gays, one giant leap for straight-kind*, I thought, decently amused by my ability to make a joke given the circumstances.

So many of those old movies start that way: with shots of feet popping out from behind sleek, black doors.

"Who is that? Better follow them!"

Pro tip: with those old movies, if the shoes are flamboyant, the character is a man, and the director is Alfred Hitchcock, then he's probably the murderer. Another breed of killer clown.

I tried to gauge character traits from the shoes I could see gathering in the parking lot, but before I could get a good enough look at anyone, I was called away by another large man dressed all in black. As I adjusted the strap on my backpack, I did see another boy leave his car, but only briefly. He held a small cloth bag tightly in his hands and found my eyes as he, too, looked for something familiar to hold on to for just another moment. The dust had just about settled when our eyes met, but suddenly, I wished it were back again—as thick if not thicker than before. I held my stare as he did too, and for one moment in time, two sets of eyes held the gaze of the other. These were eyes that had seen the naked bodies of men and walked through a world changed by the tint of the glass in front of their flesh. These were eyes that had known a love and a life that turned the gaze into something dangerous if placed on the wrong body. These were eyes that knew the gaze of the other without knowing anything else. In his look was a plea to be seen one last time. To feel a familiar gaze and understand why it had befallen him. To know he was being seen, not looked at as something out of his control. I knew because I wanted him to see me, too. I couldn't go over to him; I might never know him; but in that moment, I knew what he felt. All I could do was return his gaze and keep going. Suddenly, no funny quips came to mind, and I found myself wishing all the cars would blow up.

I was escorted over to the front yard through a small path between the church and a series of bushes set off to the side. After some time, more boys were led through the pathway and arranged into a half-moon shape just outside the front door of the main church building. From my vantage point, the church looked massive. It was painted a shade of white that made it almost disappear into the clouds the higher up I looked. Blue hydrangeas were blooming on either side of the building in huge, clumsy bundles.

The pointed finger of a Galilee staff member bounced over each of our heads, ensuring that all were accounted for. Once they were satisfied with the number, the finger retracted and the staff member nodded sharply, setting off a chain reaction of nods all around the building that was broken when the doors to the church swept open, revealing a lanky, foreboding figure. The man, who was slim and stubbled, hung in the doorway a while before stepping forward to address the crowd. As shadows parted around him, the red of his shirt made his face appear quite blotchy. The man's squinting eyes peered out over horn-rimmed glasses as he surveyed the group. Clearly, he was soaking in the moment. When it was time for him to begin the opening address, he clasped his hands together with a loud smack.

"Hello everyone and welcome to Galilee Baptist Church!" he said. "My name is Major Faunce, and I will be overseeing all activity here on our beautiful campus for the duration of your stay. So, get used to this face, right? It is my hope that through this collaborative process we will not only become *great* friends, but more than that, that you will *re*connect with the Lord Almighty." With each consonant he hit, spit gathered at his lips and flew into the front row of the audience.

The Major's words were always chosen carefully and spoken with piercing specificity. This I came to realize with time. He told us of his military background next—twelve years stationed overseas—and his desire to carry that background with him wherever he goes. For the entirety of the time I knew him, I don't remember one single utterance from The Major that didn't go through a rigorous background check in his mind. Many names fit a person like The Major well, but "unaware" isn't one of them. He knew his words went in one ear and out the other, so time was always of the essence.

"Lord, I thank you for bringing these boys to Galilee. I pray that they will be able to rid themselves of the sin they carry so deeply within them. In his name, we pray, amen."

One boy in the center of the arc repeated the final word back to The Major.

"Amen," he said.

The Major smiled upon hearing it. Amen. The rest of us, almost without meaning to, pivoted our heads slowly in his direction. I thought for a second that he might have been kidding, trying to get a rise out of either The Major or the group, but no one responded to him in a way that suggested he had done something wrong. All the men in black from before surely would have descended on him if he had done something wrong. Either way, we all looked at him as if he had a red dot on the middle of his forehead. Amen Boy looked around, too, but then started to blush after noticing the attention he was getting.

While The Major continued speaking, I looked around at the other boys and tried to determine what set of circumstances had brought them here. What made living in the straight world so difficult that they chose to be here instead? *Chose.* There goes that word again.

Some of them stood with their necks cocked, the back of a hand resting on their hip, a leg thrown out in one direction. It was easier to tell with those ones. The ones with dyed hair and painted nails didn't stand a chance, but with the others, I wondered how anyone had found them out. Had they been careless with their words like I had been, or had someone seen something and decided to complicate their lives by giving them the same ultimatum I had been given? When I overheard one of them ask one of the men in black if he could go to the bathroom, I heard in his voice the probable cause that would have been the nail in his coffin.

I was suddenly very aware of myself in a way I hadn't ever been before. Everything about me now threatened my existence here and suggested a reason for further punishment. I let my eyes roll across my body and examined myself as I had examined the others only moments ago. Did my wrists hang too much when I walked? How much did my voice give away? I knew in that moment that to survive

Galilee I was going to have to answer those questions and edit myself accordingly.

Without even entering the church, the process had begun.

The Major finished his prayer and asked us all to follow him for a tour of the grounds. The heat of the day was at its peak, and sweat was beginning to pool around my neck. To my surprise, the main church building was strictly off-limits to us. We were not to be seen or heard by any members of the congregation. They were, The Major explained, very active in their religious practices, and most attended mass—which was offered daily—three times a week at the very least. They were contributing in other ways, The Major informed us, when they were not physically participating. What that meant exactly was never explained. The congregation was opening their hearts *and* doors to us, but that didn't require knowing anything more about us.

As we passed by the main building, it was easy to see why it acted as the forbidden beating heart of Galilee. The church possessed an undeniable beauty in its coastal grandeur. For a building off the beaten path, it rose impressively high above the ground below it, which concealed a good portion of the basement level. The higher toward the sky you looked, the larger and more ornate the windows became, allowing for small glimpses into the interior, which was, unsurprisingly, just as beautiful. To some this would be a historic respite from the pressures of their everyday lives. And now it was about to cast a wide, sharp shadow over mine.

Likewise, the yard immediately in front of the church building was not for us to use, whether the congregation was on campus that day or not. If we wanted to go outside, a man in black would escort us into a car and drive us to the beach down the street. This, we were told, was a distinct privilege, and one we could easily lose access to. I wondered if Amen Boy had lost beach privileges before even hearing about it. Maybe the men in black wouldn't descend on us if we messed up, after all. Maybe the punishment would come quietly and take other forms. By the end of the tour, it was clear that we were begrudgingly accepted burdens as opposed to welcome guests.

Someone in the group made a comment about the restrictions and was swiftly reminded of the severity of his "sin." The Major's mouth coiled into a frightening smile before he focused his attention back on the tour.

We would be spending most of our time in two buildings located toward the edge of campus. One was where our activities would take place, and the other was where we would sleep. The lessons building and the dorm building, respectively. The twin buildings were raised up on brick foundations and adorned with fading white paint. Through the windows, I could see richly colored pictures of Jesus hanging on the walls. From the looks of it, neither lawnmower nor foot had braved the area in years. There was a clear line where regular landscaping had ended sometime in the past. Along the sides of the two buildings, I noticed the distinctive shine of poison ivy.

Should nature call, a small "cabin" (an outhouse) with toilets sat beside the second building, leftover from Galilee bible camps of years past. The Major stopped beside the cabin to reiterate that we would always be escorted to the bathrooms separately. A soft laugh escaped from my mouth as I considered what might have happened to make that a necessary precaution. Nature makes many calls in the middle of the night, and some itch more than others.

Afraid he might have put ideas into our heads, The Major took another moment to inform us that one guard would always be stationed inside each building. I worried he might have heard my laugh and tried hard to focus on the rest of the tour.

Our tour ended with a quick overview of our food schedule and a tentative rundown of the Galilee Baptist Church menu. We would be getting three standard meals a day to be eaten in either the dorm building or the lessons building, wherever we were when the food was ready to be served. The Major let us know that we would not be able to make any special requests—or express dietary concerns—unless they were tied to a life-threatening allergy. Luckily, I didn't have one of those. For the most part, the food was tolerable. Usually, we'd have eggs and toast for breakfast, some kind of soup and sandwich meal for lunch, and chicken for dinner. Our only drink option, The Major let us know, would be water.

Fifteen minutes were given to us after the initial grounds tour to put away our things and meet in the first of the two buildings for lesson number one, which would be followed immediately by lesson number two and then lunch. Wasting time was one of the huge no-nos of Galilee. The downside of captive minds is the constant fear of revolution, so naturally, The Major had developed a knack for keeping our days well stocked.

A small concrete porch stuck out well beyond the front door of the dorm building; an old screen door that didn't hide its age well. The wood was cracked in spots, ripping the netting that lined the panels. Teetering on the edge of the porch sat a pile of burnt pine needles, which looked to have been swept with care not long ago. It was probably someone's job to clear the area while the Escalade brigade was making its rounds. Funny how different mornings can be from person to person. One by one, each boy entered the dorm building followed by a loud creaking sound. The door didn't quite catch, so it swung back and forth until it ran out of momentum. (On windy nights the door would scream for hours.)

Inside the dorm building, there were rows of beds modestly decorated with white sheets, a teal bed skirt, and a single pillow. (Fewer layers to hide sinning hands.) Overhead, a line of fans rustled the skirts of the beds directly below them. Not the coziest sleeping arrangement, I'll say that much. As a smell precaution, lemongrass-scented diffusers sat on bar stools in each corner of the room. They all held four or five bright yellow sticks that were swelling with the smelly liquid and fanning it upwards to no great effect. The smell of sweat and dirty laundry, a cocktail of sweet-smelling rot, won out almost every day. It was bad at first, but you got used to it. Very much like the constant sniffles and ass scratches that filled the room at night, too.

Above the door hung a metal sign engraved with the phrase "When Love Is Present, All Is Possible." *Ironic*, I thought to myself. Each time the door shut behind someone, the sign rattled loudly as though reminding us of its message. *That* I never got used to. Every time the sign rattled, it startled me, and I'd snap my head toward the words written above the door. Every time it rattled, it sounded slightly different, too. If it rattled only a few times, the sound was quick and hollow. But if it rattled for a prolonged period of time, the sound reverberated, growing as it called for us to look. It was an angry sign bearing a not-so-angry message, delivered with earth-shaking anger.

As I walked further into the room, I noticed that each bed had a Bible resting on its pillow. The weight of the book caused the pillow to pucker, and so it wasn't until you walked right up to it that it jumped out at you as something out of the ordinary. I picked up the Bible on the bed closest to me and ran my fingers over the engraving on the front cover: "Louis Parsons." Not mine. The fifteen minutes were nearly up by the time I found the Bible adorned with my name: "Julien Grant."

I sat down on my bed and surveyed the room, following one boy after the other as he fumbled around looking for his Bible. Before long, the crowd of boys fumbling dwindled down to nothing. Every time one claimed a bed, the group would split off until only one boy was left. Someone was kind enough to call him over to the only remaining bed. Once everyone had found their place, it was easier to get a sense of the group. There were about twenty-five of them in total, which meant my Escalade estimation was more or less correct. They all looked to be about my age, but then again, I've never been great at guessing age. I, myself, looked easily five years younger than I actually was at the time.

Looking out over a sea of boys might sound like a dreamy free-for-all, but for me, it was overwhelming. I could see them all looking around too, anxiously sizing up the competition. Left and right they were fixing their hair and pulling their shirts out and over any little fold in their stomach that popped out when they sat down. One had even brought a mirror and was frowning into it, evaluating a red mark on the side of his nose. Even here, appearance mattered.

Each boy had a name and a story, and each one was more unlikely than the next of being known by my wandering eyes. So, I sat there imagining what each one's story might be. What their names might be. There was probably a Matthew, and there was probably a Brandon. There was probably someone who loved his parents and another who hated his. Someone loved art and someone loved football, and the only shared commonality I could think of was that they were now sitting in this room with me. I wondered to myself if any other circumstance could have brought us together. It was entirely possible that I might have passed some of them in line at a store once or beeped at one as he cut me off in traffic, and yet, here I was thinking about who they were, all because of where they were now. I wondered to myself, *I hope they're not looking at me*, and drew my backpack to my lap once more, knocking the Bible to the floor as I did. I fanned the book open and snapped it shut to see the back. Like the front, it was also engraved.

Therefore if any man be in Christ,
he is a new creature: old things
are passed away; behold,
all things are become new (2 Cor. 5:17).

CHAPTER 7

Adam and Eve, not Adam and Steve. Cliché, but effective.

As it turns out, The Major—in addition to his military credits—was also a minister. His propensity for diction made all the more sense when he started in on our two Biblical friends shortly after our first lesson: "An Introduction to Homosexuality." In his clerical collar, The Major's chin doubled as he looked toward the ground, imagining himself to be in the garden of Eden. His arms rose in sweeping motions, and with them, the trees were planted, the streams were filled, and the forbidden fruit ripened.

The lessons building was slightly smaller than the dorm building and set closer to the church itself. At night, the trees encircling the dorm building provided a cool escape from the heat of summer. Trees were sparser around the lessons building, and the metal fans did little to stir away the heat. By the time we arrived for our lessons, an arc had been created out of black folding chairs. Many of the chairs had holes in their cushions, which revealed a tan-colored padding inside. The smell of old potpourri hung in the air all around.

The arc was soon to be filled with an assortment of faces: some long and thin with sharp features; some topped by a mound of blonde or brown or red hair; others grayed by a five o'clock shadow; others still looked as though they hadn't yet hit puberty. One boy was asked to remove his hat, and a collection of dreads fell to his shoulders. Our first lesson, right before the crash course on Genesis, included a viewing of a CBS news report from the '60s entitled "The Homosexuals."

"Like anything, opinions on homosexuality have changed over time. I would like to show you a news report from a time before any of you. Before myself even! Hopefully, this will shed a light on why you're here. As you watch, pay close attention to the pain in these people's eyes. And the pain they are subjecting others to," The Major said as he rolled out a cart topped with a large box TV. A few of us exchanged quick glances when it was rolled out. The Major made no reference to it being odd, but most of us had never seen one of those box TVs outside of old movies or ads. It seemed out of place for us, but somehow it fit into the program so easily that neither the guard stationed in the lessons building nor The Major seemed to find it bizarre. I can't quite explain it, but its presence was more than a little unsettling. Leaned up against the TV was a thick rectangular box, which The Major held loosely, allowing for a black VHS tape to slide out from the bottom. I had seen these once before in the attic of our first home. The Major blew some dust off the VHS before pushing it through a panel below the TV screen. I could hear the picture firing up before it flickered onto the screen, and the sound of it sent a shiver down my arms. Deciding the picture quality wasn't up to par, The Major drew the shades closed and stood off to the side with a serious look on his face.

The report was in black and white with intercut testimonies and B-roll footage of seedy nightspots. The first man interviewed spoke eloquently about the harsh realities he and other gay men face. He also described how his sexual orientation, after years of working towards acceptance, had been incorporated into his whole self like any other piece of his identity. Mentioned in the same vein as his hair color. Simple as that.

The narrator says he's an anomaly. According to the report, the second man interviewed, obscured in shadows and shot only below the nose, represented a more accurate picture of homosexuality. This second man was indignant, explicit, and, to the interviewer, fear-inducing. Several times throughout the course of the report, the narrator highlighted the unhappiness that is bound to befall the homosexual man. Each time unhappiness was mentioned, The Major raised his hand as if to indicate that an important point had just been made.

"Most Americans are repelled by the mere notion of homosexuality," the host, a clean-cut, concerned-looking Mike Wallace, went on to say during a break between interviews.

He described a recently conducted survey next, throwing out numbers and percentages in connection to statements of general disgust and a growing interest in legal punishment. The numbers suggested that while there were more homosexuals than the girl next door might think, she could sleep soundly at night knowing that even more people wanted something done about it. Those numbers had probably been manipulated and truncated, and yet, they made it seem all the more real. In that way, numbers can be harder to dispute than words. They'd push a skeptic over the edge if they found themselves feeling torn about the conflicting testimonies presented during the interviews. Then, to really seal the deal, came a group of photos depicting late-night scenes and underground bars. These, we're told, were the places our kind could be found—bitterly aware of the condemnation from the straight world that had been so neatly summed up in those numbers just moments before.

A quick glance around the room revealed that the others were having a reaction similar to my own, which I had thought was playing out privately in my chair. Some of the boys were leaning their elbows on their knees, looking straight toward the ground, their hands pressed firmly together. They looked like they could throw up at any moment, that one more word from Mike Wallace would send them over the edge. I imagine I probably looked the same, although I couldn't tear away from the report as it crackled and burned on the screen in front of me.

"No one knows exactly how many homosexuals there are in the United States," the report continued.

The Kinsey Report, which would have been relatively breaking news at the time of the original broadcast, was still sending reverberating shock waves throughout straight America. The idea that gay men had been invading everyday life, and doing so undetected, was cause for concern. Here, the numbers were reported with significantly less confidence. Mike Wallace was unsure of how many "homosexuals", there's that word again, were skulking the streets, but the ambiguity and uncertainty achieved the same desired result. Special attention was then given to New York, Los Angeles, and San Francisco before turning, somewhat unexpectedly, to the nature of gay male relationships. In those bars and seedy underground sanctuaries would be the quick, casual sex the report had decided characterized the gay relationship. No time was given to any kind of human complexity, nor did it acknowledge the challenges that made those types of relationships more readily accessible at the time. Gay promiscuity was reported like a concrete fact—as real and quantifiable as the number of people sitting in the room.

I felt as though the eyes of the world were on me. Not only that, but I felt like they were making a judgement call I could never realistically counter. Nothing mentioned in the broadcast allowed room for response. It suddenly occurred to me that, at Galilee, it didn't matter what I thought of myself—or anybody else in the room, for that matter. All of my guesses about the nature of the people assembled around me didn't mean anything. That meant I didn't mean anything either. I wasn't the center of the story because it was a story with an already written beginning, middle, and end. What mattered started and stopped with the opinion of those running the program. Or so I thought.

As bad as everything else was, what finally broke my gaze from the TV was the accusation of promiscuity, which rang in my head: *Gays are whores. Gays are pedophiles. Gays are sickly, and they'll make you sick, too.* It reads like a secret code that has been written and rewritten, packaged and repackaged, into my head with pretty bows and false acceptances, under different names and with different faces, from every which way for as long as I can remember. The news report was no different from any other retellings of the code, but it seemed more definite. It was flipping the light on to see the cockroaches scatter for the sole purpose of reminding itself that the cockroaches are still there. More than that, it was a reminder that cockroaches get squished. I'm one of the cockroaches, scrambling to the safety of a dark corner to avoid catching the foot. I am to hide behind closets and beards, take passing as a compliment, and call the cockroach I choose to be with "partner" so as to not remind the world of the reality of my cockroach-ness.

I remember right after I came out, all I could think about was the life I would have with my future husband. I didn't know what he would look like, but I knew that he would live with me in a little home, go with me to the supermarket, and lay with me at night, watching movies in bed. It was the one thing that kept my head up sometimes—on the rainy days and Mondays. I daydreamed about the simple pleasures of life that I saw all around me, the quiet, unremarkable moments of the day that kept something inside of me looking forward. Nowhere in those daydreams was I skulking around in bars looking for dick and wishing I were dead because of it.

I wasn't the only one affected either. A boy to my left had started crying. I could see the trails of tears on his face. The Major handed him a tissue and patted him hard on the back, which only made the boy cry harder. Probably because he had reached the same conclusion as me. I started to think about what it would have been like to have seen that report when it had come out, and I started to cry too. When the video was over, The Major paused for a moment before whispering in a low, drawn-out growl: "Wow, right?"

We were all God's children, just like Adam and Eve, but like Eve, we had chosen to give in to temptation rather than do as our Father asked. We had rebelled, but unlike Eve, we were given a second chance. A chance we were to be grateful for getting at every step. In response, a sea of blank faces looked back at The Major, too afraid to move their eyes around the room. I felt my breath tighten as he continued.

"God created woman from man and intended for their union to be the beginning of a great, human civilization," he said, characteristically slowing down at the end for dramatic emphasis. "Civilization," like most of The Major's big finishes, was spoken so softly that it was practically whispered. "That is why only the union of *one* man and *one* woman can produce a child."

Line by line, The Major went through Genesis, looking up every once in a while to tell us what specific passages meant and how they proved he was justified in helping us. Early and often was the apparent policy on that one. Part one of our therapy was understanding the importance of the word of God so that we knew where the Galilee teachings came from. At one point, The Major decided that we weren't understanding the text as fully as we should and called upon us to read the lines out loud and explain what we thought they meant. I flipped through the translucent, thin pages, following the numbers as I went, until I found the passage I figured would be mine. As soon as the first boy, a soft-spoken blonde, read his line, the next to go sat to his right. My sitting on his left meant I would be going last.

Each boy before me read his line and passed the focus onto the next with factory-like precision. Their voices began to sound the same after about the fourth. There was no texture to any of the words that moved from their mouths and into the air. No one looked up either, even after they finished reading. They spoke like a child who had been caught writing something dirty in their notebook at school and was subsequently forced to read it out loud to a class of giggling peers; only no one was laughing and that was somehow worse—baritone voices singing the same note over and over. The later boys got the hint quickly: If you were stumped about what your passage meant, just talk about how you needed saving from the sin that had brought you here.

"Would you like to close us out?"

He was talking to me.

Even though I had memorized the line five people ago, I traced every word with my finger as I spoke.

"Okay, so God created man in his own image, in the image of God he created him, male and female he created them."

The Major stroked his chin and asked what I thought the passage meant. I paused to feign contemplation.

"Well, it says that we were all made in the image of God . . . so we're all God's children."

As I gave my answer, he interjected the occasional "Mm-hmm." The more pleased he seemed, the more I squirmed, making it harder to continue. Soon, I felt a burning heat rise to my face. A hum along the hazy horizon outside became a high-pitched ringing in my ears.

"And it also suggests that God is as much a woman as she is a man," I said.

This got a rise out of the other boys, who began murmuring instantly. To my surprise, The Major allowed me to continue after telling the group to calm down.

"It says right here that both man and woman were made in God's image so it only stands to reason that God would be, at least partially, female."

A loud screech broke the silence that followed, a silence which no one was brave enough to break with voice alone. Out of the corner of my eye, I noticed a wave of brown hair moving toward the center of the group. The boy who had said "Amen" at the end of The Major's introductory speech earlier that morning had now scooted his chair forward to respond.

"I disagree," he began, "because it also says that Eve was made from Adam's rib, so really woman was made in Adam's image," he said, looking pleased with himself.

"And Adam was made in God's, right?" I challenged, returning the same smug look.

I could see he wanted to respond again by the way his jaw moved around. Something was brewing and he wanted desperately to get it out; but The Major put a palm up to both of us as if to say "Slow down now" before he could. I wasn't satisfied. I wanted to fight. Here sat another gay guy believing in the very words that were being used to take him down. It infuriated me. How could he not see? I wanted us to battle back and forth until I could scream that little teacher's pet into believing I was right.

"How can you go along with any of this anyway?" I asked. "People literally use this shit to tell you you're going to hell or that you're sick or something. Stand up for yourself, dude. If this is true and we're all God's children, then you should be fine the way you are."

I spoke as fast as I could, afraid that The Major was going to cut me off, but he didn't. When I finished, he simply raised his eyebrows as if to say: "Are you done?" I felt another warm rush—this time it was embarrassment—gather on my face and rest in my ears. I shouldn't have said anything, of course I shouldn't have said anything, but I had to.

The Major's brow held its position. I tried to keep my eyes up so as to hold my ground, but the weight of the room became too much to bear. I turned my head toward the nearest window. As I turned, none of the boys in the arc dared to look at me. They weren't going to risk any kind of association with me. The Major must have known this and remained silent for quite some time, allowing me to steep in the awkwardness. When I turned back toward The Major, I noticed one of the boys had begun snickering to himself. Soon the whole arc erupted.

"I'm just interpreting the passage I was given," I said during a pause between laughter, my tongue pressed against the corner of my mouth.

The Major lowered his brow but still didn't say anything. The other boys' laughter protected them in a way because it separated them from me more than it indicated they were supportive of what I had said. Through my tongue, I could feel the heat of my face. Once again, I turned to look out the window, but this time, there was someone willing to face The Major's ire by looking at me. Sitting off toward the edge of the arc was the boy I had seen before, the one with the cloth bag.

"It's okay," he mouthed to me.

Although I knew he was being kind, the gesture made my face prickle with anger, and I spent the rest of the lesson looking down at my feet.

Day two wasn't much better than day one and only got me more concerned about how I was going to make it through the next two months. The dorm cabin had no air conditioning, but it did have plenty of flies, giving me ample opportunity to think up something horrible while drifting in and out of sleep. Just as a dream would start to come, a fly would land on my face, and I'd wake myself up with a slap. Obviously, I couldn't have another vaguely blasphemous outburst, at least not if I wanted to leave with a signed certificate of completion. The Major was an obvious complication, seeing as he was basically running the program and wouldn't be going away any time soon. *Maybe that was better? If I'm really convincing it might be more proof of how successful conversion therapy is, right? I'll be the success story. A wild homo reined in by the power of God. Hallelujah! It was bizarre how he reacted though, or rather, how he didn't. He just sat there, letting me go wild. Why?*

I was the first one up the second day and the first out of bed. Not something that could typically be said of me, but hey. Waking up at Galilee felt a little like waking up after a sleepover. There was no surefire way to shake the awkward feeling of having just done something as intimate as sleeping somewhere foreign. After taking a moment to collect myself on the edge of the bed, I waved to the guard standing by the door. It was the same guard from the night before—they rarely switched off—and we had already had our first encounter. I had needed to pee in the middle of the night and had walked over to him to ask for an escort. He tensed up immediately, never removing his hand from the baton fixed to his belt until I was back in bed and he was safe. I wouldn't have even noticed he had a baton if he wasn't so ready to use it. That was just the threat I possessed. The threat was something I carried with me to and from the cabins. It sat cradled in my arms as I moved out of my bed in the morning and took up a seat during lessons. It followed me like an evil shadow, contorting its fearsome mouth in an attempt to scare strangers when I wasn't looking. In the morning, it opened the door for me, causing the men in black who were slouched outside the chapel to perk up until I moved out of sight. We were never to be seen by the congregation and so we weren't. Only the threat that lingered behind us as we moved like ghosts through the campus was visible, and only in fleeting glances.

The guard did not return my wave, choosing instead to turn about-face and start yelling at the first person he saw.

Day two's lesson was one of the stranger ones. Not to say that any of them were particularly pleasant or thought-provoking, but even I wondered what the hell day two had to do with anything. When I walked into the lessons building, I was personally greeted by The Major

"Did you sleep alright?" he asked in a strangely warm voice.

Given my outburst during his opening lesson, I found this welcome to be more unnerving than comforting, but there was still something oddly grounded about the way he asked the question. *Did you sleep alright?* It sounded almost parental.

The group of now semi-familiar faces began to arrive and sit down in their self-assigned seats. Everybody was then handed a folder and instructed not to open it until The Major told us to do so. There was obviously a point to the activity because, a little while later, The Major looked quite happy with himself as he told us to open our folders. Behind one of the inside flaps was a piece of laminated paper explaining the activity. From the looks of it, the different paragraphs had been copied and pasted from some kind of online database. The fonts and text sizes varied almost line to line. On the other side of the folder, almost falling out onto my lap, was a collection of paper dolls. I grabbed one to inspect it. It was a woman—they were all women— barely dressed and posed with one hand on her hip and one hand pushing some of her hair back. The woman in my hands was smiling as though she knew I was looking at her, but she wasn't looking at me.

"Good morning, guys! Welcome to day two at Galilee Baptist Church. Now, we had quite the day yesterday, I believe that goes without saying, but I have something planned for today that I think you'll enjoy so I hope you're well rested and ready to go."

There was the eerie warmth again.

The Major went on to instruct us to look through the paper dolls and choose one that spoke to us in some way. He told us not to think too much about why one stood out more than another, but to pick the doll once that happened. We were to hold the doll up over our heads when we made our final choice. I picked the one on top because I figured looking through the pile would validate him in some way, which was the last thing I wanted. My doll was a thin, blonde woman in a nearly see-through bra and panties set.

"I'll give everybody another minute," he said, pausing for a moment to give the remaining boys a chance to pick a doll. "Okay, great. Now I want you to go around in a circle and tell me what you think about the girl in one word. Just one thought about her. Got it? We'll start with you."

The Major pointed to the boy nearest him, who looked down at the girl in *his* hands.

"Pretty," he said in an unconfident voice, immediately looking up for approval.

In response, The Major took a marker out of his back pocket, uncapped it, and walked over to an easel set up in the front of the room. He pressed the felt tip down and wrote "pretty" in large, sloppy letters.

"Good. Next."

"Uh . . . thin," the next boy said.

The Major shrugged and wrote "thin" on the paper and gestured with the marker for another word.

"White," a third said, sounding slightly displeased.

When my turn to speak came, most of the words I would have chosen had already been exhausted. Someone before me tried to repeat "pretty" but was asked to choose a new word. When The Major pointed at me, I looked down at the doll, tracing the outline with my finger while trying to figure out what I wanted to say about her. Finally, the word came.

"Fantasy."

"Fantasy? That's interesting. I haven't heard that one yet."

I worried that my answer wasn't to his liking, but after moving his lips around in consideration, The Major wrote "fantasy" along with the other words.

After the last few responses had been accounted for, The Major took a step back to look at the finished product on the easel. He looked happy with the collection of words, which was good for us, and told us to put away the dolls, which was even better. I put away my "fantasy" girl and handed my folder over to The Major. When all the folders had been collected, he filed them away in the big, wooden cabinet that sat in the corner of the room and returned with a set of new folders, which he distributed and instructed us to open. This folder was different from the first. Instead of a simple, flip-open school folder, this one looked more like something you'd see circulating around an office. It was a large manila envelope with a metal prong keeping the contents hidden. I opened it up and pulled out a large photo of a naked woman.

I looked down at the glossy picture, moving it around a bit with my hands to reduce the glare from the sun, and wondered what I was going to be asked to do with it. I discretely checked around the group to make sure that I wasn't the only one to have a nude photo in my folder—I wasn't—or that I wasn't the only one confused by it—I wasn't. Some of the others had a shocked grin on their faces, and one was clearly fighting back a laugh.

Like the dolls, the woman in the photo was posed like she knew she was being looked at, although her eyes were focused on something off to the side of the shot. She sat on a stool with her arms placed behind her, pushing her breasts up and out with what looked like some genuine force. Her hair was long and beautiful, with a flower-shaped clip keeping a section of it off her face.

The Major seemed to enjoy the reaction the photos were getting and waited until they dulled down to give out the next instructions. As excited as he might have been, The Major spoke clearer than he had during the paper-doll activity, carefully pausing to make sure everyone understood what he was saying.

"Okay, for the next part of the activity I'm going to have everyone go around, like we just did, and say something about the picture, but this time I'm going to give you the word instead of having you make it up. Make sense? When everyone has had a chance to go, I'll change the word. The first word is 'sexy.' Again, the first word is 'sexy.' We'll start with you. What do you think of the woman in the picture?"

The first boy looked slightly confused and jerked his head to both sides in search of some kind of help from the rest of us. We all just stared back at him, waiting to see what was going to happen. The Major repeated the question and moved behind him, looking down at the picture with a crooked smile. The boy started noticeably sweating.

"I think she's sexy, right?" the boy asked.

"Don't ask me, tell me."

"I think she's sexy."

"Very good."

The boy responded with a sigh of relief then looked around at the group again. Only this time, he was smiling. The rest of us told The Major that we thought the woman in the photo was the sexiest person we had ever seen.

"She's very sexy," I said as seriously as I could.

By the time the last few people spoke, everyone in the room was smiling, even The Major. *This is so stupid*, I thought to myself as I handed over my folder, but there was a harmlessness to the stupidity of it all. If the rest of Galilee was going to be like this, I could make it through, storing funny stories to tell back home. Knowing The Major thought he was making strides in turning me straight by forcing me to compliment a paper woman was, honestly, all that I needed to keep the rebellious comments at bay. At the end of the activity, the room felt lighter than it had when I had walked in.

After he put away the folders, The Major asked the group what we thought about the activity and smiled at the polite answers he received.

"That's great to hear!" he said. "I actually have a third activity if you'd all be interested. It's really helped some of the boys in the past."

My eyes caught his after he stopped speaking, but neither one of us broke focus. Eventually, I figured he wanted a verbal answer—from me in particular.

"Sure, why not?"

The Major gave me a thumbs up and returned for a final time to the cabinet in the corner of the room. He moved several boxes around, stacking them behind him as he continued to dig into a box I couldn't see. When The Major found what he was looking for, he turned around, revealing a large stack of loose photos. At first, I thought that these were more photos of naked women, but a heaviness soon returned to the room. The other boys soon stopped smiling, as did I when The Major handed me my photo. It was a picture of a naked man. When he was through distributing photos among the group, The Major came directly back over to me. I guess I hadn't gotten away with my comments from yesterday, after all.

"What do you think about him?" The Major asked the question knowing the answer and knowing it was different from the previous iterations of the activity.

My throat tensed up, and I could feel my heart begin to beat faster. I could also see from my peripherals that none of the boys wanted to look at their photos. They were looking everywhere but down. I didn't want to look either. Instead, I looked up at The Major and flipped over the photo, laying my hands down on top of it.

"Look at it and tell me what you think," The Major instructed.

The photo suddenly felt like it weighed several pounds, but I didn't want to keep The Major waiting. I flipped it over slowly and looked down at the man sitting in my lap. Like the woman, he was also sitting atop a stool with his hands pressed behind his back. Unlike her though, the man was looking directly at me. The photo was taken in such a way that the man's crotch was in the center of the frame. His dick was hard and extended upward toward his belly button, pointing toward a body you could, no doubt, find living in a gym somewhere. His balls rested like loose quail's eggs on his thigh. Without thinking, the words came naturally. I opened my mouth to speak, but it had run dry.

"And don't lie."

I looked back at the photo and no sooner found myself looking around the room for help, just as the other boy had done just moments ago. Everyone who I made eye contact with immediately looked away. The Major cocked his head to one side, letting me know he wanted an answer now.

"I don't know what you want me to say."

"I told you exactly what I want you to say," he said coolly. "What do you think about him?"

I felt sick to my stomach. Time had slowed down and, in the process, made my thoughts unintelligible. I felt like Alice falling down the rabbit hole, but instead of finding wonderland, I was going to just keep falling without a discernable end to the tumble in sight. I could hardly even stutter.

"I'm sorry. I can't."

"It's not your fault. You're sick."

He said it like it was a fact. As much as I wanted to look away, I couldn't look anywhere other than at his face, trying to find some indication that this was almost over. I could feel the tears beginning to well up.

"What?"

The Major narrowed his eyes and spoke almost in a whisper.

"Tell me you're sick."

I knew I wasn't sick, but I wanted the moment to end. They were just words, but they hurt like hell coming out.

"I'm sick."

CHAPTER 8

By the end of the first week, I became an expert at shutting my mouth; it wasn't surprising, and I reaped the benefits of it, too. Ever since our discussion of Genesis, Teacher's Pet didn't interact with me, and even The Major seemed to leave me alone after the naked-picture activity. He had evened out the playing field, and I was very conscious about not prompting him to do that again. Instead, I avoided participation as much as possible. Whenever I felt a comment brewing in my head, I looked upwards and counted the tiles on the ceiling, finding shapes in the indents like I used to do when I was bored in class. If I really felt as though a thought couldn't be contained, I would motion to the guard to walk me over to the bathroom, and I would sit on the toilet for a while. It was cramped and putrid, but it was also the only place I could be left alone for a minute; and so, I grew to love it.

Like most places that we were allowed to use at Galilee, the bathroom was in a state of disrepair, another abandoned space with no pressing need to update. Anything nicer might have allowed us to forget our sin. Every other morning, we were given the option to shave after brushing our teeth. When we chose to shave, the door to the bathroom was held open by the boot of one of the guards. A discolored oval in the middle of the toilet seat led me to believe that I wasn't the only bathroom refugee. There were others who found respite there, looking at the poorly painted walls, where splashes of color cut over light switches and the knobs of a coat rack, which was loosely screwed into exposed drywall. The only eyes able to see them being their own, which matched their sorrow and reflected it back in the sullen form seen in a mirror hung directly in front of the toilet.

How many of them had tested their aim and added to the dried splashes of semen strewn across it? Crusted, yellowed proof of a life still beating. I, on the other hand, chose to spend my precious few minutes alone looking out the window above the sink. If I twisted my neck just right, I could see the back of the main church building. All the important equipment needed to run the church (the rusted piping and humongous HVAC unit) that didn't keep up appearances enough to live out front was stuck in the ground in shallow holes along the siding. Apparently, we were not the only thing the congregation needed protection from.

After a few days of window shopping, I was relatively familiar with the layout of the property. Most of the dirt pathways somehow led to the main building, either by way of the dirt parking lot or a side entrance. Once I saw two men in black exchange positions from the morning to the afternoon shift. Besides the men in black though, I rarely saw any people outside. Typically, I'd spot a bird and follow it on its little journey of swooping and diving through the air and landing occasionally to call out to others nearby. I envied their freedom. One of the birds, a chickadee, I think, spent most of its time collecting debris and flying it back toward a part of the church that was out of my view. The spire was tipped with a cross that pierced upwards, and even though the squared body of the church obscured my view of the bell, I knew it was there by the shadows thrown early in the morning. The shine of the grass was disturbed every morning in the perfect shape of a bell. It started squat and rectangular and stretched beyond its recognizable form until it was nothing but a thin stripe in the grass. Somewhere near that bell must have been a little nest with a collection of squawking mouths.

Fixed to the back of the church was a decent-sized pen that held the congregation's dogs while their owners sat in nicer pens inside. I liked watching them, especially seeing their fur bounce as they frolicked with happy abandon. The sheer size of the church kept the area behind it cool and damp, and judging from the way the dogs played there, it was something they always enjoyed. I whistled at them one time, causing the commotion to screech to a halt as they looked out to find the source of the noise, but I don't think they saw me.

Another time, some kind of centipede monstrosity ran over my feet and attempted to scale my pant leg, but I brushed it off before either of us knew what was happening. The thing landed on its back and twitched for a moment, trying to flip itself over; but it had taken some serious damage from the combo hand smack and fall, and so it couldn't. I felt kind of bad for it. I don't like hurting anything, even a centipede; but it had freaked me out, so

I had smacked it. It was purely reactionary. The poor creature tried to crawl away afterward, but the back half of its body dragged lamely behind the front. For a moment, I considered whether or not centipedes get scared, and if so, whether it was scared now and trying to get to safety. Did it hate me for smacking it, or was it mad at itself for getting into that situation in the first place? My stomach lurched, but then I figured I was probably overthinking the whole thing. I was going to have to get better at controlling those feelings. To get through Galilee in one piece, I was going to have to pull strength from places I hadn't yet explored, and I would certainly have to avoid crawling up the wrong pant leg and getting swatted. I looked down at the centipede and whispered an apology before my shoe cast a wide shadow on the floor. Its remaining legs went still shortly before I stomped down my foot.

Going back to lessons after that was a challenge. Every time the wind blew sweat across my leg, I'd instinctively smack my hand down only to find there was nothing there. I'd let my hand linger on the spot longer than it had to so anyone looking at me would think it was just an itch. A totally normal itch. A nothing-to-see-here itch. In the transitional period between smack and itch, I would try to remind myself that there had been no centipede the first time, and so, obviously, there was no centipede now; but it was no use. Before long, both of my legs started shaking, slowly at first and then with increasing force. I had to lean down onto them at one point, using my weight to suppress the tremors. As I fell deeper into the fear, I imagined that the sweat on my legs had become a thick goop—a gray-green slime like the kind I had seen on the bathroom floor after I lifted up my shoe. It had dribbled down my leg onto the floor, pooling around me until the entire room was full and putrid. My mouth went dry but was no sooner filled with the taste of bile, which was as unmistakably acidic as I imagined the slime to be. I closed my eyes and swallowed hard before turning my attention back to The Major. For the rest of the lesson, my centipede nausea came in waves. The image of pooling centipede goop followed me far into the night, and after dreaming the centipede had returned to seek bloody revenge, I woke in a cold sweat and started frantically stripping my bed.

"Hey! You! Back in bed," the dorm guard said, loudly enough that some of the boys turned in their beds to see who he was talking to. I started to taste the bile again but swallowed it down before responding.

"There . . . there was a bug in the bed."

"Flip the mattress if it makes you feel any better, but there are bugs everywhere. You're in a cabin."

I hesitated, but he was obviously waiting for me to start moving. Some of the boys watched me; some watched the guard; and some of them seemed worried that their beds might also be infested with bugs. The guard widened his eyes and wound up his wrist to indicate to me that there was a time limit to the whole endeavor.

A lot of things can potentially be hiding underneath a mattress: centipedes, of course; assorted papers; hidden cash; even important family documents, like a birth certificate or someone's last will and testament. There is a whole world of potential that exists between a mattress and a box spring. I'm not sure what I expected to find underneath my mattress at Galilee when I flipped it that night, but it definitely wasn't a series of letters, which is exactly what I found.

A flurry of papers, all handwritten notes, most of them scrawled across different types of paper, dropped to the ground as soon as I hoisted up one end of the mattress. A few of them got sucked up in the quick motion of the mattress flip then came floating back when all was still again. Judging by the state of the notes—crinkled and ripped in places where someone's body weight had pressed them further into the box spring—they had to have been there for a while. Whoever wrote them didn't have a notepad sitting beside their bed either. Some of the pages look to have been ripped from a spiral notebook, although the crisp white color had begun to dull considerably. Some were scratched on small scraps of card stock—one blue piece had been torn to look like a heart. They were love letters. And they were written with a sense of frantic necessity.

"Thank you for talking to me last night. It felt so good to hear your voice, even for a moment. It's becoming harder and harder to get through the days here without it, so thank you for making me smile."

None of the letters were addressed to anyone or signed by anyone. The author must have had a hard enough time getting out the few words that they did. The words were scribbled mostly, some illegible, but even in the shortest exchanges, there was an intensity to them. Whoever wrote these messages was willing to risk getting caught just to write down a few words to the person on the other end. And now I was the person on the other end, and so the words came alive again. I collected the papers together as quietly as I could, careful not to allow even a shuffle or fold to signal to the dorm guard that something other than mattress flipping was going on. I even grunted a couple times to give the impression that I was struggling under the weight of the mattress. (It wasn't convincing.) I folded the notes as neatly as I could and shoved them into my pockets before finishing the bed.

"Alright, let's move this along now, you've had your fun," the guard complained, figuring I should be asleep by now.

"I have to use the bathroom," I responded flatly.

"You went earlier."

Well, I have to go again, dumbass.

"I mean, to wash my hands. There was something under the mattress," I said, looking down at my hands with a disgusted frown to really sell the urgency.

"Fine."

Yes!

The guard walked over to my bed, popped off one corner of the fitted sheet, and made a face as he ran his pointer finger over the plastic covering. It was hard to tell whether he didn't believe me or if he was genuinely interested, but either way, it was enough to keep the attention of the other boys—many of whom began shuffling in their beds until they were facing me. The guard rubbed his finger and thumb together vigorously while deciding if the dust was worthy of a bathroom escort. He wiped his hand along the side of his pants, leaving behind a stripe of tan-brown dust, then swiped his pant leg once more before looking over at the door and then back to me. The dust did warrant a bathroom escort after all.

The cricket chorus was well into their nightly program when the guard stepped in front of me to open the screen door. The chirping was overwhelming, erupting from everywhere and nowhere all at once. You could search the night forever and never find the source of the racket. A few fireflies flicked here and there, but they were as quiet as I was and produced only a small *zip* as they flashed on and off. The guard had a light of his own—black like his uniform—that he used to illuminate the path to the bathroom.

Sometimes as he walked, his hand would jerk a little to one side, and I'd see a bit of the property that I wasn't supposed to see, like a picnic table dressed in midnight tartan or squirrels fighting over scraps. This was a trip of necessity, not a second tour.

The only sound that competed with the crickets was that of cars moving slowly down a road just out of sight. I could guess where they were going as well as they could guess what was happening at the little church on the other side of the road. As I walked beside the guard, the sound of rumbling cars drew nearer. A pair of bright headlights flooded the walkway, causing me to tighten my grip on the letters in my pocket. The lights threw a white tint on the trees around us and caused the squirrels to dart up the nearest tree, abandoning their fight for food. The driver yelled a quick apology at the guard, probably after seeing that he was with me, and drove away, sending the light in a different direction. In response, the dorm guard raised his hand to the driver and strobed his flashlight before aiming it once again on the path in front of us. As the car drove away, I heard it creak to a stop at the entrance of the church grounds before the engine sputtering was finally replaced by the crickets continuing their song. Although I wanted to give some indication that I knew the guard had broken decorum, I kept his secret safe because I had one of my own. One that was burning a hole in my pocket.

When I got to the bathroom, I clanked the toilet seat down to warn the guard that he might have to settle in for a minute. I knelt down on the floor and spread out the letters in front of me. My eyes poured over them, trying to take in as much as I could, knowing full well the clock was ticking.

On one of the letters: "I'm sorry to hear about your aunt. From what you told me it sounds like she had a great life. I know that doesn't make it any easier, but it's something. We can talk about the funeral when you're ready, but I should probably let you know that everyone already has. You're the first person to leave and actually come back! I'm glad you did though, and thanks for the candy!"

On another: "I want to take you to the beach this weekend. Circle Yes or No." Option Yes was circled several times with a blue crayon.

I couldn't quite believe what I was looking at. The notes couldn't have been more than a few months old, but they seemed ancient. "Circle Yes or No." It was all so innocent. The guard knocked at the door, and I scrambled to pick up all the papers. As I did, I noticed a sticky note pressed to the back of one of the letters, which read: "If you're here for conversion therapy, please keep these letters safe and remember who you are. If you're a guard, fuck off."

"Times up, bud. As they say: shit or get off the pot," the guard said before rattling the doorknob.

I wanted to know so badly if the boys in the letters got together outside of Galilee, and something in that hope sparked something entirely different inside of me. The guard knocked again. As I flushed the toilet, I tore the notes up and threw them into the spiraling water. No guard was ever going to find them. Fuck off indeed.

***

Weekends at Galilee meant a break from traditional lessons in favor of more, as The Major once said, "contemporary, hands-on approaches." Basically, what that meant was they had found new ways of doing the same old thing.

The first weekend, the chairs in the lessons room were arranged around mismatched desks instead of in an arc.

Some of the desks were tall and ragged, and some were short and propped up with a book. Atop each one, a sliver of a tree trunk sat, which was carefully hollowed out to house an assortment of pens and markers, most of which barely worked. *Very rustic.*

Before The Major gave out any sort of instruction, the other boys had already broken off into groups and were happily chatting away. Most of them had already made friends with each other by that first weekend, and I can't blame them for that. Sometimes a friend is all that stands between you and the end of your rope. My strategic distancing had created the impression among the group that I was the aloof one, and no one was willing to give the aloof one much of a chance. It was too much to be here in the first place; no need to take on a desperate case. As the boys continued to talk among themselves, The Major walked around the room, passing out long pieces of cream-colored poster paper adorned with a hand-scribbled cartoon person on the front. As he snaked around the room, he explained the activity.

"Today we have something new for you guys to try," he said, reaching over someone's head to hand a stack of posters to another table. "If you'll all take a moment to look down at your paper, you'll see a blank slate." He paused. "Now, I want each of you to grab a pen and fill up the body with as many things as you've learned so far about the homosexual lifestyle. I want you to fill it as you've been filled." He pointed to each table and grinned, showing his teeth. "And . . . GO!"

I looked down at the body laid out in front of me and felt oddly protective of it. I didn't want to write anything in or outside its lines because I knew we were probably going to have to rip up the paper and burn the pieces afterward.

That's usually what happened with the weekend activities: we'd first speak ourselves into existence and then kill the imposter. I always knew which was which, but some of the other boys were losing the ability to distinguish between the two. They would become the real success stories of Galilee: the ones who'd walk away no less gay than they had come in; but they'd be shelled out and confused about who lives inside them now, doomed to walk around as an imposter in another person's reality.

I took the marker closest to my hair color and began drawing lines until the mop on the cartoon's head looked enough like the one on mine that someone else could have guessed who it was. I went on to recreate the outfit I had on—jeans with rips in the knees and an orange T-shirt—and pushed the finished product forward to indicate that I was done. While I waited for everyone else to finish, I thought carefully about how I could justify my drawing should The Major ask. I felt out of the woods for the most part, but there was always the fear that he might single me out as he had done before. I decided the drawing showed how even normal-looking people could be suffering from sin and figured he'd be at least satisfied with my effort.

Once the other boys finished their frantic scrambling, The Major asked us all to stand up and follow him outside. In response, the boys looked around their respective groups at each other and started whispering. Even my interest was piqued. I cocked my head and looked toward The Major, awaiting what was to come. This was, after all, the first time any part of *any* lesson took place beyond the walls of the second building, so none of us hesitated. I couldn't have cared less about the activity anymore, but I was very much conscious about taking every opportunity for a change of scenery that came my way. I certainly wasn't going to be the one to ruin it for everyone else either. Whatever was about to happen was a mystery, but after the week I had, the mystery was a welcome change of pace.

Everything about Galilee in some way or another was a carefully crafted mystery, with each twist put into motion by unseen hands. I never knew for sure what was happening from one day to the next, and that was the point. Life on campus began and ended by the words of eerie, enigmatic employees who moved like they either didn't exist at all or had always existed, right here, at Galilee. They were stock characters, placed by some cosmic power to inhabit an otherwise uninhabitable life, like the shoe-shine-haired old women sitting in casinos pressing the same button for the rest of time.

Besides The Major, who referred to himself as Major Faunce only once, none of us knew the names of anyone who worked at the church. The guards were simply called dorm guard and lessons guard and didn't possess any remarkable qualities that distinguished them from each other. Both were bald, hated us, and were always there. That was all we needed to know. No one was really different from anyone else in that sense. I wasn't even confident about the names of the other boys. This was something I realized as we lined up behind the lessons room door.

"The Mystery of Galilee" then continued as we made our way down a dirt path and over toward the side of the main church building. The Major spent the entire trip walking backward to keep a close eye on us. On weekends, The Major would turn in his priest garb in favor of street clothes, usually rotating between three plaid shirts: blue, darker blue, and red. More relatable, I guess. He faced away from us at one point to look for a place to stop, revealing a large sweat stain that ran the length of his back. From the looks of it, he had spent the morning huddled over a computer. After pausing for a moment at the edge of the property—at the spot where I imagined the car had waited the other night—The Major led us to a part of the grounds that was not shown to us during the tour: a large field across the street from the church.

Hearing cars was one thing, but seeing an operating road so close to Galilee was nothing short of unsettling. Everything about why I was there seemed to live in a time outside of the one I was actually living in. In the Galilee world, cars were an anachronism, and yet, there they were passing by my face. There was a short path visible from the road and flanked on both sides by thick, dry underbrush, which was mostly comprised of raked sticks and decomposing leaf litter. Eventually, the path opened up to reveal a massive field. Two circular bales of hay sat off to the corner of the field, but what I noticed immediately was something different, something numerous and frightening. At first, I thought that I was looking at bare scarecrow posts, enough to keep the property safe from furred bandits, but simple enough to save a good pair of overalls from going, well, to the birds. Once my eyes adjusted to the bright sunlight, I noticed more and more of them. They weren't scarecrows at all—they looked a lot like crosses.

By the time I had figured it out, the other boys had taken notice of them as well. They turned to each other and started chattering nervously, almost missing that The Major had stopped moving and was waiting for silence. Behind the main group, a few stragglers eventually caught up and, likewise, took on a concerned look.

The Major asked everyone to stop where we were once the group was fully accounted for, and then, he moved ahead of us, looking out into the field and then turning again to address us. The crosses in the background stood perfectly still as a breeze stirred the grass around them.

"Death is not the end," he said.

Unsurprisingly, the boys went completely silent, their chit-chat cut off in an instant. The breeze in the field continued to feather by everyone as we all tried to make sense of what we had just heard. Out of the corner of my eye, I saw the cliques shuffle closer together, which left a considerable gap on either side of me. The strands of hair that fell in my face as I looked left and right couldn't be pushed away quickly enough. *I knew it. I'm not making it out alive. I should have run when I had the chance. I should have run long ago, but I never did. And now I was going to die, alone and scared in the middle of a field.* Impending death was not a feeling I would have said I identified with before, but the feeling seemed familiar. I was actually surprised at how readily available that feeling was.

I looked down at the drawing that was still in my hands and felt myself fill up with heat once more. I was angry, but more than that, I was sad. Someone was going to find a field of half-alive bodies twitching on posts, and one of them was going to be mine. It wasn't so much the death that scared me, but the thought of dying alone, with no one there to hold me or tell me that it's going to be okay. At least the other boys had that. Who knew what would become of our bodies afterward? There could very well be nothing to identify me except for body fragments and a small drawing. I liked my drawing, too.

"It is merely the beginning," he continued.

Inside me, the heat turned to rage, washing away the feeling of death that had come with the same surprising speed and intensity. I wanted to kill him, to throw *him* on the post instead and slip his body down until the wood tip came clean through his skull.

"In a moment, I will come around and staple each of your drawings to one of the stakes out there," he said, sweeping his hand slowly across the horizon line, "and then you will take turns shooting the drawing with this BB gun to symbolize moving forward from your past." He drew a small, plastic-looking gun from inside his waistband.

I felt my body go limp. My back was drenched, which pulled my shirt tight against it, and my hands shook, hot and clammy. I thought back to the letters and to the "fuck you" written on the sticky note. I had escaped the noose once again, but I really didn't like how it felt to have death linger so near this time. I wanted it far, far away from me, and like with the Genesis reading earlier, I had a realization that said: in order to do that I had to play their game, but never at the cost of losing myself to it. I had to convince everyone but myself that I could change here. I was not going on the pole today—or any day, for that matter.

The Major drew in a huge breath and doubled over with laughter. I looked at the other boys around me—all of whom stood with death in their eyes—and realized they all had thought the same thing I had.

"Oh, you thought I was gonna . . . no!" He pointed back and forth to himself and then to us for a while as he chuckled.

"I got you there, didn't I? No, none of you are going the way of Matthew Shepard today, but you have to remember what exists out there for you if you don't take the time to seriously listen to what we're saying here." The Major quelled his laughter enough to switch to a serious tone, which ended once again in a whisper and narrowed eyes.

It was all a big joke to him. He was so far removed from the path he walked that it didn't register as anything beyond a passing joke. I tried to recall what I knew about Matthew Shepard, but nothing really came to mind. He was a body tied to a post with a bloodied face cleaned partially with tears. They always said that part, too, the bit about the tears. If only he hadn't gotten in that car. If only he hadn't been gay. Maybe there would have been more for me to remember.

Each time the BB gun fired, my body jolted a bit. My skin, cold despite the sun, ran pale, and a sickly green throbbed around the veins in my wrists. After seeing the color, I tucked them away under my arms. I used to do that with papers during college. I didn't carry a backpack and never seemed to time it right. Skies would be clear when I went into the library, but not when I came out, and so I had to tuck the freshly printed pages under my arms and hope the long trek back didn't destroy them. Where was the rain now?

Everyone quietly handed over their poster and took turns grabbing the gun with very little hesitation when The Major asked. Pressing the trigger sent some of their arms flying, but for the most part, it was smooth shooting. Before The Major came over to me, he stopped by one of the cliques and called upon the tallest person. All I saw was a jagged bob, swept neatly over an ear, move away from the group and further into the field. The Major quickly got irritated when it became obvious that this shooter was having a particularly hard time with the gun. Although I had successfully committed myself to not paying much attention to what happened to the others, I could feel my convictions wavering as The Major walked over to the shooter and leaned really close to their face. Up to that point, there had been an audible pattern to the activity. First came the clicks of the stapler, one for the top of the paper and one for the bottom; about thirty seconds later came shooting instructions from The Major; and finally, *boom*. Only, there was no *boom* with the tall one, only yelling. I avoided looking for as long as I could.

"I'm not gay, I've told you that a thousand times. I AM A GIRL!"

With that, my head snapped around. A few of the boys went over to her, and a few others stood between her and The Major. In my aloofness, I missed that one of the other boys wasn't actually a boy at all. The girl among us was shaking more than I was. She stood with her legs apart, bending her knees slightly to maintain a grounded stance. She kept the BB gun in her hand pointed at the forehead of a boy who had moved in front of The Major. She had a fierce look on her face. The boy in front of her, a friend I assumed, pleaded with her to put the gun down, but she wasn't listening. I don't know what The Major had said, but it had been enough to cause her to snap. And snapping wasn't good here. *Note to self: don't snap.*

The Major slowly craned his neck and said something into the walkie-talkie that was clipped to his belt, and almost instantly, the dorm guard and the lessons guard came charging into the field and grabbed the girl by the arms. In the resulting struggle, one of them was able to smack the BB gun from her grip.

"You fucking piece of shit, I didn't do anything to you. Why did you do that?" she cried, throwing herself to the ground. As she writhed under the weight of the dorm guard, who kept a knee pressed against her shoulder blades, the girl used one last burst of energy to throw her poster toward the crowd of onlookers. "Look what he did to my drawing," she cried out to us.

No one wanted to look. We stood as still as we possibly could.

I remember once in high school when these two girls who had developed something of a feud over the summer were placed in the same English class—my English class—at the beginning of the year. On the first day, one of them called the other one a bitch and pounced at her, pulling out her hair by the fistful and punching her ribs as she dragged her across the carpet. The whole class sat frozen in their seats. I think we would have let the girls attack us before we ran. I felt the same cool, scared feeling as the girl was dragged out of sight.

The Major took a moment to tuck his shirt back in— he wore the red one that day—and while he did, I looked down at the girl's drawing. She had ignored the assignment, which is probably why he was so mad, and had chosen instead to write positive things inside the bubble. "Beautiful. Smart. Strong. Powerful." She had written the words in a kind of bubble font and had filled them in with bright colors: yellows, oranges, pinks, and purples. That must have royally pissed off The Major because it looked like he had taken his own marker and scrawled slurs across the body in all capital letters, cutting through the words she had written for herself.

The grass was much taller in the field than it was around the church—or any of the other buildings for that matter. When the wind blew, the tips of the blades tickled my ankles. The church was still partially visible behind me, including the large bell, which had just started to toll as the girl was mounting her standoff with The Major. A flutter of wings came out from the bell tower as a family of birds flew to the nearest tree. Once The Major had stabilized himself, he walked over to me and snatched her drawing from my hands. The back of his hair was matted. During the fight, he had taken a fall trying to get out of the way. There were also chunks of dirt tumbling onto his back as he made his way to the next cross. My cross. He stapled up my body, and I looked at his face for a sign telling me that I had done the assignment correctly, something to show that he believed me. That he thought I was changing. He smoothed out the paper with a pass of his hand and moved on to the next boy. The routine had changed. The Major walked along the line and tacked up the rest of the drawings before handing me the gun.

The bell continued to toll as I took the gun in my hands. The sound of it reverberated through the field, bouncing around the branches and over the bales of hay. In my ears, the ringing knocked on my eardrums in a high-low pitch pattern. *Ding . . . dong . . . ding . . . ding.* And then it was gone. In its place came an almost electrical-sounding buzz as the sun moved out from behind a cloud. The Major was telling me something, but I couldn't hear him. The buzzing intensified, and I opened my mouth wide to clear it, popping my jaw in the process.

"Let's go faggot!" The Major's face was beet red, and he was moving quickly through the crowd and back toward me, his arms waving.

Once the ringing stopped, everything seemed to go still. I heard the sound of my heart beating and the grass moving, but everything else was silent. Even The Major, who was still yelling something at me, was muffled by the beating. *Buh boom buh boom.*

I raised the gun up, steadying myself as I did, and

turned the stout barrel toward The Major, who abruptly stopped yelling and dropped to the ground. The tall grass covered most of his body. The other boys dropped too until I was the last one standing.

Boom.

I shot the mop clean off my head.

CHAPTER 9

I needed sleep. Perhaps more than ever before, but it just wouldn't come.

My whole body felt heavy, dragged down by a constant, overwhelming fatigue that pulled at my eyelids and yet denied me of sleep. I hated how small my world had become in such a short period of time. Nothing at Galilee was in any way my own. At night, my head landed on their pillows, which were uncomfortable and thin, and I woke only to listen to their words about me, with no value assigned to the *me* they spoke of. I had become something understood only by words that were not my own. It didn't matter to them who I was; it only mattered that someone was there in front of them. In those moments of need, I was someone, but then, when those moments past, I was gone again. At night, I'd lie awake in darkness, afraid that if I fell asleep the walls would close in on me just a little bit more. I slept only when my body couldn't take it anymore and shut itself off. The little sleep I did get was spent in the fetal position with my hands stuffed down the front of my pants. I didn't want to be touched by anything. Only myself.

I thought about what went down in the field, replaying every agonizing detail in my head. The more I thought about it, the more surreal it seemed. I had come in prepared for the fire and brimstone of the first few days, but I had never expected anything to boil over into actual physical violence. I was also surprised at how readily available my own anger was. There was a line. There had to be a line, right? An un-crossable, mutually respected line. If I had expected that physical violence was possible, I wouldn't have ever smiled during the activity with the paper dolls. I had been careless, but how would I have known what awaited us on the other side of the street?

I shouldn't have pointed the gun at The Major, I know that. But then again, it's all foggy, right and wrong. I wasn't going to shoot him; I only wanted him to think I was. *Look, he threw the golden rule out the window first.* I just hated what he did to her drawing. The slurs were still stuck in my mind. That's what we were to him at the end of the day, and I don't believe he was ever going to think differently. Still, I couldn't help but wonder how things escalated so quickly.

I should have shot him when I had the chance, but I didn't. And now I can't sleep.

The look in his eyes as I held the gun to him looped in my head. He had half-smiled before taking to the ground—a thin, evil grin that said: "Do it, I dare you." It makes sense, too. Had I shot him, he would have had bountiful receipts to show how unruly we were and a concrete reason to dispense any punishment he saw fit.

If that odd smile made up for one part of my sleepless night, thinking of the impending punishment accounted for the other. Electroshock therapy was the foremost thing on my mind when I thought about punishment at Galilee. Especially after the boundaries proved themselves to be more than a little loose. There doesn't seem to be a way to separate conversion therapy from the electrodes and circus contortions associated with shock treatments. When I thought of it, it came in flashes of gray: a steel table lined with crinkling paper, to be changed when a new body took my place; dirtied, grayed-out cotton on the insoles of the electrodes; and the black-and-white images of men with their dicks out, to be shown as the shocks came.

The Major had stayed on the ground long after I shot the gun. Another boy had dislodged his poster from the cross with a near-perfect kill shot, which sent the paper fluttering toward the grass below. Its final resting place ended up being in front of where The Major would soon fall himself. While on the ground, he traced the lines on the fallen poster, looking at it as if it were the last thing in the world. I could have shot him then, too, I suppose. That's not what I wanted, though. I wanted him to see me fire the gun and to know it was him I envisioned at the other end of its barrel. Like with my first outburst, though, he didn't address me during the aftermath. He didn't even look up. *Why did that drive me crazy?* He knew I wasn't going to shoot him.

I could sense that trouble was watching me from over the horizon, so my next thought exercise was what my defense would be when trouble inevitably descended from its place high atop the hill. I tried to imagine how I would be painted. What I would be accused of. Devil-child seemed too intense, so I eventually settled on godless heathen and planned my counter accordingly.

I don't hate religion. I really don't. I don't actively

choose to seek it out either, but it's not like I dedicate time to dwelling on the subject of religion in a negative way. When I'm asked to think about it, as I was at Galilee, my feelings run more toward pain—something along the lines of a gut punch. Though I've never read the Bible in its entirety, or any religious text for that matter, the presence of its messages is nearly unavoidable. There may be a wall between church and state, but there doesn't seem to be much of anything between the church and me. This level of transparency has so solidified in my brain that I don't need to go to church to know that God hates me. (If that's what I was supposed to be learning at Galilee, they were too little too late.) I haven't heard His opinion on the matter directly, but there are hefty crowds of people claiming to have heard that exact thing. I guess I've never felt the need to read the book myself when I've got the cheat sheet at my fingers.

At Galilee, the expectation was that I could be saved through a committed attempt to gain access to the religious part of my soul that had laid dormant up to that point, tucked away in some watery cave inside of me. As if it's something inherent in me, in all of us, but I don't believe that's true.

You're getting distracted! Remember the defense!

What I do believe is that religion is a complicated thing. It means different things to different people based on a number of different factors. To me, it's a heavily weighted afterthought or a wound I've come to live with because I know how to treat it. To someone like my Aunt Patty, though, it's a constant reminder of the value of a redeemed life. *So yeah, complicated.*

Patty turned to religion after a long-fought battle with the bottle, although it might be more accurate to say "bottles," as she had not discriminated between glass and prescription. Her drinking got her all but ostracized from the family, but why that was, I'm not exactly sure. Most of that happened when I was too young to understand what was going on. That being said, I do remember that my mother and her siblings would gather in our living room every couple of months to talk quietly about "the wild one." It all sounded very exciting to little Julien, and I can remember slinking along the wall trying to avoid detection as I tried to hear more; but I always got caught and sent back to my room before the conversation of "the wild one" moved outside. There, her issues were discussed under a cloud of cigarette smoke.

I've always felt a kind of celestial kinship with Patty even though I've never really gotten to know her. She's in the back of a few early birthday photos of mine, but if you're not looking for her, she easily blends into the background. Her hair, a neglected blonde, was usually messy, although not messy enough to draw comments, and she wore shapeless, pocketed dresses, which seemed in the photos to stay perfectly still. Even the fabric she wore was hesitant to take up space. Being gay, I always feel a level of discomfort around my family because I can easily imagine them talking about me under puffs of tobacco while someone else listens on the other side of the wall. Patty was kind of the opposite because I don't think she ever knew how talked about she was. She never wanted attention, preferring instead to find ways to evade it. She liked escaping more than anything else in the world, but she would go on to choose darker and darker modes of escape.

After many failed attempts at sitting with the grown-ups while they would patronize "the wild one," I gave up eavesdropping entirely and developed something of a resentment for the way they treated her. The gatherings quickly revealed themselves to be less based in empathy and more of an attempt to distance themselves from their own problems by focusing on someone else's. It was a trade-off designed to soothe the ego. For a few hours, no one else's problems would be interrogated. Interestingly enough, I heard more of their musings when I stayed in my room. Without the threat of their words leaving the living room, my aunts and uncles would speak louder and with more confidence. I heard my mother comment once that if Patty hadn't quit her job at the bank and run off with Jimmy, she might not have lost everything and turned to "the stuff." I was confused at what "the stuff" meant, but more than that, I wondered how my mother could talk like that when we had much less money than the aunts and uncles thought. How cruel they'd be if they were to find out. In a sick way, even as a child, I started to understand why she said it and the itch those gatherings scratched for her.

Several years into early adulthood, I ran into Patty at a craft show. Seeing her in person felt like seeing a reclusive celebrity in the flesh. My heart pumped a little harder as I walked up to her table. I'm almost confident that she knew who I was, but she didn't say anything beyond a quick plug for her sea glass jewelry company, She Sells Sea Glass.

"It's all real sea glass that I recovered from a beach near Onset bay. I don't use shells or anything like that. Just taking what we put in the ocean in the first place. The settings are all recycled pieces, too."

She was wearing several pieces of the jewelry herself. In fact, everywhere you looked there was sea glass. In her ears, on her wrists, and around her neck. She could tell I was looking at her necklace and laid a tanned hand over it before launching into a quick story about the day she had found the largest piece of sea glass, which was set in the middle of the necklace.

"I used to be an alcoholic."

"I'm sorry to hear that," I said.

The stuff, I thought.

"I don't say that for sympathy or anything. It's just part of the story is all. This piece was the first one I ever found. I never thought about sea glass before that, but I saw it on the shoreline and, I don't know, I just felt compelled to take it home with me. I think maybe God put it there for me to see. I just liked how beautiful it was. Of course, I know it's a broken piece of a beer bottle, but it was so smooth. It looked like something new, you know? It's a good reminder."

Patty gave me her card and smiled as I walked away. I pulled out my phone when I got to the car and went to her website. The first thing that loaded was a large photo of her standing in front of a small trailer with a huge smile on her face. Around her neck hung a large cross made of, of course, sea glass. Both of her hands held sea glass wind chimes, which that trailed almost to the ground. They caught the light of the sun and cast a rainbow over her cheek. She didn't blend into the background at all.

At 2:15 a.m. the morning after I had pointed the gun at The Major, a shadow crept across my blanket and crawled up the wall, growing larger as its source closed in. The time stands out in my mind because watching the clock was a hobby of mine at Galilee. Any information I could take as my own helped to restore some of the power I lost daily. Not to mention, it gave me something to do at night when I grew restless. No matter what else was left to uncertainty, the clock was a constant. *Tick. Tick. Tick. Tock.* The sound, patterned and unvarying, grounded a world that traversed clock hands with an otherwise unbound carelessness.

"Get up. The Major wants to see you." The voice, belonging to the dorm guard, moved roughly through the words in an almost staccato fashion. He was in business mode. "Now," he demanded.

As warm as summer days on campus were, nights quickly moved in cold air, chilling the cement floor of the dorm building. If my body had trouble shedding the heat of the day when I laid down for bed, I'd sometimes hang a leg over the side of the mattress to nurse the heat. When my feet feathered down upon the floor next to the guard at 2:15 a.m. that fateful night, the cold cement sent goosebumps across my body.

The dorm guard didn't give me time to put on shoes, so I walked behind him with bare feet, unsure of where he was taking me. He hurried along quickly, the material of his pants swishing rapidly. The dorm guard stopped only once to nod at the lessons guard, who was standing out on the porch waiting to take over. Before stepping out, I looked up at him and then back into the dorm building—everyone else was still fast asleep. Behind me, the screen door squeaked back and forth as we made our way into the night.

Blackness extended in all directions, an open and vast world much larger than the one that lived inside the walls of the dorm building. Out here, no fan swirled over my head, and the bugs, although plentiful, couldn't be heard banging against lights plugged in here and there. The night was still and immediate, providing no time for adjustment. Under my feet, gravel shifted as I followed the outline of the guard's body across the campus. One foot sunk into a patch of wet grass, indicating that we were getting closer to the dog pens I would watch from the bathroom window. As we neared the back of the church, a light flashed on, causing the milkiness of the nighttime fog to take on a sickly glow. Quietly, the guard opened the back door of the church, the one I would see so many others walk through in the light of day, and pressed his hand between my shoulders when I hesitated.

Everything inside the lower level was dark. The hallway was lit only by a dim stream of light that escaped from underneath several closed doors. I tried to take in as much as possible, but there wasn't much to see. If I hadn't known better, I wouldn't have even suspected that I was, for the first time, in the church itself. We turned a corner at the end of the hallway and passed the only brightly lit room in the basement, a door-less half-room decorated with a blinking vending machine, a muted TV that was strobing blue light onto the wall, and a Pac-Man video game system that was looping an electronic melody. Past the snack room, at the end of the second hallway, was a partially open door. The guard knocked on it twice.

There was some shuffling on the other side as someone made their way across the room and settled into a creaky chair. After a beat, the guard knocked again and swung the door open. The Major looked up from behind a desk in the corner of a large, but mostly bare office. On the table sat the taxidermied body of a snake, which was coiled tightly and adorned with a small, leather cowboy hat. The two shared the room with space to spare. The Major looked frustrated. I wouldn't be surprised if the dorm guard had received the message to fetch me hours before he actually did and made me late to be sure The Major was *juust* the right amount of angry by the time I was delivered. I suddenly longed for my bed, not the one there, but the one at home; soft and plush and smelling like something familiar.

"Thank you, Andrew," he said, dismissing the guard before turning to me. "Now, why don't you take a seat?"

Andrew. He had a name after all. A common name. One that I have known since childhood. There was Andrew Miller, who I went to school with—a quiet, wiry boy whose knees threatened to knock him over when he walked. And Andrew Laurel of course, who built sets for a theatre company I spent a summer with. He was a handsome guy; his hair was always styled, but never greasy. Odd how Andrew fit them all, although worn very differently.

Once Andrew left, The Major turned his eyes toward me. They were bright blue, but it was easy enough to miss the color since it was usually concealed by squinting lids. Whatever his bright blue eyes landed upon was studied carefully—archived maybe—for an undetermined later use. I averted my attention down to the snake on his desk. It was a peculiar thing to have on a desk. A peculiar thing to have in general. Keeping my eyes low, I wondered, not about its origin, but in what setting it—and its little cowboy hat—would fit in. Is there a desk somewhere on this planet or the next where the coils and leather wouldn't elicit the same questions?

"I got it when I came back from my second tour," he said. "The snake I mean." The Major picked it up and spun its muzzle around to face him as though he had forgotten what it looked like from my angle. "Me and some of the guys would go out and hunt snakes when there wasn't anything else to do over there. It became a daily thing after a while—there was never really much to *do* besides that. One of the guys got this for me one Christmas after we got back because he said it reminded him of the snakes we caught." He studied it carefully for a moment before returning it to its original position, with the muzzle facing me—another set of eyes watching. "No diamondbacks where we were though."

He adjusted its hat before continuing. "You're quite the troublemaker, aren't you?" he said with a chuckle. "No! I'm not blaming you for lashing out. I actually think you're one of the smart ones. That's why I've asked you here tonight." He corrected himself halfway through speaking to adjust his tone, adding in a laugh to break the tension. "You see, many of the boys here just *stew*. You know what I mean by that, don't you? They sit and boil when I talk to them, but they never actually say a thing. They never move, some of them! But you spilled over in the field, didn't you? You react because you listen and that's what we need. You're getting the message and I thank you for that."

I shifted in my seat as he spoke. He was lying; he had to be. There was something else to come that he was buttering me up for; I just couldn't figure out what it could be. I had seen that girl get dragged away with my own two eyes, and there was no way that she had been dragged to the same chair I now sat in to be complemented by Major Faunce. Punishment was the point of Galilee, and it would be stupid of me to think otherwise.

"I listen because I have to," I responded.

Silence.

"I'm sorry Major Faunce, I'm . . . I'm just a little defensive because I don't know why I'm here. I appreciate the compliment, but I'm looking to get out of Galilee as soon as I can. No offense."

He smiled again. The Major always waited until you had submitted to him in some way before he would smile.

"My first name is actually Gerald. It's an old family name. You can call me that from now on if you want," he said quietly. As if I were the first person he had granted this permission to. "What do you like to be called?"

"Julien is fine."

Silence again. Only this time, it was broken by The Major, who told me that I was being removed from my scheduled lessons to be put into a more rigorous program. One that, he was sure, would prove more beneficial to me since I was obviously in need of something more intensive.

This program, called Understanding Sin, was designed for men who demonstrated an inability to work within the basic program. Basically, Understanding Sin (which they called UnSin for short) was for the loud ones who needed more force and less freedom for Galilee to work properly. It sounded like detention, at the least, and at the most, like added time.

I asked if I had a choice. I didn't.

"Unfortunately, you made your choice when you spoke up. We let it slide the first time, however, we're running a program here and the success of that program is our biggest responsibility," he continued, very matter-of-fact. "Tomorrow you will meet me at the front steps of the church for your work assignment."

"Work assignment?"

The Major's mouth moved into a tight smile before he answered.

"Yes. We find that UnSin works best when coupled with routine volunteer work. Keeps the hands busy while the mind is adrift. You know what they say about idle hands." He pantomimed as he spoke, wiggling his fingers around.

The Major must have somehow alerted the guard that our time was almost over because, shortly after he told me about the work assignment, the double knock came again. Neither The Major nor the guard said anything, so I stood up and waited to see if anyone pounced, but no one moved. I made my way over to the door and whispered something under my breath about forced labor.

The Major must have heard because just as the door was closing his voice boomed: "Galilee is the world, Julien. Better get used to it."

The following morning, the sun rose on a somber scene. The other boys watched as I made my bed and left the dorm building through the broken screen door, instead of following them to lessons like usual. I could feel their stares boring through the back of my head. No doubt, I would be the hot piece of gossip for the day.

"Did you see Julien this morning?" one would ask.

"I heard he told off The Major, so now he gets taken to the church to be beaten by the congregation," another would offer.

The story would grow farther from the truth by the minute. I would be a hero to some, a traitor to others.

"Why does he get special treatment?"

Outside, the campus looked different than usual. The grass had been cut sometime during the night and now lay in alternating stripes of light and dark across the lawn. The cool air I had walked in just hours ago had been replaced by a soft heat, which dried the small patches of mud hidden in the grass and on the edges of the walkways. All around was the tingle of newness.

I was allowed to walk myself over to the front of the church and took my time doing so. Great, white clouds moved across the sky, their tails breaking off in pieces around a sun that was shining down on the green morning grass, still slicked with dew. In the moments when the cloud trails were at their thinnest, wide swatches of sunlight flickered in my eyes. Even after rubbing them away, remnants in the form of floating dots lingered.

Around the front of the church, a group of familiar faces had gathered: the boy with the cloth bag who had smiled at me before; Teacher's Pet; the boy who had stood between the girl and her gun; and the girl herself. UnSin certainly boasted an interesting assortment of people. When I turned the corner, the group broke into pleasant nods and half-smiles before turning their attention back down to their feet. Every so often, someone would wave their hand around to swat a mayfly, and everyone would look up and then back down again. Even though no guard was there to enforce anything, no one from the group dared to speak a word. I assumed everyone had the same sleepless night I had, trying to answer the same impossible question: What comes next? Something had fundamentally changed at Galilee, and everyone was on their best possible behavior because of it.

We all politely ignored the existence of the person next to us, which I accomplished by staring at a long flowerbed next to the stairs of the church. The garden was neat, no weeds or dead leaves in sight, only bushels of green dotted occasionally with the dark-red heads of the Galilee dahlias. In between glances at the flowers, I flashed my eyes over to the girl several times to see how she looked. She didn't look bruised or anything, but she did look scared. Her face was mostly red, and patches of hair were sticking out of different parts of her face. We were allowed to shave, but it looked like someone had taken that privilege away from her. I looked down at her legs to find that a layer of peach fuzz was growing there as well. Even when I could only see her from my peripherals, I could tell she was crossing and uncrossing her legs, lifting them up to scratch away the discomfort of growing hair. The girl looked as though she was hoping the ground would open up and swallow her whole.

I wondered what each of them had done to get placed in UnSin. For a few, it was fairly obvious. With those few, I felt I could guess their crime like I had guessed it the first day. But what had Bag Boy and Teacher's Pet done? Something crazy, probably. I knew Teacher's Pet wasn't all he let on to be. He was most likely trolling us because he knew of no other way to survive. *Maybe I should have been nicer to him?* Even so, it was a smug personal victory to see him down on the same level as the rest of us. He still managed to maintain an air of smugness while standing outside of the front porch, though, choosing to position himself furthest from the group and closest to the church. I wasn't the only one who noticed. The girl and her friend kept looking at him and then turning away to talk about what they had just seen. He hated us for being the same as him, but then would hate himself into being different. His hatred was so mixed up that he probably wouldn't have been able to tell you who it was he really hated. It didn't make sense. So, I decided to adopt the same policy about him that I assumed the others had of me: don't bother with a lost cause.

After some time had passed, more boys began to arrive at the front steps, one after the other in evenly spaced chunks of time. Every five minutes or so, another face would join the crowd and imitate the blankness worn by the others. It seemed as though the staff members didn't want us talking to each other—or, worse yet, conspiring in head-lowered whispers—but that was hardly an issue. If as much as a single fly had landed on those front steps that morning, we would have heard the creaking of the wood beneath its spindly limbs.

After the twelfth person had arrived, the pattern was broken. The passage of five minutes brought not another face, but the first words of the day.

"So, which one of you is Judas?" the girl asked abruptly, her voice dark and low.

"What are you talking about?" Bag Boy responded, scrunching up his face as if he caught a whiff of something foul.

"I mean, there are twelve of us, right? So, either some Agatha Christie shit's about to go down, or we're headed to the last suppa," she said, running her tongue over her teeth. "And I'm not about to be sold out by none of you bitches neither." After making an I'm-watching-you gesture and sending it our way, the girl laughed wildly to herself.

"Warmer!"

The voice took me by surprise. It surprised the girl, too, based on the way she jumped. The voice possessed the unmistakable cadence of The Major, but I couldn't see exactly where it was coming from. Moments later, the panel to a window near the front door of the church came slamming down. He had been watching us the whole time from behind a window no bigger in size than his head, and for the first time, his presence didn't fill me with immediate dread. She was the one that made the choice—to use The Major's term—to draw attention to herself, and so I felt less inclined to keep choosing after that. Part two of the "don't bother with a lost cause" philosophy is, of course: better you than me. It wasn't that I wanted the attention off of me enough to wish it on her, but I was happy with where it rested. And happier that it found her before I had to think of ways to deflect the attention myself.

The front of the church was much nicer than the rest of it, since it had been painted recently enough to maintain the illusion of being done by the stroke of one humongous brush. Not a chip in sight, although the sun would make short work of that. The railing, which was supporting my weight as I leaned against it, led up the steps to a square porch decorated on one side with a large pot of marigolds and on the other with a rocking chair, which was swaying in the summer breeze. In all, it was clean and neat, and one could easily forgive the neglect seen on the other three sides because of the church. The jangling of keys from behind the door preceded another grand entrance from The Major. Orientation number two.

"I'm going to jump right into it and answer some frequently asked questions about UnSin," he said, really milking the frequently asked questions part. "One: UnSin is a more advanced program, and so more advanced techniques will be employed to teach it. Two: complete compliance with instructions is expected. I will not tolerate anything less. Three: if you plan on leaving here with something from us, you will need to remind yourself of why you are here." The Major wagged his finger and cleared his throat before continuing. "Lastly: you will be working inside the church on days our congregation will be present. I'm sorry, let me repeat that: you'll be around when the congregation is present. You are not to be seen or heard by *any* member of the congregation. To aid this, all of your activities will take place below the first level of the church sanctuary. Got it?"

We all said yes—quickly and without attitude. There was something different about his delivery that morning, something in the military directness that was more reminiscent of The Major who had sat with the taxidermy snake than the one from day one. There were fewer theatrics, fewer attempts to move us with soft hands, and fewer things that remained hidden in the bright light of the morning.

"Good. Follow me."

I caught a glimpse of the church's interior from behind the head of the Bag Boy, who took his place ahead of me in line. The walls didn't appear to end, rather, they stretched farther than my eyes could strain from the porch. As the portal swallowed up more bodies and as I neared the front of the line, a crystal chandelier dropped into view. At my feet lay a perfectly clean carpet, red and new, which stretched to the far end of the room where an organ sat, covered by a leather duster on a shallow stage. All around me was a blue paint so light I could imagine the swatch reading "Periwinkle Prayers." We were now in the first few feet of the room, the only portion not taken up by long lines of wooden pews. Years of shuffling feet had lightened the wood floor below me, which creaked and moaned as we made our way to the first row of pews. The Major asked us to take a seat and explained that we would each receive further UnSin debriefing momentarily, but in private for legal reasons.

"So, who's going first?"

In response, we all shrank as far into the pews as possible. I didn't want to go first. I knew I had to go eventually, but somehow, first seemed like the worst option. The Major clasped his hands behind his back and moved his face into a quick frown before pacing the floor in front of the stage. Beneath his feet, the wood continued to moan, the sound of which set my teeth on edge. With each step, The Major looked at us intensely, trying to discern who should be picked to go first. The dynamic seemed to amuse him. He chuckled several times to himself before throwing his arms down to feign surprise, as if the heat from his stare was supposed to compel our arms to rise in unison. I knew The Major was capable of moving from laughing to screaming in a matter of seconds, so before the wood had the chance to creak again, I lifted my hand into the air. As I did, The Major brought his hands back up and clapped them in my direction. He was pleased. That was good.

I rose from the pew to the thunderous cracking of wood, both from the floor and the bench itself. The sound sent everyone's head snapping in my direction in a rush of equal parts relief and pity. When the room is full of people, I imagine the creaking sound travels unnoticed through the chants and songs and right out the nearest window, never heard by anyone. But since the room was filled that day with silence and dead air, the noise was finally able to be heard. In the empty air, it flipped and swelled as it pleased. The Major thanked me for volunteering and pointed toward a patch of carpeting that ran the length of the front of the stage. A set of stairs on stage left met up with the carpeting—most likely to ensure smooth transitions between speakers during mass. A few feet away, not visible upon entering the building, was a large door that he opened for me. Beyond the door was a short landing followed by seven steps leading down to the lower level of the church. My eyes wandered down to my feet and noticed they covered a grouping of carefully painted letters. When I moved to the next step, I looked back at the now legible writing.

"Sloth," it read.

On each stair in front of me—in slightly different handwriting—were the rest.

"Wrath."

"Pride."

"Gluttony."

"Greed."

"Envy."

"Lust."

The seven deadly steps to the basement.

We walked down a familiar hallway, past the room with the singing game system, and into The Major's office. This time the room wasn't bare like before. Instead, it housed a large, plum-colored leather examination table, which sat upon four locked metal wheels. There was a wet shine to the material, especially where it puckered away from the buttons that were pushed in throughout the cushions. On one end, a section of the padding curled upwards and rested on a feeble-looking metal arm. There was something glamorous about the look of it. It was like something you might see roped off in a bedroom of a Newport mansion, some exotic fainting couch from a time long past when entire lives were thrown against the feeble arms of beautiful furniture. *But why is it here now*?

The Major instructed me to sit down on the cushions, which I did, then called in a guard I had never seen before. At least I thought he was a guard at first. He wasn't dressed in black like the rest of them; he wore a long, white lab coat and carried a ratty briefcase. The cushion sank as I placed my weight against it, crinkling in spots as it made room for my body. The flesh I laid against the leather and paper twitched once it felt the wet chill underneath. I sat upright and tried to the best of my ability to focus on my breathing, which was now staggered and tense, sending a shudder to my jaw that clamped it shut. My eyes moved slowly back and forth between the two men, making sure they knew the terms of my surrender—namely, that I could still fight if that's what it came to. I had an exit strategy all planned out too. If anything happened, I would kick the nearest set of balls and make a run for it. I figured the lab-coat guard would be busy fingering through his briefcase and might not even notice what was happening until it was too late. I tucked away this image and hoped I wouldn't have to use it. Strike number three was not happening today.

I never thought that way before Galilee—never considered what weapons surrounded me, concealed, but dangerous nevertheless. However, I was now intimately familiar with images of heads pounded in by loose bricks and eyes pulled from their sockets, resting, bloodied and disconnected, in between my bony fingers. Sometimes the visions would come to me and stay until I mistook the sweat in my palms for blood. I had a secret stash of defenses hidden in plain sight: rocks, books, shoes, sticks. You just had to need them for their usefulness to become clear.

I would never have the chance to actualize my plan, though, because the lab-coat guard asked me to lay down, and as soon as I complied, The Major moved out from behind him and slapped ankle restraints on me so fast I didn't even see them come out of the briefcase. Within seconds, I was a wild animal. I twisted and jerked my legs, trying to break free. I wanted nothing more than to claw his eyes out. Strike three was less scary than what was currently happening. I kept kicking, or at least trying to, but the energy I expended just twisted my legs around. I could see my ankles turning red from the thrashing, but I kept going anyway. Looking somewhat irritated, The Major stepped back and waited until I had accepted my immobility.

"I never finished the snake story," he said when I finally stopped moving, "the other day when we spoke."

I looked at him confused, wondering what the snake had to do with anything. In response, he smiled and continued smoothly, pacing around the room as he spoke.

"The guy who gave it to me, his name was Dan, right? Well, Dan came back from his deployment that last time with one thing on his mind: going home to his *loving* wife, Ashley. He talked about her constantly, even kept her photo with him. Can you believe that? Fifty friggin' pounds of weight on his back and he's worried about carrying a picture. You want to know what happened when Dan went back home to Ashley? I'll tell you. They sit down for dinner and she's uncharacteristically quiet. *That's okay,* Dan thinks, *she's just going through a lot. I can relate to that. We'll talk about it and it'll be okay.* Well, Ashley was going through a lot alright. She was going through a list of about three different women while Dan was away. Damn near destroyed that family, too. Is that what you want? Because it's what you're gonna get!"

The Major's face grew increasingly more red. Something had happened to him while he recounted the story of Dan and Ashley that prevented him from keeping a distance from the different sides of himself. They were all blurring into one as the real Faunce came into clearer focus. This Faunce swore and, more than that, fanned a fire lit out of fear and anger that had been simmering in his belly longer than there was a snake on his desk. The anger was desert snakes, their bodies ripped open and left to bleed in the sand; it was living vicariously through unfulfilled promises and wounds that were unable to be healed. It was easier, now, to pile the snakes a little higher.

"I'm gonna say the same thing I tell my two-year-old: we can do this the easy way, or we can do this the hard way."

I stopped moving. He walked closer. My hands were still free, so I swung them at his face, striking the side of his nose and sending him reeling backward onto the floor.

"Easy-peasy," I said.

I didn't know if I should sit up or not, so I remained in the position I had just landed in after punching The Major, which was kind of slumped over. Blood streamed onto the collar of his shirt—it was the blue one this time—and squished into the floor as he pushed himself up. His dignity was still worth something, so being on the ground again enraged him. He struggled for a moment before finding his footing. He kept the back of his hand pressed firmly into the right side of his nose, but even that couldn't keep the blood from pouring out over his knuckles. I could feel my stomach rising up to my throat and moved into a more contained position, one I felt granted me more control over the situation. The Major stood for a second, his free nostril flaring, until finally he moved closer to me. My eyes widened at the sight of his nose once he removed his hand, which he twisted into a fist. He wanted to say something, but the blood was running into his mouth too quickly to wipe it away long enough to get a word out. He returned his hand to his face and stormed out of the room.

I felt old at ten. *Seriously*. I remember sitting with my grandparents at my mom's kitchen table, listening to them tell stories about living through national financial crises and major wars, and realizing how different their childhoods were from mine. Their pockets were weighed down with stories; their lives wrapped, like their hands, neatly around the handles of coffee mugs. They could have sat and told me their stories until I was as old as they were. I have never felt younger than I did in that moment when The Major was on the ground, when I realized for the first time that I wasn't—and might never get the chance to be—old.

"Tie down his hands and do whatever you need to do to shut. Him. Up," he had said before leaving the room. The sound of a slamming door followed not long afterward.

The man in white pulled out a stool from beneath the table and flopped his briefcase down on top, sifting through the contents without speaking. The chains around my ankles rattled. The man removed a small box from inside his briefcase, closed it tightly, and spun around to open the smaller box. When he turned back toward me, he was holding a set of arm restraints in one hand and a vial of liquid topped with a long needle in his other. *Easy way or hard way.* The man swished the liquid around in the vial before strapping it back into the small box and returning it to the briefcase. I raised my arms slowly and allowed him to restrain my arms, staring at the briefcase the whole time. With my arms up, I felt more helpless than before. There was no way to fight back. All my hidden weapons had now disappeared.

A moment later, the man's chair squeaked as he pushed himself away from the stool in front of him. He set the briefcase down on the edge of The Major's desk and began to assemble something out of view. I started to realize what it was as he took more pieces out of the case. At first, it looked to be a stethoscope with two prongs connected to a thin, metallic base. Unlike a stethoscope, however, this instrument had tips like huge Q-Tips: metal knobs wrapped in a white material and held together by a rubber band, which had been twisted and turned around and around until it held everything together so tightly that the ends of the fabric flared out like a peplum.

As the man began walking toward me, I could finally see the interior of the briefcase. Inside was a bizarre, 1960s-looking contraption with two vacant spaces for the electrodes to snap back into once they were off my head. The man in white moved mechanically, his robe trailing lightly after him as he drew an off-white headband with yellow sweat stains along the edges from the briefcase. Six silver knobs ran the length of the headband, spaced maybe an inch apart from each other. As the man got closer, I could see that his lab coat was embroidered with a name that had been covered with several strips of masking tape. Despite the security measure, the name was still clearly legible: "Dr. Markmann."

As he slipped the band over my head, I began to cry. Partly because I was scared and partly because I didn't want to be alone. I longed for a hand to push my hair back into place or to hold the fingers that were peeking out beyond the metal cuffs. I instinctively jerked my hands down in an attempt to cover my stomach, which was now exposed from the writhing, but the restraints prevented me from moving. My flesh was there for the taking in any way anyone else saw fit, and there was nothing I could do about it. Now it was my body I saw carved and strewn about the room.

Without any hesitation or warning, white sleeves draped over my face as Dr. Markmann hooked two electrodes onto the metal rings resting above my temples. A quiet, electronic knocking signaled the machine was on. Pushing my stomach upwards in hard, jerking motions, I begged for him to stop. My voice grew more frantic as he walked back over to the briefcase—my window of opportunity was closing fast. The fear he carried in his eyes when my wrists were freed had faded away into a look of stark indifference. It was the look of someone well used to causing pain. I was a nameless pig up for slaughter and with no clout to save my own life. The moment was one of strange clarity as I realized instantaneously, in something of a cool rush, that everything is carried out by human, not divine, hands. Electroshock therapy, like the hatred that fueled its usage, was as human as the man currently gearing up the machine.

My pleas were, I realize this only now, for me and me alone.

Under my writhing, the leather cushions squeaked and crinkled. The man looked into my eyes only once as he secured the knobs to my head. I went to scream, but my mouth was no sooner filled with a rubber mouth guard that tasted strongly of dust. Moving away from me, Dr. Markmann sat down on the stool, parting his coat to rest the briefcase contraption on his lap. He flipped a switch after turning around to face the wall opposite me, and with the turn came the sound of a power grid switching on. I braced myself against the restraints at full force, hoping to snap my limbs and stop the coming shock. Nothing broke free from me except a small squeak in response to a sharp pain in my teeth from grinding them against the mouth guard. When I couldn't hold the position anymore, my body slumped into the cushions under it. My eyes had shut. From the other side of my closed lids came the drooping sound of a machine powering down.

I must have passed out or, at least, forgotten the pain of the shock because my brain had been scrambled. I thought quickly of how much I could still remember. My name: Julien Grant. Where I was: Galilee. There was no memory of the shock, though. The man in white removed the band from my forehead and tucked it into the side of the briefcase before snapping the electrodes back into the velvet interior of the briefcase and vanishing through a door I could not see.

The only movement I could manage after Dr. Markmann left was rubbing my ankles together. A sickness was gathering at my Adam's apple, but not the kind that threatened to burst forth. It was the kind that would soon sink and settle, maintaining its hold for the foreseeable future.

As I started to come to my senses a bit and felt confident that I hadn't suffered any cognitive damage, I tried to recall what just happened in greater detail. That's when another detail cropped up. When Dr. Markmann had removed the headband, the electric knocking started again, only this time it sounded hollow and cheap. I saw the knobs as they clicked into place and noticed, just behind the thin layer of cloth, that there was a grid similar to the one you'd find on a pair of cheap over-the-head headphones. The whole apparatus was nothing more than a toy.

I was still shackled when the doctor left, and as the adrenaline began to wear off, I assessed the damage my thrashing had caused. My wrists and ankles ached from the constant banging, and I could feel at least two places where the skin had broken on my ankles and leaked blood onto my toes.

Alone on the table, I allowed myself to fully weep.

The blood on my toes had just about dried when the dorm guard came a few hours later. He hesitated at the door when he saw me on the table, but came over and unshackled me a moment later. His hesitation read to me more as surprise—like he genuinely didn't expect to walk into what he had just walked into. My body was weak, and I had to lean against him as he walked me back to the dorm building. Rain had come while I was inside, spreading grass seed into the gravel pathway and filling the holes in the ground with cool, brown water. The mud felt good against the cuts on my ankles. Once we neared the entrance, the guard transferred my weight to the side of the building and reached down into his pocket. He pulled out a card and instructed me to start using the name that was printed on it. I looked down at the card to find the name "Peter" written in messy handwriting. On the other side of the card, in the same handwriting, was the following note: "Disciple. Fisherman in the ancient sea of Galilee."

I held the card in my hand and pushed away from the side of the building. When the guard saw I could walk on my own, he went ahead of me into the building and started yelling at someone inside.

Peter.

I stared at the letters as I made my way down the center aisle toward my bed, while everyone else looked at me wondering what had happened to me and whether it was about to happen to them.

CHAPTER 10

My work assignment was in the rec hall located in the basement of the church.

The Major was being generous when he called it a "hall." The room was no bigger than most of the other offices on the floor, which themselves looked to be converted classrooms of some kind or another. Light tan patches of color in the rec hall's otherwise golden carpet gave away where desks or bookshelves had once been placed and never moved. The whole room smelled of unwashed curtains and dried flowers. Every step drew the smells closer until they were all but unavoidable. Stale lavender burned in my nose most days. There were live flies buzzing around the curtains trying to get out, and dead flies laid on their backs along the windowsills, which sat above a lengthy, dusty shelving unit with books and DVDs scattered across it. The windows would open with some effort and stir the air (and the lavender), but most of them slowly closed on their own unless otherwise propped up with one of the many yellowed books.

UnSin, to my understanding at least, didn't really exist as a part of the national conversion therapy program. It was more of a Galilee-unique byproduct of the system, something thrown together to quell any murmuring uprisings, which it seemed to do to great success by removing the troublemakers and placing them underground. The Major told me there had been several waves of UnSin participants in the past, including some who had been stationed in the very rec hall I was soon to call home. Others, and this was true of the UnSin wave I was a part of, worked in various locations around campus, some in the kitchen and some on the grounds, but the work generally seemed to be centralized around the basement of the main building—close enough that we could be monitored at the staff's discretion. That being said, staff infrequently—if ever—actually checked up on us. UnSin allowed them to dedicate their full attention to the more malleable minds in the program while simultaneously delegating unwanted in-house chores, like maintaining the rec hall or organizing the church's archives, to the mouthy ones.

Almost all twelve of us worked in and around the basement except for Teacher's Pet who worked with The Major cleaning the chapel sanctuary for worship services, something I knew about only by word of mouth, but believed anyway. As our contact with Teacher's Pet lessened, his presence among us grew stronger. We gossiped almost daily about what he could have done to get that placement as we made our way down the seven deadly steps to the first-floor basement every morning, way before any other heads had risen from their pillows. I welcomed the gossip when it came. Gossip meant fewer things would remain hidden, and even fewer moments would be available for the others to ask about what had happened to me in The Major's office—and I wasn't going to be talking about that to anyone. *Ever.* Gossiping granted me space to think beyond myself for a moment, and for those couple of seconds, I could worry about Teacher's Pet and put off worrying about what else might happen to me that I would have to keep hidden forever. And truth be told, I was a little curious—maybe morbidly so—about the whole thing. Hitting The Major in the face after pointing a gun at him didn't warrant anything even remotely as bad as more contact with him. *Jeez, what did Teacher's Pet do anyway?*

The rec hall was longer than it was deep, with windows running the length of the outside wall. It was actually one of the few windowed rooms in the whole basement due to its being situated lower within the hill that the church grew out of. Toward the flowerpots and railings at the front of the church, the hill hugged the building so tightly you'd never know there was anything beneath it.

In the middle of the room, there was a table topped with a large, colorful puzzle, which itself was topped with a sheet of Plexiglas intended to preserve the completed image. Rather, images. It was actually a collage made up of several classic movie posters: *The Wizard of Oz, Gone with the Wind, Casablanca, All About Eve, Vertigo, Sunset Boulevard, 2001: A Space Odyssey, Gentlemen Prefer Blondes*—all the ancient classics you'd expect, repeated across the rectangle. I trailed my fingers over the glass, and in the cleared streaks, I saw the ruby red of Dorothy's slippers: technicolor beauties that have survived fallen houses, worlds changed by war, and the death of their most famous host.

I remember reading once about Judy Garland's life and how she was forced in and out of relationships as a part of her studio contract, which also obligated her to get an abortion because if she was too young to play a mother, well then, she was certainly too young to be one. This same system, of course, bred the Production Code that dictated what was moral while turning a blind eye to real acts of immorality: lavender marriages, blackmail, and in some cases, rape.

I moved my hands more and swept clean a puzzle piece bearing the red lips and bare legs of Miss Marilyn Monroe, perched atop the sweeping title *Gentlemen Prefer Blondes*. I tried to picture what she would have looked like as an old lady, but somehow the image wouldn't form. She died young, robbed of old age in mind and memory. Seems like a kind of curse if you ask me. Although, what's the alternative? Judy Garland lived long enough to become an audience member of her own demise and pilled herself to death because of it. Can't be old, can't be young.

Seeing Marilyn in *The Seven Year Itch*, seeing her move around in that white dress, brought up a similar feeling. The image of her standing over the subway grate might be matched in fame only by *American Gothic* in the West's collective consciousness. Seeing the stark white material twist and flutter on screen is like if the Mona Lisa ripped herself from her canvas to join the crowd growing around her broken frame. There's always some form of tragedy lurking underneath the surface of beauty, but only a select few get the luxury of scratching off the metallic covering to reveal the truth. I think that's why the Marilyns and Judys of the world are so beloved, especially among gay people. (I mean, without Judy and Dorothy, there wouldn't be a rainbow flag.) We get them because they get us. One life here; one life there; a real life lost somewhere between the two.

I had two main duties to complete in the rec hall every day. One: clean. Two: check for a delivery. If there was a delivery, there was also more to do. Namely, to organize the donations (all the deliveries were donations) in alphabetical order, then log them in the big, dusty record books that came along with the boxes. The deliveries were always donated novels, board games, VHSs, DVDs, and vinyl records, and they were always carried in under the sun-tanned arms of Sheila Duffy from the Narragansett Public Library. Sheila was, for lack of a better description, the most conspicuous creature to ever walk through the front doors of Galilee.

After a couple days of working in the basement, I had memorized everyone's footsteps. The Major walked hard on his heels, but he also took wide steps, creating a step–echo–silence– step pattern. I hadn't seen The Major since I punched him, so I always froze when I heard that particular stride. On the other side of things, if the footfall could be described as a pitter-patter, it was probably one of the other boys. All Galilee staff walked with clear purpose: destination only. Scurrying feet were often closely followed by the considerably slower clopping of a staff member.

Sheila's footsteps were something special. I knew she was coming solely by the noises reverberating up and down the hallway—subtlety was not her strong suit. Sheila caused a raucous no one else could have mustered, even with genuine effort. The woman walked like a statue come to life: awkwardly, but with an undeniable sense of personality. She wore long, silken skirts, and her hair was twisted—most days at least—up into a clip, which allowed a few strands of dyed-blonde hair to fall into her face, giving her something to do when she talked. And boy could she talk! Sheila could tell a story like no one else, drawing you in with the words that spilled out of her mouth, a mouth encased by deep-cut parentheses formed by years of turning tobacco to smoke. White eyeshadow covered her eyes, sweet eyes that looked at you when you talked. For a while, she was my only friend, and I'd feel my cheeks glow when I heard her come barreling down the hallway.

The first time I met Sheila Duffy, she had leaned down to place a cardboard box on the ground and stayed hunched over for a while. I worried she might have gotten stuck until she turned her face toward me, and while looking directly into my eyes, said she was sorry I was there. That it was wrong, but she didn't know what to do to change any of it.

"I'm just a library aide," she said while looking down at the box.

On top of the pile was Emmylou Harris' *Roses in the Snow* album, which Sheila picked up and looked at while trying not to cry. Emmylou stared back at her from a bed of wildflowers. I was so surprised by the encounter that I didn't have anything to say at first. Part of me worried it was a trap, but when the tears started flowing onto Emmylou's garden (Sheila wiped the tears nervously and placed her hand on the front cover), I knew it wasn't. Sheila held the album up to her face and sniveled hard. I told her it was okay even though it wasn't, and we mutually agreed to forget about where we both were when she came with the donations. We elected instead to talk shit.

Sheila would tell me little things about Galilee when she'd come. About how the previous group that owned it saw such a decline in weekly attendance that they were forced to sell to the current owners, all of whom had close ties to The Society. At least that was her suspicion. She couldn't think of any other explanation as to why the congregation grew as much as it did. Another time, she talked about how they had asked the library to send donations so they could write off UnSin as charity work, but discarded most of what was donated before it ever reached the rec hall. What remained in the boxes Sheila brought were dusty relics that passed what she called "The Faunce Test." Major Faunce would go through the donations one by one and toss out anything even remotely gay. She said that one time a copy of *Cabaret* had slipped by him and later screened for a movie night. The craziest part is that one of the boys got up during "Mein Herr" and started dancing on his chair, mimicking Liza to near perfection. Needless to say, he got thrown to the basement like I had. He was the last person to run the rec hall, actually.

After the *Cabaret* incident, the library had to get creative with what they sent over. The selections became more obscure and harder for The Major to judge. *Cabaret* turned to more covertly queer films, like *Grey Gardens, Strangers on a Train,* and *Death Becomes Her*; things we'd understand, but The Major couldn't detect. The ones with campy women in feather boas and more than a dash of subtext. On one occasion, Sheila personally brought me a copy of *The Best Little Whorehouse in Texas.*

"Come fah Dolly Pahton, stay fah the jockstraps, hunny," she said in her Fall River drawl and then punched my shoulder lightly.

She was one of the first people I had ever met who made me feel normal like that, who made jokes about boys that I was in on. Without any sort of weight to the comment or need to explain anything.

Sheila told me The Major specifically asked for VHSs and vinyl records because he thought they would torture us. Nothing new or enjoyable was the mindset there, but the joke was on him. All my favorite music lived in the vinyl age, so, unexpectedly, The Major delivered new friends to me almost weekly in the damp darkness of a cardboard box.

Stevie Nicks is my favorite, always has been, and I told Sheila that. The last time I saw her, she clip-clopped down the hallway in a manner I can only describe as akin to a sentient hurricane, which was a slightly more organized chaos than was characteristic of her. Her heels met the floor one after another in an even, song-like pattern. When she finally made her way to the rec hall, I heard the clopping abruptly end. She was checking to see if I was alone in the room before barging in with that week's donations. I couldn't help but laugh at how hard she was trying to seem nonchalant and how badly she was failing at it. If anything, she came off as more suspicious than usual.

Up to that point, the routine was that Sheila would put down the box, and I'd begin organizing it. She'd chat at the mouth of the door for a while until one of us started worrying too much about eavesdroppers and ended the conversation. The last time, however, she put the box down and said nothing. It was only after Sheila rattled her jewelry in the direction of the box that I realized she was waiting for me to look over. When I did, I had to clasp my hands over my mouth to keep from squeaking. Laying on top of the cardboard box was a freshly wrapped copy of Stevie Nicks' *The Wild Heart*—it had a price sticker on it and everything. I looked back to see Sheila watching me for approval. She had gone out and bought the album for me because it was the only thing she could do to help make Galilee a little more bearable. And in an odd way, it did. Seeing Stevie in Galilee opened up something in me, something that transcended the words that can be used to describe it. It marked the beginning of the one small rebellion I could carry out while I was there—a rebellion of music that could heal the growing battle wounds and thrust me back to the pages of my mom's world record book.

The album came out when Sheila was a much younger woman. She reminisced fondly about going out with her friends and hearing "Stand Back" at every club they snuck into. Somewhere in that memory, and in the mutual space Stevie Nicks occupied in our consciousnesses, existed the unnamable reason why that gift changed my outlook. Sheila slinked out for the last time with a wave and a mimed kiss, and I continued my work, excited to slip the album under my mattress when I left, excited to have a secret only we knew about.

No one had verified the record log after the first round of donations, so my method of organization quickly changed to flicking through the covers until I ran across one I liked. I had found a box cutter while snooping around during my first shift, which I used to carefully break through the packing tape that held the boxes together. The donations themselves were pretty stuffed, but I devised an easy method for sorting, which involved taking the records out in chunks and putting them back into the box chunk by chunk, taking out the ones I liked to make room for easy flipping. I stored these "keepers" in a nearly empty fabric bin I had found toppled over in the closet during my first shift. The last time I saw Sheila, the box of records was particularly packed. At the front of the stack laid the slightly busy, but ever-intriguing, cover art of Kenny Rogers' *The Gambler*. The cover looks like one of those souvenir photos you get at an amusement park dress-up booth. Everyone is posed around a poker table in saloon-style clothing for some reason, eagerly awaiting Kenny's next move, but he's too busy looking at the camera to make it. From the top corner, an old woman in opera glasses peers over the action, not one to miss any good drama.

A smile broke out across my face as I held the album in my hand, remembering a story my mom had told me about her childhood. Way back when, Mrs. Kaiser had instructed each student in her fourth-grade class to bring in something to share for show-and-tell. Some kids brought in their favorite toy, with ragged, spit-covered fuzz serving as proof of their love for it, and some—the rich ones—brought in souvenirs from far-off places. My mom had never left New England at that point. When it was her turn for show-and-tell, she walked up to the front of the class holding, yes, Kenny Rogers' *The Gambler* tightly to her stomach. She even played the class a song on the record player that was usually reserved for music class. It's probably safe to say that neither the record player nor the class had ever been exposed to the wild ways of Kenny Rogers before: smoking, drinking, womanizing, and all that. When the song ended, Mrs. Kaiser accused my mom of trying to pull something on her, but in reality, she just wanted to share some music she liked with her friends. Regardless, there was no show-and-tell after that. As they say, it only takes one to ruin it for everyone else—sometimes it's "Mein Herr" and sometimes it's *The Gambler*.

Behind Kenny Rogers was Elton John, who had somehow passed the sensors. Apparently, no amount of Donald Duck costumes or feathers and Muppets can dissuade straight people from bopping to "Tiny Dancer." This time it was *Goodbye Yellow Brick Road*, which has an album cover I've always liked. On the side of a brick building, chipped and forgotten, hangs a poster depicting the yellow brick road to Oz. On Elton's feet are platform versions of Dorothy's ruby-red slippers, one on the ground in front of the building and one about to take its first step down the road before the building crumbles for good. The songs, odes to Marilyn and sequined cowboys, to a love left bleeding and solid walls of sound, desperately piece together an image, like the tattered poster on the album's cover, of the balance between reality and beautiful, beautiful fantasy. I placed the needle down on "Roy Rogers" and out came Elton's warning that complaining won't do any good.

Touché, Elton, touché.

* * *

The last time I saw Sheila was also the first day a second boy was assigned a work detail in the rec hall. I'm pretty sure I was listening to folk music at the time—either Peter, Paul, and Mary or Melanie Safka, I don't really remember anymore—when he walked in. He moved quietly; I can only assume because he was scared of how I would react to someone new coming onto my turf. The boys of Galilee kept a respectful distance from each other for the most part. It was one of the few kindnesses we could show each other. So much of our day was spent under a microscope that it was refreshing to be left alone. To the other boys I was just another gay guy, nothing special, and I liked that.

The reason I'm almost confident it was folk music that I was listening to when the second boy arrived was because, after taking his seat, he told me that Joni Mitchell was his favorite singer. Since I hadn't heard him come in, I jumped when he spoke.

"OMIGOD I love Joni," he exclaimed, having found a copy of *Ladies of the Canyon* in one of the boxes. When he saw how surprised I was, he put his hands up in an apologetic pose and continued quietly. "I actually sang "Big Yellow Taxi" in a school choir once and I've been listening to her ever since," he said, lightly singing a few words for me. "I just didn't think anyone else my age liked that kind of stuff, that's cool. I didn't mean to spook you."

Who was this person to walk in, scare me in the process, and then go on talking as if I had asked his opinion on Joni Mitchell? The boy finished and paused for a response, growing red as he waited. As his embarrassment mounted, he retreated back a few steps, allowing me a chance to see him fully. He moved his mouth around like he wanted to say something but was obviously waiting for me to go first. He wore a large, striped T-shirt, which was tucked into a pair of seersucker shorts and kept safe by a belt wrapped tightly around his thin frame. I thought to myself that he looked very much like a sailor—even his hair stayed high and tight despite the summer breeze. Up toward his chest, the boy broadened out a bit, eventually giving way to what was now a flushed face. His cheeks weren't red so much as rosy, which illuminated the freckles underneath. My fear began to wane after taking stock of the situation, so I figured it was only fair to lessen his fear along with my own.

"So, what's your name?" I offered after some time. Not the best opener but the best I could come up with—I was still a little jumpy.

"Like, my real name, or my fake name?" he replied, smiling wide.

The lingering jumpiness faded away. He referenced a fake name, which meant he had suffered through the same electroshock prank that I had. We belonged to the same macabre fraternity, of which only a few could ever speak of their membership. His smile showed his teeth, but not in the way The Major's did. The boy's lips parted gently to a flash of white and then clasped together again, revealing two small dimples in his cheeks. His smile made me want to smile back.

"Either, whoever you feel like being today," I offered.

"Well, according to my card I'm Thomas, the one who didn't believe Jesus was resurrected at first. What about you?"

"Peter. Disciple and fisherman in the ancient sea of Galilee, or something like that," I said, exaggerating the brief resume with sweeping vocal changes.

"Well, it's nice to meet you, Peter," he said.

"You too, Thomas," I replied.

His name wasn't Thomas, obviously, just as mine wasn't Peter, but as we continued talking, we used the names as if they had been given to us long before then. We textured them as we saw fit, adding color and warmth until the heart within the name beat with life. With the new names, we could decide what was and wasn't connected to them. I was Julien, but I was also Peter; and Peter was both the one The Major knew, as well as the one Thomas was getting to know. And not a one of them was the same. We could be as much like ourselves as we wanted or as far from that person as possible. And there was no way of knowing which he was choosing, but when he spoke, I believed him.

As the back and forth continued, the fantasy world around me began to dissolve. *What am I doing?* I couldn't believe I had allowed myself to let my guard down for the first boy who walked in, but then again, how could I not? It was dangerous, no doubt, but something about him drew me in—disarmed me even. He talked to me like I was an old friend, sometimes tripping on one word as he tried to get to the next. Every card he had he kept out for all to see.

Time was a funny thing in the rec hall. Once the door

shut behind me—and I always shut it behind me—there was this sense that time took a look around and decided its powers could be put to better use elsewhere. Typically, its choice was to recede to the hallway and look for a new target to either drag along with it or hurry forward with a firm hand on the back. This is not to say that the days spent underground didn't drag on sometimes in the same way, and it's not to say there weren't days that moved quicker than you'd think they could. But the music and, later, Thomas shook something from my brain that had been intertwined with time so intensely that the marriage was slowly suffocating the very thoughts inside of me. Thomas once asked why I hadn't cleared away the dust on the top of the shelves or swept the dead flies into the trash. The truth of the matter is that I hadn't even thought to do it. Dust and death were as welcome in the rec hall as I was, or at least that's what I thought until the day Thomas came.

With each day that passed, I tried to find out something new about him, and after about a week, I had gathered that he was from Mass, like me, but unlike me, had a huge family.

"My mom has the cousins and everything over a couple times a month for a dinner party," he told me once. "It's fun. She promised me she wouldn't have one while I was gone, but she probably did. My ears have been ringing so I know they're talking about me. What's your family like, Peter?"

Thomas had the habit of asking unexpected questions like that without any of the pretenses that usually come with the territory. He'd ask, like he did then, about my family in the middle of discussing the weather, or about religion as we Windex-ed the windows. He usually didn't even look up when he asked his questions. It was always casual—as if he had never been told that you're not supposed to ask about such things; as if the questions just popped into his head innocently, so he could ask them just as innocently. Thomas was a collector of information, forever curating a back stock of useless tidbits that he deemed useful for, well, for what I'm not exactly sure. I always wondered what it was he was thinking about when he grew quiet, trying to anticipate his next question, but I was always wrong. Perhaps it was because of the way he asked the questions (almost as an aside) that made me answer them without hesitation. Or maybe it was because I wanted him to keep asking me things. I liked that he talked about the things you're told to never talk about. Even in those first few days, I knew I wanted to answer his questions so he'd keep asking them.

To answer the family question, I come from a complicated family lineage. Half the family doesn't associate with the other half, and in the half I belong to, everyone ignores history so as to avoid becoming part of a fourth. The branches of my Charlie Brown family tree have been pulled to the ground so many times we'd rather just not address it. I have people I'm related to who are known to me only by names written on the backs of black-and-white pictures and the inside flaps of birthday cards from years I don't really remember very well. Not having a huge family used to drive me crazy, and I took out the anger primarily on my mom—as a lot of people do when they're young and don't know better. It wasn't until I did some maturing that I became aware of the pain those scribbled names and black-and-white faces can cause. Old doesn't mean forgotten. *How do I sum that up without sounding crazy?*

"Normal," I said before rolling my eyes and laughing. "Just kidding, they're insane."

The questions about family and religion went about as quickly as they came—just as fast and just as innocently.

Before I knew it and while still thinking about my family, Thomas would start asking if I remembered the name of the plant from *Little Shop of Horrors*, the one that ate everyone. Or which character sings the song in *Mamma Mia!* when all the groomsmen come out of the water? Asked as earnestly as anything else.

No one told me why Thomas was placed in the rec hall, but then again, I never asked him directly. I knew his questions interested me, and I knew, despite how hard I tried to deny it, that I was becoming more and more attracted to him to the point where I was afraid of the answer he might give. I felt a kinship developing almost immediately, which put us both at great risk. His answer to that particular question might have either alienated us from each other or drawn us together so closely there would be no clear path out of Galilee anymore. He didn't ask why I was there either, and I assumed it was for the same reason. Sometimes not knowing is better.

Another question there will never be an answer to is why I never saw Sheila again. I told Thomas about her one day, of her gait and kindness, and I wanted so badly for him to meet her; but she never came back. In her place came a tall, lifeless man whose only contact with us was a knock on the door and a quickly shouted "Delivery."

By the second week of shared rec hall duties, I came to know a good deal more about Thomas, and he of me. I woke up one particular day to the sound of a constant, pounding rain on the roof of the dorm building. I usually couldn't sleep through the night, even with the help of my earplugs. My sleep at Galilee was more a series of restless naps—the kind of sleep you get when you're coming out of a cold. However, I opened my eyes on this one rainy day and remembered only that I had shut them what seemed like seconds beforehand when the night was still hot and flat. The rain did little to break the heat, but it cast a blue hue over the campus, which made the yellow of the marigolds vibrate with a sleek glow. The clouds overhead rose in great, jagged columns, which showed the height of the sky. At their tips, bulbous rays of light peeked out, too afraid to spill downwards. It was a day in conflict with itself.

I woke to an acute feeling of excitement that confused me. I crossed my arms over my stomach, but it did little to reduce the flutter of butterflies underneath. I tried to brush the feeling away like the smell of sleep on my teeth, to swirl it around and spit it out, but there was no denying that I was feeling butterflies for a boy I had just gotten to know. And at Galilee of all places. The feeling was a difficult one to manage, so I tried to distance myself from it without being too obvious about it, but Thomas caught on right away and kindly kept to himself as best he could. He allowed me a few hours of silence before finally asking what was wrong.

"I'm hot," I said, which wasn't a lie, although not entirely true either.

"Come here," he responded. Thomas was sitting on the storage shelves that ran along the windows and was pressing himself up against the glass pane. His cheek created an imprint as he pulled away to repeat himself. "Come here, Peter."

The rain was coming down harder than I had ever seen rain come down before. Everything outside the window melded together in running streaks of blue and green. It was as if the rain was reducing the whole world to just a few necessary shapes. Thomas was the only clear thing in my view, his profile illuminated by the wet shine created by the rain behind him. I submitted to his request but walked slowly, waiting for something to stop me, although nothing did. As quickly as time had moved since I had met him, it slowed as I neared him.

Thomas slapped the shelf to invite me to sit alongside him. Dust rose into the air and settled back down before another firm pat kicked them up again. As my shoulder brushed against the window, I realized why he had asked me to come over to him. My arm pressed lightly against the glass at first, but then the chill drew me in closer. The rain had cooled both the glass and my arm in the process. Thomas laughed, knowing he had given me some release, and took on a smile that showed his dimples again. I closed my eyes and pressed my face against the glass until I felt the chill settle into my jaw. As my body cooled, I began to feel myself relax into the seat. A moment passed, and I opened my eyes to find Thomas looking at me peacefully. Without speaking he drew his hand over to mine, allowing his fingers to hover over my fist until I moved it to take his. Once intertwined, he pressed the back of my hand into the glass and smiled once more.

Young love had hit and hit hard. In its glow, everything looked new and fresh: skin pulled taut over muscles and sharp chin bones, plunging down into hair and veins. Everything was inviting and dreamt over, from the wrinkles under his arms to his nose and Adam's apple. The thought of what they'd taste like, perhaps, would cross my mind from time to time. He was something fresh in a world that had long ago gone stale.

According to Galilee staff, the rec hall was supposed to be a space for anyone to come and hang out. However, there was never any free time for the other boys to visit, so it was always just the two of us—with the occasional guard checking in. We played board games and I Spy if it wasn't too warm, but mostly, we sat around the record player putting on songs for each other and explaining why we liked them, listening with more care than either of us had ever done before. Whenever he'd play me a song, I'd feel my voice start to tremble. We didn't so much as hug by that point, but somehow, the sharing of music was more intimate than anything we could have been caught doing together. And the thought of being caught listening to music together was almost too much to bear. It would have been easier to have been found naked together. Or at least easier to explain. The world hollowed out when the needle cast down. I'd sit and wait for the line Thomas had excitedly told me about—even if I knew the song and where the line was—and rock back and forth, drumming on my kneecaps to the beat.

Summer in New England is always hot, even bizarrely so, but the summer I spent at Galilee was one for the record books. No one slept much to begin with, but I heard the groans and discontented shifting of bodies trying to find rest growing more desperate as the days passed by. The guards put box fans in the windows of the dorm hall, but it didn't do much. Eventually, it got so bad that they let us sleep on the floor because the cement retained a nice chill. I thought about Thomas while I laid out on the floor, imagining his hand was pressing me into the cold ground, until I drifted off to sleep. During the day, the window trick continued to work for a little while longer, but even that became fruitless labor in the heat.

"This sucks," Thomas said one day, slapping both sides of his hand against the window in frustration.

I was preoccupied with a humming sound coming from beyond the glass and didn't hear him. He propped the windows open with some books, and at first, it was great. The wind was just starting to pick up, and there was a momentary release; but then the wind stopped, and it wasn't great anymore. Even the birds didn't move much in the heat. They sat on their perches waiting for a breeze to motivate them. When the wind did come, it came in random gusts like humongous breaths, rattling the pages of the books whose stories held the weight of the windows. Thomas eventually moved away from the windowpane, but I kept looking out even though the sun filling his place was shining directly in my eyes. After fishing through the box of records, Thomas pulled out one and tapped his fingers along its sides before laying it down on the record player. Linda Ronstadt's voice boomed out a song about a heatwave.

I turned my head toward Thomas to a kaleidoscope of dots that flashed every time I blinked my eyes. He took my hands, but instead of pressing them against the window, he lured me off the windowsill with a gentle heave-ho. I rubbed my eyes to stop the room from spinning, but it only stretched the dots into fractured bolts. Through them, I saw Thomas twisting his hips and moving around his hands to the beat of the music—or as close as he could get. When my eyes regained control a bit, I saw that he was turning red and not from the heat.

"Come on!" he demanded. "I don't want to dance alone."

There was only him and me in the room, and yet, I still felt a hesitation. *Always a hesitation.* The warmth of the sun was making me itchy under my clothes, but the song pulsed on.

Thomas' arms went limp, his arms swinging dead by his sides as he continued to twist—now at half speed—to the music. As Linda kept singing, Thomas' face drooped more and more into a pout, which was quickly overtaking his face. I rolled my eyes and swallowed hard before reaching down to find the courage to dance. It started with me moving my shoulders opposite my hips and ended with us jumping and shaking our hair in each other's faces. When the song ended, Thomas collapsed against the windowsill, his face slicked with sweat. He fanned himself before throwing the back of his head against the window, which knocked the book by his elbow out of place. The window slammed shut with a *boom*. Thomas was so startled by the noise that he jumped up and grabbed my hands before falling to the floor in a fit of laughter. I knelt down beside him and covered his mouth with my hands to prevent anyone from hearing him. The more I tried to suppress his laughter, the more furiously he laughed. I started giggling too. He pointed at me, and soon his laughter turned to silent wheezing, with only a few squeaks coming up from his throat. He covered my mouth with his hand, and I slapped his cheek. Then I started to wheeze, and the only sound to be heard came from the birds outside, whose wing beats thundered as they leapt from their branches and took to the sky.

CHAPTER 11

As summer wore on and heat continued to sweep swiftly and intensely through Galilee, more boys began requesting trips to the beach down the street. The beach was called Clamshell Bay, so named because at low tide all the clams signal their location by heaving streams of water through pores they create in the sand. All is still until—*whoosh*—another one squirts into the air. When enough of them spit, it looks like the ground is pouring water back into the sky.

No rain had fallen for a few days on campus, and the heat had dried up the ground until the wind threatened to blow it all away—even the red dahlias on the front porch of the church were wilting. As protected by the shade of the forest as it was, Galilee was not well equipped to handle the rising temperatures. Things slowed to a near stop as everyone found it harder to move their bodies from A to B. The heat affected The Major's lessons most of all. Where once he bounced around talking, now, if he moved at all, he did so lamely in the soupy air. At times, sweat covered so much of his face that it looked like the skin was sliding right off. Eventually, he gave his lessons more or less from one position and spent significant spans of time staring down at his watch. He looked slightly possessed, occasionally wincing or snapping his neck to one side as if responding to something only he could hear. The pressure continued to mount as the number on the thermostat rose closer to its metal top, threatening to pop it right off and fill the room with a mercury ooze. The Major started stuttering through his lessons more often, too, which he would end earlier and earlier, choosing instead to assign pages in an old workbook for those not enrolled in UnSin before stumbling out of the lessons building to the air-conditioned safety of his office.

There were fewer participants than there were copies of the workbook, so I grabbed a copy out of curiosity. The workbook consisted mostly of lengthy Bible passages and reflection questions, all spiral-bound with a clear plastic cover. There were also comic book-like text bubbles with quotes from Galilee staff and former participants of the program. How real they were I'll never know, but they were certainly convincing.

"My time in the program was a wake-up call. I realized how unhappy I was and how that wasn't going to change unless I took the necessary steps toward addressing my unhappiness," one of them read.

The themes of the quotes, which ranged from abandonment to loneliness, were very targeted to the gay experience. The part of the program that I think drew people in was this idea that Galilee was willing to acknowledge the suffering of its participant. The workbook told them, through its carefully selected passages and pointed reflections, that it saw and empathized with their pain. It just disagreed on what was responsible for it. Considering the alternative of having to fill in the blank lines of the book, I found myself more content with my placement in the rec hall.

I tried to suppress the feelings of excitement that would bubble up inside me when The Major ended his lessons early—this wasn't school after all—but the feeling wasn't so easily dissuaded. Sometimes I would feel a pang of guilt knock around and replace the excitement in my core for a while. I had to pick one to lean into, which I didn't think was a fair mental game to be put into, so I chose to interpret the unease as excitement. Thomas and I did a good job of maintaining a professional distance during the diminishing lessons, but once we got to the rec hall, we'd finish the little work there was to do as fast as possible. That way, we'd have more time to sit and listen to music. From there, there was no mistaking what my stomach was telling me.

The records did a good job of keeping us company, but more importantly, they were good at filling space that would have otherwise driven us apart, either by heat or anger or, maybe, a healthy combination of the two. The first prickles of the needle cooled me in a way nothing else could. A calm coolness, like the feeling of a blanket fort in a rainstorm or swimming underwater. There was a broken clock in the room that I switched to say 12:30 one day and played "Twelve Thirty" by the Mamas & the Papas for Thomas. I liked the line about beauty laying there stagnant. He liked the one about vibrations bouncing in no direction.

We moved the record player onto a frayed piece of carpeting that Thomas had found rolled up and leaning against the corner of the rec hall a few days into our placement in UnSin. When we sat on either side of it, our heads fell just below the windowsill and clean out of sight to anyone passing by. Sitting relieved some of the weight the heat had piled on and allowed me to find genuine enjoyment in the music. Not only because of Thomas but because the songs provided more room for interpretation than was typical for the other recitations happening daily at Galilee. I could sit there, leaning forward with my eyes fixed on the spinning record, and just listen—with no expectation, condemnation, or praise.

When the donations would arrive, I'd pop up from the floor and engage in a brief conversation with the library assistant, usually about the weather, giving Thomas enough time to look busy just in case the assistant was looking for some proof of work.

"Here are the donations," the assistant would say, quickly adding, "Nice weather out there!"

"Must be nice," I'd reply with a monotone and look over at Thomas as if to say, "I've gotta help him, please leave."

After that, we'd return to the floor and take turns flipping through the records while periodically telling the other person to close their eyes so as to keep the next pick a surprise.

Sometimes, if there wasn't a song I really had a burning desire to play, I would find the longest one I could and move around the room, slowly if the song called for it, or quickly for the same reason, raising my arms to dance in between sweeping for the upteenth time. Thomas's go-to long song was "Hotel California." He'd act out the whole thing, too, from the Tiffany-twisted mind of the mysterious woman to the steely knives of the big feasts. It was all fun, but it became apparent that the music and dancing were only prolonging the inevitable.

One day, I picked out "Sunday Morning Coming Down" to play from an album whose title had worn off but still featured a clear picture of Willie Nelson. The needle touched down and out came a sound like rushing sink water. Then the water went still, and Willie's voice began. It was a cover of a cover of a song written by Kris Kristofferson, although most people attribute it to Johnny Cash. I, myself, didn't know there was another version. Sometimes with those long songs, it's easy to get carried away to someplace else in your mind; that happened with "Sunday Morning Coming Down," which ended with me sitting against the window-sill, looking out into the backwoods of the church.

I looked out and tried, as the narrator in the song does, to connect to the beauty and life of the outside world. Everything beautiful I had in that moment existed only in that one room, alongside the soured lavender and dead flies. There was a door closed on it and great care was taken that no one ever see it. Comfort is important, but it's also a lie. A pretty lie, yes, but a lie nonetheless. And one with the power to lull unsuspecting people into ease only to snatch it out from under them. There is no stability in comfort, only temporary sedation. My comfort wasn't a blooming rose for all to see, but something to be sutured and stitched away. It was the dahlias outside wilting petal by petal every day. My comfort was a fake name and a feeling of hatred mixed in equal parts with a growing feeling of love that had a fast-approaching expiration date. "Sunday Morning Coming Down" tells the story of a destitute narrator torn and comforted in equal measure by substances and voids that have become all too consuming. He passes by strangers whose lives entangle with his for a fleeting moment, and in that moment, he is reminded of the space between them. In the chirps of the birds and the billowing gusts of wind around Galilee, I felt that space, too. The space told me: *don't get too comfortable.*

Thomas never bothered me when I was in one of my moods. He would see me sitting and find work for himself to do somewhere in the room, maybe running a hand across my back every once in a while. I appreciated that—the space he created for me to *be* without explanation. He understood what I was feeling better when it went unexplained, passed instead through the air around us. I pictured it hugging the sound escaping from the record player and penetrating his brain. *Oh, I get that,* he'd think. To attempt an explanation would have confused the whole situation. Watching Thomas work without asking for any help made me feel guilty, and so I'd usually come around before too much time had passed.

"Clamshell Bay" became the buzzword of Galilee immediately after The Major first told us about it one day before ending lessons early. He had hinted at it during our first day, but now that it had a name, it seemed all the more real. Clamshell Bay, The Major said, was a beach down the street that we would be allowed to go to so long as we understood that such trips were an easily revocable privilege and *not* a God-given right. Beach trips were organized around a request slip that had to be turned in to the dorm guard and later approved by the lessons guard, both of whom had to agree you were in good standing with the program. Regardless of the caveat, from that point on all you heard from any of the boys was "Clamshell Bay" this and "Clamshell Bay" that. Some of the boys in one particular clique, which had boomed in size after the twelve of us were removed from lessons, referred to it only as "CB."

"Wanna go to CB tomorrow?" they'd say, loudly enough for the UnSin losers to hear and start sulking. Requests from us were accepted far less frequently than those in the general program.

The clique was too big for them all go to CB at the same time. So, from that day on, I saw a never-ending line of rolled-up T-shirts and sweat-drenched hair pass by the rec hall windows and file into a stout, white bus that would drive off every couple of hours. I watched as wind weaved through the line and messed up hair here and there. Some of the boys quickly moved their displaced bangs back into place, but most of them let their hair go wild in the breeze. Were it not for the flurrying hair, I would have thought the swaying caravan of boys was moving in slow motion, or maybe that it was primordially, even supernaturally, attracted to CB. When the boys came back several hours later—cooled and dripping, hair washed clean by the salty seawater—I saw what so rarely came across the faces of the other boys—smiles.

"You think they change in front of each other?" Thomas said lazily one day as one group lined up outside. He kept his cheek pressed against the window but turned his face slightly to hear my response.

"I don't think they change at all, they're still in their regular clothes when they come back," I answered.

Embarrassingly enough, the thought had crossed my mind too. The beach would have been a great excuse to get around some of the restrictions of the church. Even with a guard standing by, changing is changing. At once a horrid exploration of one of the most deplorable forms of voyeurism possible, but at the same time, a space to invite consenting eyes to peek around and window-shop. A towel dropped and not immediately picked back up, for example, or a figure facing toward the group while pushing his manhood down into the netted lining of a swimsuit.

"Would you want to go to the beach with me?" Thomas asked, much to my surprise. "I may or may not have an approved request slip in my pocket for the two of us." His face was still squished against the glass. I paused for a minute and turned away to hide a widening smile before looking back toward the window. Thomas was now using his right hand to press his face harder against the window.

It was a date, right? I mean, I knew it *wasn't* a date, but was it really? I decided it was, and more importantly than that, I decided it was a date I was going to go on. All the lessons—short as they were—were really starting to get to me. I wanted—maybe even needed—to feel some attraction to another man to remind myself that this was all a ruse.

"Sure. But no dick slips, accidental or otherwise," I joked.

"Wouldn't dream of it," he responded, returning his gaze to the van as it coughed out some exhaust and pulled away toward Clamshell Bay.

Even though up to that point we were fairly sure no one knew or even suspected anything was happening between us, Thomas and I took every precaution possible to ensure that no one ever caught wind of what was going on in the rec hall. The approved request slip to Clamshell Bay was only further proof that the plan was working, so best to keep it going.

If we absolutely had to talk about matters beyond work, which happened increasingly more often, we'd first make sure no one was listening outside the door. Then, we'd whisper what it was we wanted to talk about, making sure the music was loud enough to drown out any noise. Whatever topic we wanted to talk about then became something we just so happened to know about only because of a person on the outside—definitely not us. Hours would pass discussing dates we heard our friends had gone on or the qualities of some girl back home we had suddenly developed undying feelings for. It was fun having a language between us that no one else understood, even if they happened to hear it flat out. And the music was a great facilitator. At night, I would lay awake thinking of which songs I wanted to show Thomas the next day and what I could tell him through the lyrics. At the end of each day, when the last song has been sung, one of us would leave the rec hall first, and whoever was left behind would stay put until the door down the hall slammed shut.

After our beach trip had been approved, the waiting came—an almost unbearable feat, I might add. I've never been particularly good at waiting. I'm hesitant to admit it because when I do, I hear my mother's voice rasp: "Kids today need instant gratification;" but it's true, we really do. Before the beach, the only thing I had to look forward to was leaving Galilee. That was a dangerous wait to sit through, one that made me sweat through my sheets and jolt awake at night. Clamshell Bay was different. It was bubbly and intoxicating like the breed of butterfly that comes Christmas morning and flutters around, making you unsure if you want to open the gifts underneath the tree for fear of setting them free. This feeling was also all-consuming. It followed me around, sometimes too close for comfort.

As the days ticked by, the effects of the waiting picked away at our nerves to the point where Thomas' request to not play music the hottest day of the summer enraged me. A furiously whispered fight ensued in which he said he took back the invitation. I told him that was fine because *this* was all temporary anyway, and if he thought otherwise, he was just kidding himself. I regretted the words as soon as they came out, and when his lip started to quiver in a mix of angry sadness, I told him that we could still go because I was inviting him to make up for it. We took turns apologizing and hugged for the first time shortly afterward, and he let me play him the song I wanted him to hear that day: "All Through the Night" by Cyndi Lauper. He liked the synth bridge, which was the part I wanted him to like. Fast to fight, fast to make up. Not a first fight I ever could have imagined, but hey.

The night before Clamshell Bay, I had the worst nightmare of my life. I couldn't get the butterflies to settle no matter how hard I tried. In my sleep, they roamed up to my brain to wreak havoc. As is the case with most nightmares, I was in it before I could help it. Oddly enough, it was the first time I dreamt while at Galilee, or at least the first time I'm aware of. All around me were the workings of a nightmare, and I had finally fallen into it.

In the dream, Thomas and I were already on the beach, and the sun above us was shining at full force. I remember that—the brightness of the sun and how it distorted everything—more clearly than any other part of the dream. The guard who had taken us to the beach in the dream left us with the warning that he'd be back in an hour.

"No more, no less," he said.

Once the engine of his car started, Thomas and I walked down to the water and sank our hands into the cooler sand just before the waterline. What we didn't know was that the guard didn't actually drive away; he only drove out of sight, stopping behind a humongous, rusty dumpster that was overflowing with coffee cups and plastic bags. Seagulls sat atop it all, picking at the pieces as they blew away to begin their adventure out to sea.

Thinking we were safe, we laid down together by the water and watched the clouds overhead until they all turned gray. All at once, the brightness of the sun was gone, and I realized, only in its absence, just how bright it had actually been. It started to rain then, only it wasn't rain so much as a solid wall of water pouring into the ocean. Before we knew it, the tide started rising, creeping closer and closer to us by the second until we were lifted up by the force of the water running underneath our bodies. I held onto Thomas and made my way toward the only dry part of the beach left. When we reached the patch of dry sand, the rain suddenly and inexplicably stopped, and the sun was bright once again, maybe even more so than before.

The rising water had left only a few islands of sand exposed. On one of them, the guard sat in his car, his high beams on, shouting something about a plague of water. The plastic litter was strewn all around him; the dumpster was nowhere in sight. The guard continued to shout, and as he did, the water began to recede as quickly as it had come, leaving fish gasping for air all around our feet. I'm not sure why, but I distinctly remember feeling an overwhelming urge to get the fish back into the water, so I told Thomas to grab as many as he could and to follow the receding water. We ran hard, following the current, but couldn't catch up to the deeper water. In my hands, the fish turned gray, their skin rotting away as they were reduced to skeletons, and yet, I still ran toward the water with the bones in my hands. I ran with such urgency that I didn't see Thomas behind me screaming at the sight of the dead fish in his hands.

He shouted my name, and when I turned around, he was buried knee-deep in sand. The force of the current rushing by his feet caused him to start sinking. I ran toward him as he screamed out my name again. The water burying Thomas was also exposing hundreds of clams that had dug themselves into the ground for safety. The sand kept moving, but it never finished exposing the clams; they kept growing deeper with the hole until Thomas was surrounded by towering walls of sun-bleached clam shells. He yelled my name a final time and warned me of the shells at my feet, but it was too late. Each time my feet hit the ground and pushed off to get closer to him, they were sliced by the razor-sharp edges of the clamshells in the ground. I kicked the shell nearest Thomas when I finally got to him, leaving behind a bloody footprint. I kicked in my sleep, too, and woke myself up with a start.

Night passed slowly after that until, finally, the sun started to rise. At first, it came in only where the curtains parted, whispering the light into the room until it was full and soft. Sometimes the morning breeze would flutter the curtains open, and light would stream in with more intensity. When the sun had fully risen, no curtain on planet Earth could keep back its light. The inside of the dorm hall was an off-white color that caught and intensified any sunlight that hit it. It was impossible to sleep when morning came.

Soon, the dorm guard collected me and, as he walked me out the door and around to the bathroom, he made a brief mention of the fact that he would be the one driving us to the beach later on. I half-listened to him recite a list of beach rules as several men leapt from a landscaping van set off near the back of the church.

"You couldn't bury a body here if you wanted to with all the roots growing under the ground," one man exclaimed.

Another said something under his breath, made his

fingers into the shape of a gun, and drew it up to his mouth before pulling the fake trigger. The man who had made the comment about the roots underground stopped talking immediately, but periodically looked over at me in between pulling shovels from the van and handing them to the other one.

When I got to the rec hall, Thomas was in a markedly chipper mood, which his music choices reflected. I asked him if he was excited about the beach. In response, he frowned and told me he wanted it to feel like a spur of the moment thing.

"Let's not talk about it, Peter. I wanna ask you later and we can pretend like we just decided to go. Like we wanted to, so we did," he said.

I obliged his request although it tore me up inside. This was the day the waiting was supposed to be over; I didn't want to have to wait anymore. The only thing he did tell me was that he had asked the guard, during an escort to the bathroom the other day, to put us in the last van. Going last meant we would more than likely be alone. There was no way of knowing for sure who had been approved to travel to Clamshell Bay on any given day; however, everyone usually wanted to go to the beach in the middle of the day when the sun was high and work could be skipped. The guard had asked Thomas if he was sure, which he was, and just like that, we were all set.

The day lumbered on slower than usual, but on the whole, it was unremarkable; one of those lost days of Galilee, I guess. Thomas would periodically crack his knuckles in between smacking down Uno cards, but other than that, we were both pretty quiet. It was hard to think up anything meaningful to talk about with Clamshell Bay weighing so heavily on our minds. At one point, with nothing else to do, I stood up from the puzzle table and sighed loudly, which Thomas responded to by standing and sighing even louder. We spent a good couple of minutes trying to outdo the other's discontented sighs until I looked at the clock and found it wasn't anywhere near where I wanted it to be. Even the music was heavier when mixed with anticipation. Thomas put on something I hadn't heard before and got irritated when I spent most of the song staring above his head at the clock on the wall.

"You're not paying any attention, Peter," he said, "and you're not making the clock go any faster either. Stop it!"

He was right, but I couldn't help myself, and as the hours ticked by, the excitement of our impending trip began to sour. By the time the van was ready to take us to Clamshell Bay, I was almost ready to call the whole thing off. Our Un-Sin work typically ended around six, but we were in the last of the vans, which left from outside the rec hall, so we were told to stay put until it picked us up at eight.

Adding to the frustration of waiting was the fact that I had been wearing my bathing suit all day, which was both riding up my ass and squeezing my balls at the same time. I could tell Thomas' bathing suit was causing him the same grief because he was always reaching down and adjusting his balls when he thought I wasn't looking, but there aren't too many places to hide when you're in the same open room. The first time he did it—quickly, while turning to grab something—he left it, maybe intentionally, maybe not, in a way that accentuated the outline of his bulge. He caught me staring while he was moving boxes and blushed before turning away and adjusting again. Later, when I stood up from Uno and began the sigh-off, I was the one left blushing when I caught him staring at a mess of flesh that had slipped below the netting of my suit sometime during the game. But even that excitement wore away as Clamshell Bay taunted us from afar.

A large school bus pulled up in front of the rec hall at about five minutes past eight—much larger than the Escalade I was expecting to see. It was clunky, with a roof that extended way out over the front windshield almost like a baseball cap. The bus appeared to have once worn the mustard-yellow uniform of a local school bus but was now painted a dull shade of gray. The paint was thin, though, and the yellow underneath shone through, making the bus look ill. Its doors swiveled open after the bus itself let out a great, big steamy sigh announcing the lessons guard, who was making his way to the rec hall to gather us up. Thomas adjusted his balls one last time and turned to me with a huge smile on his face.

"Peter, I was wondering if you might want to go out sometime?"

Some of the sour excitement began to pass at the sight of his smile.

"When were you thinking, Thomas? This is all so sudden!"

"Right now!"

"You know what? I think I'm free right now."

When we got to the beach I realized, in all the uncanny tree roots and dunes of sand, that my reason for choosing a conversion program in Narragansett—because I didn't have an important memory there—wasn't altogether accurate. I had been to Clamshell Bay once before. The trip lived somewhere in my past, but a line of eerily familiar houses sat a little ways off in the distance pulled the memory from that faraway place in my mind. Although it was growing dark, I could suddenly remember specific details about the houses across the water.

I had been alone, I remember that. I had driven myself, too. Having just received my license, I was adamant to enjoy as much freedom as possible. In the memory, I stood at the water's edge, a wave had cast a clamshell onto my foot, which I swiftly kicked off and watched as it filled with loose, dampened sand. Some people call those shells Rhode Island ashtrays. During the summer, people will sit outside in their long tank tops and put out cigarette butts in the overturned bellies of those clamshells while they ponder their life and wring their burnt hands in anger—not in Newport or anyplace like that, of course, but where the everyday people live.

I had felt a buzz in my pocket shortly afterward. It was my mother calling to tell me that my father had just died. Her voice was hoarse, but a tired kind of hoarse; the kind that comes from a lack of sleep rather than from tears. My father was not a sickly man, but when he did get sick at the end, I knew he was going to die. I think my mother did, too. We visited him together most of the time, but I stopped going with her after it became too much to manage emotionally. Visiting him was like prolonging the inevitable. He was unresponsive most of the time anyway. My mother never made me feel bad about how I handled my grief, but I knew it hurt her to have to face the end all alone. To her, it was not prolonging the inevitable, it was allowing his still-beating heart to haunt her one last time. I heard all of that in her voice when she called. I looked down at the Rhode Island ashtray at my feet and told her I'd be there as soon as I could.

The headlights kicked off when Thomas and I reached the parking lot, and with it, the memory started to fade away. My window had fogged up, too, around where my mouth had been a few moments before. I looked over at Thomas, who smiled and touched my hand. I opened my door with the throw of an elbow, swiping at the fogginess with a quick wave of my hand.

It was approaching nighttime, but life was all around us. Had it been winter, everything would have been quiet, but the few extra hours of daylight kept the bugs out in full force. Croaks, chirps, buzzes, and rustling leaves suggested that we were not the only ones safer under the cover of darkness. Things crawled over footprints and stones, leaving behind a slime that would disappear without a trace before the sun had a chance to notice it was ever there. These were creatures nearly blinded by evolution; sight wasn't necessary because light didn't often hit their eyes. Night is still when contemplated from rocking chairs made of wicker, but in reality, it moves when others do.

Before long, the underbrush in the parking lot gave way to growing mounds of sand. The lessons guard walked alongside us, kicking up rocks he found with his foot and grunting to fill the silence. Not exactly the date you dream of, but beggars can't be choosers.

"You go on ahead," he said, pointing his flashlight toward a dock a few yards in front of us. "I gotta piss," he added before clicking off the light and leaving us in relative darkness.

I could feel my heart beating in my throat. Thomas took my hand and led me down to the dock while I kept turning around to see if the guard was watching. Clamshell Bay was situated just close enough to the road that the transition from pavement to sand was almost seamless. The sand from the beach traveled organically across the parking lot in thin, dust-like clouds close to the ground. Pavement turned to underbrush and then to sand and finally to ocean with almost no discernable interruptions. Once we sat down at the edge of the dock, Thomas released my hand from his grip and began rubbing his knees hard, pausing to run his hands through his hair and look over his shoulder. I thought at first that he was looking for the guard until he turned to me with a worried look on his face.

"My name isn't Thomas," he said, as if I hadn't even suspected it.

"Yeah, I know that. What's wrong?" I replied.

He looked over his shoulder one last time and then blurted it out all at once.

"My name is Finn . . . Finn Lavette. I don't know why, but I really want you to know that. It's important to me that you know my real name. I don't know what that means . . . I don't know what any of this means actually. And you don't have to tell me yours. I just . . . I had to tell you."

Finn Lavette. I rolled the name around in my mouth for a moment. I looked over and saw Thomas slowly crumbling away, with just a few of the details I had attached to the old name remaining to form the new one. *Finn.* Something as simple as a name and I was beginning to feel sick at the taste of my own as it made its way toward the front of my tongue. Once I said it, there would be no hiding it away again, and something about the finality of that was frightening. The sand, the crashing of the water—all of it was suddenly very real in a way it wasn't just a second ago. I felt the weight of my body and the tickle of a mosquito landing on my leg. I slapped it before responding.

"Finn," I said to myself, hearing the name in my own voice for the first time. "My name is Julien Grant."

"Julien," he repeated.

I liked the way it sounded when he said it. It sounded new.

"I like that name," Finn said.

We sat in silence for a while after that, looking out over the sea. The water below us was relatively still, rolling slowly onto the rocks surrounding us. Every once in a while, a row of waves would rise higher than their predecessors and crash with some force, spraying our legs before receding back again. It was all cyclical. That's the great thing about the ocean, it keeps coming back. *Rise. Crash. Fall. Rise. Crash. Fall.* Finn rubbed the water into his skin and let his legs swing. I wanted more than anything to relax into the moment with him, but I was too worried about everything happening around us. Telling him my name made everything more serious. Not only our relationship, but the nature of its origin. I really was *here*. At Galilee. There was also the matter of the guard, who was somewhere behind us. I was pulled between an urge to rest my head on Finn's shoulder and a need to locate the guard so I could keep an eye on him. Finn didn't seem as worried, which doubly freaked me out. He should have been just as antsy, but he seemed so damn calm as he watched the waves in utter peace. He even stopped to look at me a few times and smiled before looking back out over the ocean and bouncing his legs a bit faster.

"Hey!" It was the guard calling from the edge of the beach.

His voice made me jump a little.

"I gotta go back to the church. Someone cut their hand opening a window. I'll be back as soon as I'm done." He paused for a moment before saying in all seriousness, "No funny business."

"Aye, aye captain," Finn responded, saluting the guard, who I'm sure was too far away to see or hear him.

The guard walked back to the car, rattled it on, and drove away. The sound of the engine grew quiet and was soon replaced by the crashing of the waves. *Whoosh.* Back and forth over and over again. Finn and I looked at each other as if some miracle had just happened right in front of our eyes, some sort of warped burning bush telling us this was our one moment.

Don't blow it!

Finn jumped to his feet and started smacking his thighs as he howled with laughter.

"I can't believe it," I whispered as I drew my hands up to my mouth.

Eventually, Finn got very serious and leaned over my shoulders.

"What should we do?" he asked. "We can do whatever we want."

"I'm so stunned I don't know what to think right now," I said.

"I know what I'm thinking," he said and started walking toward the edge of the road.

The further he got from the dock, the more I started to worry that he'd ask to run away. Why not, right? But there was something inside me that secretly hoped he wouldn't ask to leave. I hate that about myself, if I'm being honest. I never run. Like a dog, I sit and I stay, never running from anything. Adventure movies always scared me as a kid because I knew I wouldn't be brave enough to run and fight the powers that held me back.

Finn stopped walking when he reached the parking lot. One leg remained planted in the sand while the other teetered onto the pavement. I watched him from the dock as he looked out over the white-lined parking spaces that would soon fill with carloads of happy people with their pastel umbrellas and polka-dot bathing suits. A late-night wind lifted his hair and dropped it back down in a messy heap. For a couple minutes, Finn stared without so much as moving his fingers until all at once he snapped around and took off running back toward the dock, throwing himself into the lapping water below and almost pushing me over in the process. He moved so fast that I didn't even see him take off his shirt, which was now in a pile by my side. Flashes of reflected white moonlight rippled away from his body as he rose to the surface, giggling and pushing his hair back. He bobbed around another couple minutes, bathed in white moonlight, before he started speaking.

"Julien, come in!" The air lifted his voice high, swirling it around in the night air before returning it to me like a freshly concocted potion, brewed and bubbling over. "Julien!"

I wanted to give in to his call, but I imagined the rocks by the dock and whatever shared the ocean with them. My feet carried me to the edge of the dock, but no further.

Why can't I run just this once?

My toes hung over the edge of the dock, wiggling a bit, but not budging. Defeated, I sat back down and buried my head in my knees.

"You don't have to do anything you don't wanna do," Finn said, more seriously now. "I'll just come out and we can sit in the sand if you want."

In that moment, the world around me came into focus. The night, in all its black expansiveness, had been reduced to just Finn's concerned face, which itself was reflected in the water below his chin. He had given me permission to pause or not pause, jump or not jump, but the choice was mine to make. It didn't matter what came before or after. All that mattered was the choice I was about to make. As a person, I face as inward as I can. I wring my hands when I talk and chew the tips of my fingers until they bleed, but something in those words made me rise to my feet again. Finn had brought me outward, made me pause longer to enjoy every moment, and made me angrier that I had to be here.

I had made my choice.

Finn started to clap as I swung my arms in anticipation. I pulled my shirt up over my head and paused, looking at Finn's chest and then down at my own. With a scream and a leap, I flung myself into the water below.

"He did it, ladies and gentlemen! A solid 10 . . . for effort!" Finn exclaimed.

Even in the depths of summer, the freezing water stung my body in painful ripples. Finn paddled over to me and splashed my face.

"Look up," he said between gasps.

I tilted my head back to see but sank under the surface before I could bring my legs up to balance out my weight and float. The waves slapped against my ears until they filled, and the sounds of the night grew distant. From under the water, a hand moved onto my lower back and hurried me upwards to see the sky. Finn was holding me close to his body, spreading his hands wide across my back so I wouldn't go under again. With our hands pressed into each other for support, it felt as though we had finally obtained some unobtainable golden idol, one that sent sparks through every cell in my body until they sang to the tune of some ancient, wordless song.

The sky above us was turning gray, with some stars and airplanes shining through the scrim of darkness. I bobbed gently with the waves and extended one arm to rest my palm flat against the water. The other held Finn around his neck. The water reflected the sky, creating one, all-encompassing mass of white-dotted gray. Looking up at the sky, I felt like we were alone; the only living things in the entire world, and yet I wasn't afraid. When I closed my eyes, I imagined I was moving with the waves toward the shore. I felt myself spray against the rocks and then retreat back, becoming whole again in his arms. I continued floating for a while until Finn's legs grew weak from kicking and he suggested we swim to shore. When I was left to support my own weight, I went under a few more times until I stabilized myself with a doggy paddle that carried me safely to shallow waters.

The waves washed over our feet as we stood and began to make our way to the beach in front of us. The ripples we created in the water behind us were beginning to grow still. Eventually, there would be no proof of what happened just a few precious seconds ago. Walking toward Finn, I felt an ancient pull, one that tried, as the ocean current ran opposite me, to call me back toward something different. I got the sense that the water below me had once washed up— that same wave even—on the shore of a beach that didn't know the feeling of water that is so cold it takes your breath away; on land where people spoke, ate, dressed differently than me. People who never thought of the ocean as only temporarily warm. To them, it would always be without vacancy and without a dusting of snow each winter. These would be foreign thoughts.

"Julien, do you ever think about being gay?" Finn asked as we laid down in the sand together.

"What do you mean?"

"Just that. Do you ever *think* about it? Because I don't

think about it, at least not all the time. They seem to think that's all we ever think about, but I don't know. I don't know if I ever think about it, actually. Well, now I am because they've got me thinking about it. I just didn't know if you ever did."

"No, not really."

"I don't even know what it means anymore. I mean, I know what it *is* and I know I'm . . . *that*. But I don't know what it *means*, you know?"

"Well, when I find out, I'll let you know," I said.

Finn laughed lightly in response before going serious again.

"What did you want to be when you were little?" he said, twirling a strand of my hair around in his fingers.

"I wanted to be a paleontologist. I saw *Jurassic Park* on TV, and it was over. I read every single dinosaur book my parents gave me. But, you know, those dreams don't come true."

"What do you mean? I think they can."

"Oh yeah," I said, detecting my own pessimism, "and what did you want to be?"

"A teacher," he said.

We both laughed.

"I think you maybe set your sights too high, Julien."

"Why is that the first question people ask anyway? *What do you do?*"

"They want to know if they're gonna have to respect you or not."

"It's just . . . we pick what we want to be, but almost no one does it, you know? And then we just sort of pick something else to, what, impress strangers we meet?"

"I guess."

"I don't know what I want to do anymore."

"Me either."

A moment passed where neither of us spoke a word. I moved my fingers through the sand, following the coolness underneath us. I looked over at Finn, who wasn't moving the sand around. He was laid out perfectly straight, with his hands cupped together on his chest—there was something on his mind. Finn broke the silence with a cough before speaking.

"What did he ask you?" he said, keeping perfectly still, his eyes directed upwards.

I didn't know what he meant, so I asked him.

"Before you were put in UnSin," he said.

I stopped digging in the sand.

"They didn't ask me anything, Finn, they just put the straps on my head and did the shock thing."

"The shock thing?" His whole body turned to me, although awkwardly in his haste. It was as if his body moved before he had asked it to. He leaned over me slowly, placing his fingertips on my temples and telling me that he was sorry.

My jaw started trembling, and soon, I was the one staring blankly into the night sky.

"Finn, it wasn't a real shock. Remember?"

"They didn't do that to me," he said, joining me in staring at the stars.

As he laid his head on my chest, Finn started telling me what had happened to him, which was vastly different from what had happened to me, and which was probably different for every member of UnSin. The Major had brought Finn into his office, which was populated by an audience of men in black; some he recognized and others he didn't. He told me that they sat him down in a funny-looking chair and told him he would be taking a lie detector test.

They told him it would help him understand that what he wanted was different from what his body really wanted. His body, they said, was with God. It was his mind that was the origin point of sin.

"They asked me if I was ever molested. How many men I've slept with. If my father left us. If I thought I could have a family. And no matter what I said, it told me I was lying."

Every word he spoke left his mouth and disappeared into the air in front of him. The words dissipated and became one with the ocean's rise and fall. There was nothing I could say, and so we laid together in silence, looking only upwards, trying to make sense of the mess of stars up above us. After a while, I could feel the sand around me moving as Finn's hand made its way toward mine.

The moon was shining high against the night sky when we got back from the beach. The guard had returned to find us sitting on the dock as though we had never moved. We filed into the bus and were no sooner back at Galilee. The moon was the largest thing in the sky that night. So much so that a group of men in black gathered around the front of the church to admire it, commenting on how much closer it seemed to Earth. Around the moon's many craters sat a milky fog that pulsed down onto the ground underfoot so far below it. Stillness had returned with us to campus.

Inside the dorm building, some of the other boys were in various stages of their respective nighttime routines, others were trying to sleep, and the ones closest to the window barely turned to see who opened the door because they were too wrapped up in trying to catch a glimpse of the deer someone had claimed to have seen a few days before. Apparently, the boy who vacuumed the hallway carpets had said that he had run right into a deer while he was outside emptying the filter. A lot of lies were fed to us at Galilee, but that one ranked among the biggest. If he really had gone outside, which he hadn't, he would have passed by the rec hall window because directly outside it was the only trash can that was accessible from the basement. Finn and I had been in the rec hall all day and hadn't seen anything. I wasn't going to say anything to those who got excited about it, though. What would that do?

The boys who weren't fortunate enough to have been placed by a window spent their time finding new ways to distribute their body weight across the mattress lying dead underneath them. Legs dangled over one side or another, periodically banging against the bed frame, while others rested, propped up on the metal bars at the foot of the beds. On all counts, these feet were connected to eyes more concerned with catching a glimpse of something out of the ordinary walking in or out of the swinging front door than they were with spotting a deer behind cheap, foggy glass.

Feeling bigger and better than I was, I walked into the room of wandering eyes ready to take them all on. I wanted them to look and to suspect and to guess what went on when the guard had come back to campus while we were alone on the beach. Had I been given the opportunity to go back in time, I would have forgone drying off in favor of sucking Finn's neck until it swelled, purple and tender. Unfortunately, with the exception of a few, brief glances, no one really stirred much at our entrance. So much for feeling smug.

Down the main aisle of the dorm building was the bed that marked our point of divergence, the place where Finn and I would go our separate ways and reality would set back in. Even with him being in the same room, nights never got any easier. His being in my life neither removed me from where I was nor lessened the length of the days I spent there. Alone at night, I really was alone. As we neared that bed, I felt the overwhelming urge to take Finn's hand and lead him back to my bed. I wanted nothing more than to go to sleep believing, however fleeting the comfort, that I wasn't alone after all. I thought maybe I'd dream of us at the beach and of my body floating in his arms—a different kind of alone and one I knew was possible to feel. Since no one was watching, I moved my hand over to his and squeezed it quickly before breaking away and continuing on to my bed.

"Hey!"

The voice came almost immediately.

"Hey!"

It sounded again, this time more urgently.

"What!?" I said, turning around to see who was trying to get my attention so badly.

It was Teacher's Pet.

"Did you go to the beach with Thomas?"

Finally someone noticed! *Yes, I did! And are you jealous?* I thought about what I wanted to say, how I wanted to play it. *Better play it cool.*

"Yeah . . ."

"He's cute. Don't you think?"

That I didn't expect. Teacher's Pet laughed nervously as he waited for my answer.

"Yeah . . . I guess he's cute," I said, as if stating a scientific fact rather than an opinion on something superficial.

I could see my hesitation was making him nervous, and he apologized for asking in the first place, saying that he thought he would try to make conversation since he doesn't ever see the other boys. I thought back to the gossipy mornings the twelve of us spent making up stories about him on our way to the seven deadly steps, the tall tales bred from the little we knew—or thought we knew—about him. His face maintained a smile that said: I will leave if you ask, but I want so badly to know what it was like. I felt bad for him, so I told him what happened at the beach with Thomas—well, more or less. He looked happier. My good deed for the day was done.

When I was through talking to Teacher's Pet, I returned to my bed and sat down, thinking about the beach. I closed my eyes to the sound of rushing water and screeching gulls. After taking a moment to revel in the memory, I tried to grab Finn's attention, but he was hidden behind a group of boys on the other side of the room. I could hear him fending off questions like the ones Teacher's Pet had asked me. The boys occupied Finn for quite some time, asking about the temperature of the water and if we skinny-dipped. He responded by asking how that could be possible if his trunks were still wet.

"I don't know, to cover for yourself," one of them said with some attitude, obviously wanting to keep the story going.

I closed my eyes, listening to the conversation go back and forth. It was easier to focus on what they were saying without the visual distractions. The world narrowed down to just a few voices telling stories. At one point, Finn was clearly exasperated and slapped his hands against his thighs before jokingly conceding to a delighted audience: "Ya got me."

When I hopped back off the bed sometime later, I noticed a wet mark spreading across the blanket from where my ass had just been. It stretched across the fabric, breaking and converging like tree branches until finally stopping at the edge of the mattress. In my haste, I had completely forgotten to change out of my bathing suit. At that point, the dorm guard was resting against the wall with his eyes narrowing in on me.

I tried to blot the dampness with a dirty shirt, but it was no use. *Ah well, it'll keep me cool tonight at least*, I thought to myself. My clean clothes were folded in a pile under my bed, and I grabbed a fresh set of pajamas to change into in the bathroom. I asked the dorm guard to walk me over, but to my surprise, he told me to go ahead by myself. I looked over my shoulder to make sure no one else had heard and asked him if what he was saying was actually what he meant. It was. His face sunk a bit when he repeated himself. I didn't dare hesitate for fear of him changing his mind. I tucked the clothes under my arm and darted past him and out the door, hoping no one saw me.

For the first time, it seemed like the heat was on the verge of breaking. There was a chill in the air when it breezed past me, and I could hear more rustling in the taller grass behind the buildings. *A rabbit*, I thought. I sucked in a deep breath, raising my chest upwards to swallow as much of the coolness as I could, hoping it would stay inside me. I thought of Finn and the feeling of his hand under the sand. More than anything, I thought of his name, picturing the curves and edges of it as I repeated it in my mind.

During the day, it was mostly the sound of birds that you'd hear, with the occasional barking from the congregation's dogs, but in the night, the sound of frogs croaking and the buzzing of a million little bugs—some that flickered green—filled the void that was left when the birds went back to their nests or to their tiny holes in the trees.

Only, there was another sound coming from behind the outhouse that night after Clamshell Bay. Not the sound of any old animal, either. This sound was distinctly human.

I froze dead in my tracks, clutching my pajamas closer to my body, and moved carefully to investigate the noise, making sure to stay out of sight. The closer I listened, the more voices I could detect. First one, then two, and then finally three. Three voices were mumbling behind the outhouse. *Why?* And if I didn't know any better, it sounded like one, or maybe two of them, were crying. Between a few garbled words, there would be a heaving sound followed by a tiny squeak like that of a dog that had just had its paw stepped on but didn't want to upset its owner by howling in pain. Someone was trying hard not to be heard. I pressed on silently. The grass under me was starting to creep farther up my leg. I was about as close to the back of the outhouse as I was going to get before totally exposing myself to whoever was back there.

"I'm not gonna say it again. Do it!"

One of the voices belonged to the lessons guard.

Why is he outside?

I started to feel really warm again. Almost as if at any moment the heat would burn through me and fly out of my mouth. I pressed myself up against the side of the outhouse and brought a pajama leg up to my mouth, biting down as hard as I could. A sharp pain ricocheted through my mouth. The lessons guard continued to get louder (as did the crying) until finally I heard a loud smack, and the crying turned to screaming. The grass around my feet twitched as I contorted my ankles, hoping a pit would open up that I could jump into. Another smack resonated in the air shortly afterward, and that was enough to get me to move toward the front of the outhouse. *Forget changing, I'll sleep in a wet bed. Just get me out of this.*

When I got around to the front, two of the voices were standing there. Simultaneously I felt waves of heat and freezing cold prickle across my shoulders and down my spine. They were naked and crying, and they were two of the others from UnSin: the girl and her friend. I recognized her friend as the boy who had stood between her and The Major when she had pointed the gun at him. The girl covered herself, but her friend reached out to me and begged me to get help. I saw that his nose was bleeding pretty hard. There were scrapes on both of their bodies.

"Please," he said, "there's no time."

And he was right. As soon as the boy started talking to me, the lessons guard came out from behind the building. His pants were down around his ankles. He looked at me and then over to the girl, extending his hand onto her shoulder and smiling back at me. She turned away and cried to herself again, this time leaning against the door so no one would see her penis. The boy raised his hand, but then covered himself before he did anything with the fist he had made.

I expected the guard to chase me down, or even to scream at me, but he stayed perfectly still during the brief exchange. He didn't even reach down to pull up his pants. His eyes showed no fear that he would be caught because there was no possible way for that to happen. He knew he could get away with what he was doing, and it was making him smile ear to ear. It was me who started running in the end. I ran back to the dorm building, dropping my pajamas in the mad rush toward the creaking screen door and my only hope of help.

The dorm guard must have heard me running because he was outside of the building by the time I got there. *Good,* I thought, *maybe he saw what had just happened.* At the very least, that increased my chances of him believing me. Which, I should say now, I really believed he would.

Stupid.

I started to tell him what happened, but I could feel the tears growing in my eyes. In between hiccupped breaths, I wiped them away as fast as they fell—I was only going to recount the story once. I didn't want to cry through an important section and have him either ask me to repeat it, or worse, for him to decide it wasn't important enough to ask for clarification. Before I could finish, he put his hand on my shoulder and told me to calm down. It was at this point I noticed that I had dropped my pajamas. I wanted something to hold onto, and suddenly that thing was gone.

"What you're saying is impossible. Now, be honest, what were you and Thomas doing at the beach?" he asked, smirking to suggest we had done something that would have made me imagine the whole assault.

"What?" I said, somewhat surprised. "Nothing, you have to believe me. Please go over there, you'll see them. Please."

He looked at me with wide-eyed sympathy before finally whispering, "You couldn't have seen anything because you didn't go to the bathroom. You need *me* to take you to the bathroom, remember, and I've been *here* the whole time. So, either you imagined all that, or I just caught you sneaking away from camp. And you know what? That would be a pretty big strike three for you, Peter."

"What," I whimpered, completely dumbfounded.

"So, I would suggest you get back in bed before you get yourself, or Thomas, into any more trouble."

A feeling came over me in that moment that hadn't surfaced since I was a child and my parents would say I couldn't do that one thing I really wanted to do. Maybe they had even promised earlier in the day that I could, and now I couldn't. I felt like somehow the dorm guard would listen to me if I really clenched my kneecaps hard enough and begged through stutters, so I kept whispering "please" as he looked on with increasing anger. He lifted his arm and let his hand fall firmly on my shoulder, his fingers spreading and gripping me tight. As his arm was lifting, I noticed he had a tattoo on his wrist, which upon further inspection revealed itself to be the shield emblem of The Social Preservation Society. My tears started flowing faster than I could wipe them away. I looked over to find that the girl, her friend, and the lessons guard were gone from the vicinity of the outhouse. The dorm guard removed his hand from my shoulder as I looked back at him to continue pleading. In one fluid motion, he reached behind his back before swinging his hand around again, this time plunging the baton from his belt into the side of my face.

CHAPTER 12

"Blood brings attention."

It was the first thing I heard when I started coming to. The voice that said it spoke with frightened intensity, as if at any point the speaker would break into a full-bellied scream. It was a voice teetering on its edge and about to fall.

"You fucking know that, and this is what you do to prove it? Huh? Real fucking smart. Real fucking smart, Jimmy!" The voice, which had to that point maintained a sense of professional indignation to keep the jitters from overtaking the situation, soon cracked as it roared out: "Fix this, or I swear to God I'll bash your fucking face in."

The outburst was followed by the hollow sound of something metal thrown against tile and the slamming of a door.

All around me were what seemed in my altered state to be disembodied hands. Some were carefully attending to a wound on the outside of my mouth, while others held something against my teeth on the inside. I tried to get a sense of whether or not I was in pain, but I couldn't tap into any specific part of me no matter how hard I tried. I was adrift in the air like soft music. The taste of blood pooled around my tongue, waning in intensity as a tube came in to suck the goop away. The instrument gurgled and coughed through its attempts to swallow the mess of spit and blood.

My senses came back to me in short, violent bursts; first taste, then touch. It felt like my jaw was broken in several spots. I could imagine the crushed bones that their gloved fingers were desperately holding in place. So many of the hands around me had probably wished for the chance to use the power that was resting, burning in their belt loops, but now that someone had, they wanted it all put back. But it was too late; the dam was crumbling beneath them, leaving only a sea of blood for them to drown in.

Should my blood be their downfall, let it flow freely from me, I thought.

Pain intensified in a few of the spots where I determined the damage was probably the worst. I tried to move my tongue over to investigate, but as I did, the hands around me stopped moving. I was encircled by figures frozen in tableau. The stillness of it all allowed me to make out a few of the bodies that were holding perfectly still behind the fingers.

"I think he's awake. What do we do?" said one of the hands.

"Here," another shouted.

A sharp pain pricked in my shoulder, and I started to float again, this time dipping in and out of consciousness. The figures behind the gloves faded and, with them, so did the desire to move my tongue. I tried to hold on to the pain, hoping that it would snap me awake again, but it didn't. I was too far gone.

Through the fog, I was only able to pick out bits of information, short snippets of words, which grew more disparate and languished as I, myself, faded faster and faster. Someone was talking about The Major someone else was yelling about me; and I thought I heard someone crying, too. Each time something stuck in my mind, it took several minutes to make sense of. I had to think hard about the sound of each word that I was trying to make clear in my head. The curves and cadences of the voices that spoke them only added to the difficulty of the task. I started to forget what I had heard versus what I had made up in my mind while trying to understand what was happening around me at the same time. After a while, I could only make out the sound of air leaving my body in long, labored gusts.

My eyes grew heavy soon after the shot had been administered, but I used my last bit of strength to try and keep them open. I wanted some glimpse into what was happening inside my mouth. For the most part, the hands drew pieces of white chips in and out of my mouth. At first, I thought all of my teeth had been shattered, but soon enough I realized the chips were not my own. They were comparing colors for a crown.

"Don't touch that," I heard a voice say. "You never know what he might have."

While I floated above the table and looked down at the body below, as much a foreign entity as my own possession, I saw a misplaced confusion on the faces of those surrounding me. They didn't know whether to fear me or to hate me. Medical oaths and cultural practices converged below the fog, making me once again more enigmatic than reality would have revealed to them if they chose to look beyond their gloves. If they chose to fear me, even that registered as confusion on their faces. They hated me without knowing me because of something that told them my blood, mysterious in its purity, was worthy of hatred.

I've always known what I am and what it means to *be* what I am. Only to those who hate is the body of one confident in self-definition made hazy and confused. A few moments later, I lost the battle with the drugs they had pumped into my veins. I fell back into my body from my vantage point in the air and into a deep, deep sleep.

The next day my mouth was sore, but I moved quickly to the rec hall so I could tell Finn what had happened.

"What the fuck?" He was never one to mince words.

"Yeah, so basically jokes on them because they fixed my teeth for free," I responded, clicking my teeth together while trying to keep a lightness in my eyes.

Finn kept his eyebrows furrowed as I talked. Below them, his eyes locked onto mine trying to discover what he missed in the story that warranted joking. I so wanted him to laugh and for his body to push it out without any effort. It was a horrible thing that had happened, but I was running out of strength. Before long his face relaxed as he began howling with laughter. *Yes!* Every time I moved to shush him, we fell further into the fit, eventually collapsing onto the floor. We were both afraid, of course, and the pressure was beginning to mount in ways we had no way of predicting when we had first been driven onto campus in the black Escalades, but right now, there was no reason to fall into fear when it was just as easy to fall into laughter. Once we picked ourselves up and sat down at the puzzle table, Finn's eyes narrowed after some moments of stabling silence. The seriousness was inevitable, and I had pushed it back about as far as I could.

"Why did he hit you?" Finn was wringing his hands nervously.

I didn't want to tell him. I wanted to keep that horror as far from us as I possibly could; But then I thought of the two people outside the outhouse, being forced to take their clothes off for—I didn't even want to think about what for. I responded clearly and monotone, staring down at the puzzle table. HAL's eye from *2001: A Space Odyssey* stared back at me.

"I forgot to change after we got back from the beach, and he let me go to the bathroom alone, which I thought was odd, but I went anyway. When I got over near the outhouse, I heard three voices. The guard had two of the others off in the back. I think he was raping them."

"Julien." My name was all that came to him. Whatever Finn thought I was about to say, that wasn't it. He was truly, genuinely lost for words. He just kept whispering to himself and shaking his head to reset the images flashing through his brain. As I continued, he grabbed my hands gently.

"And," I said, interrupting his mumbling because I could feel the tears welling, "I told the dorm guard what was happening, but he knew. He had it all planned out. He said that he didn't walk me over so either I broke the rules and left without asking, or I imagined the whole thing, but I didn't Finn, I didn't imagine it. I saw everything."

"I'm so sorry, Jules . . ."

"I was so scared and I didn't know what to do so I just started crying and begging him to do something, but he just hit me instead." Finn moved over to hold me as I started crying. "It hurt so bad, Finn. I thought I was gonna die."

Despite the pain and fear that sat by my side at Galilee, crying into Finn's chest was the first time I felt truly defeated. I couldn't help but succumb to the enormity of it all. I buried my face deeply, inhaling his smell in each breath. I couldn't look at him while I was crying. He could see me bleed and he could see me laugh, but I didn't want him to see me cry. To cry meant that I had buckled under the weight they put on me, and I didn't want to lose my strength.

"We don't have to talk about it if you don't want to," he said tenderly.

"I wish I could have helped them."

Finn asked me to look at him, but I shook my head and buried it deeper into his shirt. He asked again, shifting his body around until I was holding myself up, crooked and shaking. I looked over at his chest at the wet spots I had left.

"I'm sorry about your shirt," I said, finally looking at him.

"It's okay, Jules," he said, running his fingers through my hair, trying to put each section back into place. "If you want, we can report them when we get out of here."

We. It was the first time Finn referenced a we outside of Galilee. I hesitated to respond because I wanted to hold on to that word for just a moment more. It was selfish given the circumstances, but I needed to sit with it. Crying hadn't removed my strength; it had brought Finn to speak *we* into existence. It was no longer a faraway hope in my mind. And it meant that maybe we really could report it after the fact. Strength in numbers, right?

"Promise?"

"I promise."

Later in the day, there was an unusually large delivery from the Narragansett Library. The personality-devoid delivery-man dropped off two boxes and came back a few minutes later with two more, grunting as he stood back up.

"Sorry about the load today guys, we got a donation from a nursing home that closed recently. It's mostly good stuff I think," he said from behind the cardboard before taking off a final time.

Finn told me I could sit down if I wanted to and that he would handle everything, but I decided to help him put away the donations anyway. Partly because there was just so much to sort through, but mostly because I was beginning to feel antsy and wanted a distraction.

I opened up a box which was filled to the brim with old copies of *People* magazine. On the bottom left-hand corner of each cover was a hole in the shape of a rectangle, where an address had once been. Laying in the box, it looked like the magazines were printed with a large hole in them. It didn't seem at all like anyone had taken scissors to them. The incision was so small you wouldn't even have known it was there unless you opened the front cover and the rectangle parted across your knuckles. I snickered to myself while flipping through the pages of the magazine on top of the pile. It was dated March 19th, 2018 and featured a large photo of two seemingly happy straight people with the caption "The Bachelor BETRAYAL!" Exclamation point and all. Above the photo was a small line of dialogue about the shooting at Parkland, and next to that was a collage of photos from that year's Oscars. I imagined the copy from 2019—which was probably somewhere in the boxes we were sifting through—looked very similar, just with some different contextual notes. Almost thirty years later and the same headlines still run, selling left and right. The reason for my chuckle was because at one point this had been breaking news to those who followed the pop culture of the time closely: the moms in line at grocery stores across America; the young gay men taking mental pictures of the Sexiest Man Alive issue before anyone caught them looking. Now, it was decades-old news: read, remembered for a time, and then largely forgotten. The music Finn and I listened to outdated the news stories by several more decades, and yet the magazines seemed so much older.

Before showing it to Finn, who was sitting in a pile of board games, I picked up a *World Wildlife Federation* magazine that was under the first few issues of *People*. The pages opened with little effort to a photo that had been dog-eared. "Adopt A Tiger Today" was written in above the photo, which featured a tiger posed on a rock with a stuffed animal version of itself off to the side. For a few payments a month, you could sponsor conservation efforts that would supposedly help raise the number of tigers in the wild. Whoever had dog-eared the page had also scribbled some numbers in the margins.

At the zoo near where I grew up, they used to have a tiger exhibit with a pair of white Bengal tigers that had been rescued from somewhere far off and exotic. The specifics are hazy now, but I think it was somewhere in the Indian subcontinent. Anyway, they were at risk of being hunted, so they could never be re-released—something the zoo was pretty good about with the other animals they rescued. At first, the pair of tigers were fine, great even, as they acclimated to their new surroundings, but one winter the snow really got to them. New England winters often bring bitter chills, and that was the case that year. When the snow finally melted, the tigers refused to leave the cages they were kept in over the winter. A zookeeper tried to coax them out and nearly lost an arm in the process. Over time, the zoo gave up hope of making the tigers comfortable until one spring day, right when the tulips were in full bloom, the tigers emerged from their winter cages into their outside enclosure. Down the protective barrier surrounding their exhibit, past the clicking wire of the fence and the bulletproof glass, was a seizure-support dog whose owner was distracted by a squirrel and looking in the opposite direction. Both tigers walked over as close as they could get and sat down, mirroring the position of the dog. If the dog stood up, so did the tigers. When the dog finally whined to get the attention of its owner, the tigers roared so loudly it's said that the zoo shook. This startled the owner, who hurried the dog away.

"Anything good?" I asked Finn.

"I think if we put the pieces together from all these, we might have one game we can play," he responded.

I didn't tell him about the tigers, but we had some fun with the *People*, filling out the leftover crossword puzzle answers and critiquing the clothes people had worn to big premieres and book launches. The laughter continued until we saw the next magazine in the pile—not *People* this time. This magazine's cover featured a photo of a young man who had killed himself after going to conversion therapy. Finn moved to take it from me, but I yelled at him that I wanted to read it, and he quickly relented.

"Julien, I really don't think that's a good idea."

"Don't tell me what's good for me."

The boy's name was Cody, and he was from a small town in the southernmost part of Georgia. He had been raised by a well-to-do family with deep connections to the local church scene. He knew from an early age, of course, but there were a lot of things he knew; for the first time, some of those things were in conflict with each other. It was easy enough to avoid as a topic for a while, but when his peers began dating, Cody began to get interrogated as to why he *wasn't* dating. He told his parents the truth, which they were fine with so long as he agreed to never tell another soul.

I've seen these stories before. The in-depth beginning and ending, and the vague, specter of a middle, which is like toes skimmed across the surface of water trying hard not to get wet. Cody eventually developed a friendship with another boy from the area, who he spent hours talking to about everything from religion to favorite foods. One day, the other boy sent Cody a naked picture, which scared and attracted Cody at the same time. Which came first, I don't know, but the article went on to mention that Cody was the one who brought up the idea of conversion therapy to his family. His family sent him off to a camp in Jacksonville, Florida, and Cody deleted the boy from his life. Everyone was content believing they had done the right thing. Only, when Cody came back, nothing changed, so he changed it himself. *A grievous loss of life.* It was both what I thought, and how the article ended.

I put down the magazine and stood up quickly, looking for the next thing to occupy my mind. Finn stayed seated in his pile of board games and watched me walk around in circles.

"Julien, sit down. We can talk about it."

"I don't want to talk, Finn! What's there to say? He killed himself. It's over." My forehead began to sweat, and I lifted my wrist to dab away the beads. I tried to clear my throat as well, but all that came out was a whimper. And then I saw red. "He killed himself and I'm here with you and it's not right. It's not fair."

"You're right," he said. "It's not fair, but there's a lot that's unfair and you work through it. That's what we're doing here, right?"

"I don't know what we're doing here, Finn. I mean, what are we doing? We're sitting around and pretending like what's happening isn't what's happening. Look around, this isn't camp!"

"You think I don't know that?"

"I don't know!"

As I said it, I tripped on one of the board games. My body came tumbling down in a heap. Finn was silent and my ears were ringing. It was hard to tell if I felt more like I was about to throw up or pass out. I sat up and started kicking the board games, one of which knocked into the pile Finn was working on. The pile crashed and sent the disparate pieces scattering across the floor.

"I'm trying to help you, but you can't let yourself go like this," Finn said in a measured tone.

"Why not, *hmm*? Because then this is gonna happen!?" I threw the magazine with Cody's face on it at Finn. The pages hit his lap with enough force to create permanent creases in the paper. Finn picked up the magazine and bend it a few times, trying to make it lay flat again. When he looked back at me, his eyes communicated that his patience was wearing thin.

"Yes! Because it *could* happen," he said. "It could happen to you, it could happen to me, it could happen to any one of those people who sleep in that dorm with us. Look at where we are, Julien. Don't you remember how we ended up here? Neither one of us could keep our heads down long enough to stay out of trouble. You getting mad at me right now is exactly what they would want. Do you really want to be alone here? That's not going to make the world change. It's not going to bring the Codys of the world back, either."

"I not going to stop fighting, Finn. If you want me to give this place a pass to kill us, that's not gonna happen."

"I didn't say that. What I'm saying is that you have something Cody didn't, and I'm sorry he didn't have that, I really am, but you can't live in that pity forever. You have to decide who you're fighting and who you're not."

I looked around at the scattered pieces of the board game and felt a wave of embarrassment crash over me. Finn was right in what he was saying, but I wasn't ready to concede. I wanted him to organize the pieces into neat little piles again and ask me to help him figure out what empty boxes they belonged in. It was becoming more clear, though, that the mess was mine, in more ways than one, and, therefore, mine to pick up.

"How can you be so sure of that, Finn? I don't want to be angry and I don't want to be mad at you, but I don't see how that's going to do anything."

Finn picked up the magazine again, looked at the cover as though it might say something, then put it face down and moved to the puzzle table. I joined him there and repeated my question. The look in his eyes afterward, one of silent connection, sparked something familiar. Something I hadn't felt since the day I had arrived on campus and had seen Finn with his cloth bag stepping out of his Escalade into a cloud of dust.

"When I found out I had to come here," Finn said, "I felt like the world was ending. I had been so mad all the time and I felt like if nothing had come from that anger yet, then nothing ever would. I just wanted someone to look me in the eyes and tell me they got it. That they really, really understood what I was going through. But no one ever did that. I didn't even tell anyone I was coming here because I didn't plan on coming here."

"Finn, I'm so sorry."

"I waited until my roommate left and then I swallowed as many pills as I could get my hands on. I mean I took everything that looked like it could kill me. I thought it was the angriest thing I could do to get back at everything that had ever hurt me. I realized I was wrong probably ten seconds later and threw them up. Julien, when I tell you I have never felt worse in my life. I sat there and cried all night." Finn paused for a moment to collect himself, and then, bizarrely given the circumstances, he smiled over at me. "But then I woke up and I was alive. And I thought to myself that the biggest fuck you I could give all of them is to keep on living and sucking up their air."

The wave of embarrassment returned, but this time quickly washed itself away. I didn't know exactly what I wanted to say, but it involved taking more responsibility than I was willing to take a moment ago.

"I'm so sorry I got angry, Finn. It's just everything is so hard to handle right now, and I thought if I could just let it out. If I could just release it. I'm guess I'm not sure what I thought. But I wasn't thinking of you and I'm sorry. I do know that I don't want to think of a world where you're not in it. You're special and valuable, and I'm so sorry that happened to you."

The pain of recollecting the story stayed in Finn's eyes, but he smiled and cleared his throat abruptly before turning to look at the game pieces all over the floor. I told him that I would clean it up if he wanted to rest, but he responded—somewhat firmly—that he wanted to do it.

"I think it might be good to focus on something else for a while. Why don't you take the trash out and get some air, too? Kinda looks like you're gonna puke or cry."

Some people have "resting bitch face," but I have something even worse: "resting deer-In-the-headlights face." If I'm not focusing on what my face is doing, it communicates some great sadness to everyone around me, even if I'm nearly bursting with happiness. At the very least, my face meant that I was listening to what Finn was saying. It was going in one ear and sticking, which isn't always the case when I'm confronted with something. Finn didn't look like he was going to puke or cry, but I could definitely see that he needed some space for a minute. I told him that taking out the trash was a great idea and twirled the top of the trash bag into a tight double knot before heading toward the door.

As I was just about to walk out into the hallway, from behind me Finn said, "Just so you know, Jules, listening to music here with you is everything I was looking for before that I couldn't find."

I closed the door to the rec hall and felt my emotions, all of them maybe, rising to the surface. Finn's story kept repeating in my head, and I thought of all the times when similar thoughts had risen in me. I dropped the trash bag and broke into a run, running through the downstairs hall, up the seven deadly stairs, out the front door, and across the field to the dorm hall feeling much like I had when I had fumbled through the halls of the dentist's office. I couldn't move fast enough, but there was nowhere for me to go. It felt like the ground underneath me was breaking apart behind me. When I finally made it to my bed, I fell into my pillow, and everything went dark.

CHAPTER 13

Outside the dorm window, a family of giant, gray clouds gathered and changed the hue of the day. Streaks of light that reached the church grounds wavered soft and dull, a nightlight in perpetual darkness. When I woke up, I could feel the coolness of it all in the breezes that passed over my body. The screen door clapped against its frame as if dancing in the wind. I looked down at my shirt to find it darkened not with rain, but sweat. I was still alone in the room, but I was already getting ready to leave it empty again.

I was lucky that no one had found me. My guess was that The Major had found a surge of energy from the rain and was prolonging his lesson. Even if someone had found me, I could have easily explained away my presence as sickness.

I grabbed my backpack, dusted it off a bit, and threw it on top of my bed. When Sheila had given me *The Wild*

Heart album, I had taken it back to my room and hidden it under the mattress at the foot of my bed, where the weight wouldn't crush it. I had kept it in its plastic wrapping, hoping maybe it would be opened outside of Galilee. Maybe even with Finn. I tucked it deep into my backpack and darted through the door on a back swing.

The grass outside was slicked with dew and sprayed my ankles as I made my way back to the basement, hoping Finn was still there. All around me was the perfume of wet pavement, fresh and damp. The closer I got to the main building of the church, the faster I ran. Finn was right; I was no use to me or him acting like that. The rain had caused the basement door to swell. I knew that opening it would cause a considerable squeak to ring out into the campus. Once inside, I turned around to shut it quietly, pressing a firm shoulder against the swollen wood, but my body weight sent it slamming instead. There was no doubt they had heard me up above. I paused for a second just to be sure no one was coming down the stairs to scold me and made my way into the room. To my dismay, Finn was gone.

The scene I had walked into behind the outhouse played through my head again, pinging the sides of my skull as the images zoomed past—the girl holding herself and the look of desperate fear on the boy's face. The images laid upon piles of guilt and regret over my own inaction and fear over what else had been made possible by the actions of the powerful in the night. It was words the guard used to command two innocent souls to engage in what had been condemned by thousands of years of other words uttered through similar teeth; years and voices that called out in a cacophony of sound for damned souls to perform their sin in front of judging eyes. Words fall in expectation, creating lines in the sand. There is no crossing lines which words have made so. If bodies fall on the other side, there's no saving them.

It's a feeling I know well. My life is lived at the end of strings. Sometimes they are held clearly within my own grip, and sometimes they have no visible ends. Being at Galilee, the hands that hold them had become clearer to me. I can always feel myself being pulled. There is rarely a time I feel my actions, my body, are solely mine. So often, I find myself caught somewhere between what others want from me and what I want for myself, and I never seem to satisfy either. The more time I spent at Galilee, though, the more I realized that the postulating that had consumed my every waking moment was not unique to me. Everyone in there, even The Major, was carefully crafting each movement for no reason other than that he was afraid, afraid of the same thing I had now acquired the fear of. This was, of course, because he was one un-cautious movement away from taking my place, and if I played my cards right, I was one cautious movement away from deriving enough power to drag myself out of there.

I slouched my backpack onto the puzzle table and stared down at the unzipped pouch housing *The Wild Heart* album. I needed to hear it now. To know there was still something alive in this world that rang louder in my head than the scene behind the outhouse. The air here was lifeless and stale. The combination of which had placed an ache in my head, which only worsened each day I lifted it off my pillow. I needed something to break through the constant ringing.

The purples of the cover photo appeared deeper in the sullen lighting, the three Stevies moving like ghosts through a red-tinted mist. Years spent between stacks of vinyl had muted the crispness of the photo, and it laid in my hands like an artifact from an ancient time. I sat listening to her voice and let the day grow dark.

I had spent many nights like this in the past, sitting with a glowing screen to my face, watching old videos of Stevie performing. She was the most intense person I had ever seen captured on film, powerful enough to push out near inhuman bellows, but soft enough to warble almost to breaking. As much as her voice could summon, it could also soothe. Her hands threw shawls off her body as she spun but drew them in tightly during moments of stillness. She was barely self-contained. If a shawl spun loose, she would have surely disappeared. I watched the same videos over and over again, but that tension was never gone from them. I had spent so much time in the closet. I hid so much I started to believe there was a reason to hide. When everyone was asleep in the still of the night, I would swipe the blankets off my bed and spin like she did. *Free.* My closet doors were kicked down through blue-lit screens by a witch with suede boots and demons of her own.

I opened the blinds that had closed out stares earlier in the day and let the orange flood in and bathe the room. By the time the sun started to sink further, the album had made several revolutions around my world. Normally I would have sung along with the first rotation, but it was too risky. There was no telling what would happen if I were caught. But several loops later, the lyrics began to eat away at me until they could no longer be contained. "Nightbird" was the song that tipped me over the edge. It's mystical, ethereal, and odd. Quintessential Stevie. By the time the chorus hit for the first time and the castanets clipped away, I was unstoppable. In my excitement, I missed someone walking in who was protected from my sight by the growing shadows.

"And when I call you."

A line sung by Sharon Celani and repeated back by Stevie. Only this time it wasn't Stevie who answered the call, but a different voice.

I opened my mouth to scream but stopped when he stepped into the light. Finn was in his pajama shirt, which was buttoned just below his collarbone, exposing a small patch of hair. He hadn't intended to startle me but was entertained by it nonetheless.

"*Shhhhh*. It's only me. I'm sorry," he said, laughing as he placed a hand on my shoulder. "I figured you'd be here. I told the guard about the big delivery and said you were still working on it. He told me I was a bastard to let you do it alone. Sent me right to you."

Finn's hand gripped harder on my shoulder until we were swaying together in the orange glow. I thought of the many things I wanted to do right then. I wanted to tell someone about what the guard did, I wanted to get out of there, and I wanted to dance with Finn. Three completely opposed wants of varying validity, and yet, there they were. I was going to get out of there and I was going to tell someone—everyone—about what I saw by the outhouse.

I sang along to the music softly. To myself mostly, to keep away the thoughts that were fighting for attention in my head. There was nothing but myself keeping me from giving in to the urge to dance with Finn. I slipped my hands around his waist, and he pulled me close to him as we rocked to the beat of a piano solo halfway through the song. When the chorus started up again, I broke from him, grabbed a blanket from the floor, and swung it around the two of us, pulling it tightly around us like a cape. He laughed, throwing his head back, grabbed the cape, and flourished it like a matador.

Stevie's voice came back, but Finn just stared at me without moving. I paused, thinking something was wrong, and then all in a rush, Finn moved towards me. I grabbed his hands, squeezing them quickly, and pulled him in for a kiss that lasted until the end of the song.

One thing became clear to me after our dance in the night—I was no longer alone there. I had someone whom I now felt responsible to protect and was emboldened by the drive within me to do so. Even in Galilee, there was still a spark that could not be so easily blown out. Something in me had called for Finn, and something within him understood enough to take my waist and sway to the music. It was that spark that I now needed to protect. I was prepared to do so at any cost. Nothing more could be taken from me, but I still had something to give.

When the song ended, the silence took me by surprise. There was a brief moment right before the next track started, Sheila's beloved "Stand Back," that was steeped in complete, deafening silence. We broke from the kiss, and looked at each other without speaking. It was the kind of silence that can only follow something wholly unique, when the high is broken and reality shifts ever so slowly back into focus. We could do nothing besides look at each other as if to acknowledge the passing nature of the moment. Soon we'd have to move in silence back into the roles we were expected to play, happily and without complaint. It was the only way to ensure the call of the nightbird could be heard again. Somehow that was enough.

Following our routine, Finn and I left in stages, with me being the first to go. I slipped the album back into its sleeve and set it down against the record player. It was too special to sit packed between records we'd never get to.

Making my way toward the door, I felt a feeling of

contentment deep within me, which hadn't existed at Galilee before. Or anywhere else for that matter. I reached for the door, and as I did, the following thought crossed my mind: *how weird that the door seems so near.* I expected a hesitation as I moved to leave, or a *Poltergeist* situation where the space between myself and the door became wider with every step, but neither happened. The distance bridged during our dance also served to solidify one important thing: the value of our lives, together and apart. With it, the hesitation was gone because I finally knew that whatever was waiting for me beyond the doors wasn't going to make me question my worth again.

I slept better than I had ever slept before. Gone were the images of centipede goo and, in their place, came a wonderful stillness. My dreams were black enough to keep me asleep the whole night. Not to the point where I had forgotten where I was, but enough to make that reality seem just a few inches further than it actually was. If I were to extend my arm as far as it would go, my fingertips would just barely graze the surface of reality, parting the cosmos before retracting safely back to the security of my blanket.

I rose with less hesitation than usual, even taking a minute to enjoy the sunlight that was just beginning to fill the room. It was warm, but not too hot. Just warm enough to make you stretch extra high during your morning yawn. The dorm guard was characteristically quiet as he led me out to brush my teeth in the bathroom sink. He didn't talk much to begin with, especially not early in the morning. I paused for a moment at the mouth of the door and turned my head back to find Finn, but he had already left.

The congregation's dogs were playing outside again.

This time they were playing fetch with a woman in yoga pants and a high ponytail, which spun like a propeller each time she threw the ball. The dogs would come bounding back to her, and then she'd repeat the process, arching herself back before throwing herself forward with a swallowed grunt. The dogs didn't seem to mind the repetitiveness of it all, but she did. The woman eventually threw the ball into the pen, which the dogs ran into, before she closed the gate and disappeared to the front of the church. Soon after she left, a group of young kids came around the corner of the church and started a game of tag. It was a sunny day, and most wore strips of white sunblock across their faces as proof. One of the kids was slower than the rest and so the one most often "it." He got so fed up with it that when he got tagged the last time, he threw his arms up in defeat and declared a time out. The other kids all agreed a time out was needed and plopped down on the grass. Some of them laid down, stretched out on the grass, and others sat cross-legged, rocking back and forth, but they all waited to move until the time out was over. As important as the chase was, it could begin and end at the speaking of two words. "Time out" sent it all screeching to a halt.

When I was done brushing—and checking the corners of my mouth for lingering toothpaste—I shoved the brush back into the plastic bag The Major had given us all on the first day and crunched across the gravel path back to the dorm building. In the new day sun, the dried water stains along the bottom of the plastic bag brought a nasty taste to the back of my mouth which I promptly tried to smack away with a few disgusted flicks of my tongue. *I wonder if they'd give me a new one if I asked? Better not.* I tightened my grip around the toothbrush and followed the guard back to the dorm.

The calendar on the wall read July 18 in black lettering. July 17 now existed only in the serrated edges of a page someone had ripped off while I was brushing my teeth. I avoided the calendar with great success after the first week. There was more time on the other side then, but now there were only a few more days until I'd be out. That was somehow more manageable.

At one point, my only priority was to fake it until a certificate was handed to me, and I could finish my root canal in relative peace. It would have been impossible to tell that version of myself that before my time at Galilee was even over, my own health would be the third thing on my to-do list. UnSin was just another unbelievable curve in the road. The me that woke up on July 18th made sure my priorities were in order as I walked to the rec hall to see Finn.

One: As soon as I get out, I'm going directly to the police and reporting what the guards did to the girl and her friend. I don't know their names, but maybe I could ask them before I leave. Maybe a description will be enough. Someone must have a log of everyone that was sent to Galilee. *How hard can it possibly be to get retroactive justice?*

Two: After the police, I'm going to sit down with Finn and write down every single thing we can remember that happened to us and compile it in a book. After that, I'm not sure what we'll do with the stories, but they'll be there when we need them. Maybe we'll find The Major's address and send it to him just so he knows we know and will never not know. The thought only then occurred to me that nothing Finn and I had was entirely set in stone. It might even be circumstantial, although I didn't want to believe that. *I'll ask him today.*

Three: I will frame my certificate and bring the whole thing down to the dentist's office, through the glass doors, and hang the proof of my excursion on their wall when they're not looking. Then I'd set up a follow-up appointment for the surgery I no longer needed just to tell everyone in person that they can fuck completely off. I'd laugh and peel out of the parking lot feeling triumphant and when I got home, I would go immediately to my computer, pick a new dentist, and *RESEARCH THEIR POLITICS*!

When I arrived at item number four, I found myself at the door of the rec hall full of spit and vinegar.

Four: I will walk through this door and forget about 1-3 for the time being. Finn brings me peace and I deserve a moment of peace.

I could hear him moving around on the other side of the door and paused for a moment to listen. He was lifting something from the ground and walking it over to the puzzle table. I heard the distinctive sound of heavy cardboard boxes landing against Plexiglas. Unable to wait any longer, I opened the door and slinked around it, closing it quickly to avoid anyone seeing the excitement on my face.

The rec hall was brighter than it usually was. The curtains were drawn open as far as they could go, and several of the window panels were resting on books to allow a steady stream of morning air to pulse in. *Strange*. Finn was always careful to keep them shut so that no one would hear us talking or listening to music, even if that meant the room ran hot for the day. The records we finished and kept by the record player had also been tampered with. This wasn't Finn.

"Hello," I said, markedly more as a question than an invitation for politeness.

The boy snapped his head up. A few strands of hair fell into his face, which he promptly pushed back into place.

"Oh, hi! I'm Judas," the boy said nervously, extending his hand to me as he came out from behind the table.

I stared down at it for a moment. Judas nervously flicked his eyes up at me and then down at his hand before letting his arm go limp and swing by his side.

"I don't know what happened, but this morning The Major told me that he was moving some people around. He said I was here now."

For some reason, I very vividly pictured my fist grinding Judas' face into the ground. *Why? He hadn't done anything wrong. Who knows, maybe he did?*

"Look, I'm sorry. I know I shouldn't say this, but I saw you coming back from the beach with that other boy. We all did. I'm . . . I'm sorry they moved him."

The nicer he was, the more vivid the image became.

"None of us said anything if that's what you're thinking. I'm not really Judas, remember?"

He was right. He wasn't Judas. But then again, I didn't know who he really was, so he might as well have been Judas. Or Voldemort, or the wicked witch of the west, or Hannibal Lecter. He could be any combination of any number of anythings, and I was angry that I didn't know for sure. I looked away from Judas to keep from choking him, and suddenly, the familiarities of the rec hall started melting away. The harder I tried to keep them in my mind—how Finn's shadow moved with the sun, or how carefully he set the needle down on the records—the quicker they fell away from my memory. I started seeing spots on the wall I never noticed before, and I found it harder and harder to picture the way the records spun. The little blips and burps that came with every revolution were beginning to fade. The sunlight coming from outside was almost blinding as the light streamed into the room, a microscope light flickering on to see the slide held between metal clamps better.

"Shut the curtains," I said quickly.

He did, just as quickly. When he was finished, his hands lingered on the fabric as if to offer additional adjustments. Anything that would make me less angry with him. He stood like a servant waiting for orders, even opening his eyes really widely, raising his eyebrows dramatically, and pursing his lips into a tight smile to show fearful, angry subservience. He was only going to put up with my venom for so long.

The intensity of the sunlight was gone now. I looked at him, feeling an apology tingling in my mouth, but I couldn't bring myself to say it. Maybe I didn't want it to come out. Without speaking, I moved over to the box of records and began sifting through them. I pulled out the ones that Finn and I had listened to and set them against the record player, but not before checking to make sure nothing had happened to them. Judas watched from the windows as I examined each one. First the front cover, then the back, and finally, squeezing the sides, I made sure the record itself was still intact. I didn't want anything to be wrong, and there was no real indication that anything *would* be wrong with them, but I checked anyway. Partly looking for a reason to stay angry, maybe. At Judas. At Galilee. At everything. I turned around to look at Judas when I was finished. He was still holding the curtain, but now I could see he was also holding his breath.

"Don't ever touch those again," I said. "I'll handle the records."

Judas nodded, finally releasing the curtain from his grip.

Slowly, the room started to look familiar again. As I began to cool down from my anger toward Judas, I decided to strike up a conversation with him. Getting on his good side, I reasoned, would bring me one step closer to finding Finn. Either I could convince him to do the little work there was to do while I figured out a plan, or I could quietly come up with that plan and then use him to see it through. It even passed my mind to share the eventual plan with him. Whatever would get me answers faster. In any case, whatever was to come was going to require a certain willingness from Judas, so I had to build at least a semi-positive rapport.

Judas was what I would call a hopeless optimist. As soon as I asked him the most basic of introductory questions, his face lit up, and he couldn't stop himself from oversharing. As if the events of only a few moments ago were long buried away. I half listened, half schemed through Judas' responses, but what I was able to gather was that he was from Connecticut and came from a broken home. Burying animosity, it seemed, was a talent of his, and he seemed to have made a habit of it in his youth to great success. His parents would fight loudly in the kitchen, and then, after being confronted by a confused, innocent Judas, they would move the fighting to the bedroom. When they were done, they'd apologize to Judas and take him for ice cream, which he ate happily. It was around this point that I started leaning more into the listening, if only out of pity. Here he was, in conversion therapy, and still looking to make someone happy. All at once though, he moved away from talking about high school, and a look of worry washed over him.

"When I was moved here, the guard said something about me having to get a delivery from the library. Do you know anything about that? I'm not sure where anything would be," he said out of the blue. Waiting for my response, he anxiously clapped his hands together.

"I'll get it!" I said excitedly.

Judas smiled back, grinning hard, thinking he had buried yet another hatchet. In reality, he was giving me an opportunity to go looking for Finn.

When I left the rec hall, I closed the door behind me without catching it with my heel to stop the noise. I was, technically, doing what I was supposed to be doing, so best not look too suspicious while doing it. Once in the hallway, the openness of the church became horridly apparent. There were plenty of places Finn could be on this floor alone, and I only had a little bit of time to walk around before it *did* become suspicious. Luckily, there were small windows on most of the basement doors, so I could quickly glance in to see if anyone were there. They all ended up being empty except for the room with the video games and The Major's office, where I could hear feet pacing back and forth. No voices, though. I began moving faster to each window, just to keep picking away at the list of possible places. Each time I pressed my face into the glass, my heart pounded to the point where I was exhausted after the first side of the hallway. The anticipation would be so great that I imagined what he could be doing in each room. I pictured him with a broom in one and folding clothes in another, and in each vision, Finn ran to the door to greet me with a kiss. I wanted that kiss. Now I was running.

Finn wasn't in the basement, which meant one of two things was going to have to happen in order for me to find him. One: I would have to go outside, look for the package, and *really* stretch out the search time. Or two: walk back up the seven deadly steps and look in the rooms upstairs. After remembering the woman with the ponytail from that morning, I decided to go with option two. Option one came with too many negative possibilities, from being caught by a guard to running into someone from the congregation. I figured they probably know everyone, so a new face out in broad daylight would draw too much attention. In the pews, however, everyone would be sitting, maybe even looking down at the Bibles in their laps, so it would, theoretically, be easier to sneak through undetected. As I thought about this, I practiced my casual walk down the hallway to the stairs, pausing to swallow my heart back down. The first step creaked when I stepped down on it, so I retracted my foot and wondered if what I was doing was worth it. And then I remembered the music. The image of the vinyl spinning came back instantly. As straight as they looked, they always warbled as they whirled round and round. That image that I couldn't keep straight in my mind earlier was a clear memory now, playing out in front of me as if I were back in time. I could even hear the songs if I closed my eyes. And then I remembered Finn's questions and how stuck they must be now. I decided I had no alternative.

The stairs led to a small landing just behind the door that led into the sanctuary of the church. In that moment, it was anything but a sanctuary. Pressing my ear to the door, I listened to the people on the other side. The particleboard vibrated with their voices. At first, I could pick out bits and pieces of someone talking about their son studying microbiology in college, but they must have walked away because it drained to nothing. Those voices were then replaced by a woman complaining about her new baby, and how the baby kept her from going to the gym. Whoever she was talking to apparently agreed that this was a shame because she kept submitting *hms* of varying pitches. Unless I pressed my ear against the door, there was total silence on my side, with only the vibrating particleboard as proof of life on the other side. And one of those lives could be Finn's. I opened the door with a sharp twist of the wrist and broke the barrier between worlds, moving out into the noisy space. All at once, the conversations became clear.

"So I was, like, it's no big deal, but a little appreciation goes a long way," someone said, clearly implying that whatever favor they had graced somebody with was, indeed, a big deal.

"Phi Beta Kappa!" said a father vigorously engaged in a one-up battle with another man who replied, "Brett's finishing up his internship, and then it's back to MIT for grad school," followed by an abrupt, violent laugh.

It was as if I had never been in a situation like that before, which, of course, I had. Only now, I looked around and saw a room full of people passing around miseries while real misery was being run right beneath them. But because it was beneath them, they didn't have to think about it. People started to look over at me, so I moved quickly to the middle of the room to scope out where to start. I had to sidestep to avoid people, shimming my shoulders to fit the spaces so graciously provided by people who had to pause their very important conversations to let someone through they didn't recognize. I stunk of irregularity. Far down the aisle lined the pews, where an organ sat on a stage, soon came the distinct ringing of vocal scales. The choir was about to perform.

The congregation flew into a frenzy, their words spilling

out faster than they could control to get in a final word about grocery shopping before finally taking their places in the pews and settling in to watch the performance. Before long, I was the only one standing, and people started to take notice. A harmony of voices filled the room, and I sank deep into a seat I hadn't expected to take. I listened to the song with a pit in my stomach, which grew with every passing moment. Finn wasn't here, and now I had put myself and Judas in danger by being selfish. *Why couldn't I have waited to see him that night? To see him lay peacefully in bed?* To distract from my thoughts, I scanned over each face in the choir, focusing as hard as I could to keep my nerves at bay. *What color is her shirt? Red. His bangs are too long. She's trying too hard; you can see it in the way she holds her mouth open.* Each observation gave me greater control over the last thing I was able to control. Myself.

Eventually, my eye began jumping to whoever stuck out. Whether that was someone fidgeting, or someone proudly shuffling forward to sing a solo, then afterward, retreating back with a smugness that would stay on their face long into the next song. One boy in particular kept catching my eye. It wasn't that I found him attractive, rather the opposite. There was something repulsive about him that I couldn't quite place. A sickly feeling began to reappear the more I looked at him. A sinking feeling that observation alone only served to worsen. There was something eerily familiar about him that became both more familiar and distant at the same time. He carried in his face a look of omniscience. He didn't sing any solos. He was actually hard to spot, and yet there he was, looking like he knew my deepest, darkest secrets.

Almost as if by fate, the boy in the choir who I'd been

looking at flashed his eyes into the audience and caught me looking at him. As soon as he looked at me, I knew immediately who he was. No amount of hair changes or cleaning up could wipe from my memory the look of pure indignation that had befallen Teacher's Pet on that first day of classes.

What the fuck is going on? My mouth dropped as his snapped shut.

A look of pure terror broke the smugness Teacher's Pet carried in his eyes. A look I feared now registered in mine. To the surprise of many in the choir, Teacher's Pet bolted down the risers and ran off behind the stage looking like he was about to throw up. The singing continued after an impromptu "when nature calls" joke from the conductor, starting with a roar that only grew and grew. I could hear all the conversations again, more clearly than before, although now they were coming from inside my head. If Judas knew about me and Finn, then clearly Teacher's Pet did too. *I knew something was off about him! And I told him about the beach! I gave him everything he needed to destroy us.* The voices began competing with the choir, which was now reaching the big finish of their program, "His Eye is on The Sparrow." There was a mole, that much was true. And if there was one, there were bound to be more. I needed to find Finn and find him fast. My mind held tight to the thought of finding him, and soon I could hear his voice in the mix, calling my name.

"Julien," the voice said.

"Julien," it repeated.

"Jules are you okay?"

It sounded so real. Like it was coming from the room. I looked down at my hands. They were shaking and sweating.

When I felt a hand touch my shoulder, a horrible coolness washed over me. I turned my head toward the hand, and as I did, I heard the voice again.

"Jules . . ."

I followed the arm trying not to believe what I was seeing. Finn put down his tray, revealing a rectangular Galilee staff badge, and asked again if I was okay.

CHAPTER 14

Wrath. Envy. Pride. Greed. Gluttony. Sloth. Lust. I found myself in a pile on the floor before I was able to comport myself normally again. In my haste, I had forgotten to close the portal that kept the worlds separate, which now allowed a stream of light and chatter to spill out and slowly loom toward me. I could hear Finn calling out to me still. His voice grew as he made his way through the crowd and to the top of the stairs. It was Finn who finally closed it shut.

Wrath. Envy. Pride. Greed. Gluttony. Sloth. Lust.

Finn joined me on the floor.

"Hey, hey, hey . . . Look at me, Julien. Look at me," he said with a sense of frantic urgency. "I'm in the kitchen now, they made me wear this so no one would ask questions. The other kid you saw, his name is Eli. He's the son of a couple in the congregation. I don't know what you told him, but he knows everything. I wanted to say something, or slip a note, but I just couldn't. He's got them watching everywhere."

The thought was a frightening one: the quiet players who once loomed in the dust outside my Escalade could just as quickly jump into action. Against me of all people. All they needed was a reason to act. It was that very reason, the promise of action, that made their stagnant waiting worth the effort. I quickly came to feel as though I had been caught. As a child, there is this unmistakable chill that runs through your nose, burning with each breath you draw in, when you're caught red-handed. Humpty Dumpty has broken in front of you, and no matter how hard you try, there is no putting him back together again. I felt the same burning coolness watching Finn unravel before me.

"I don't believe you," I responded quietly.

He paused for a moment and took on a look like he had gotten the wind knocked out of him.

"I know how this looks, Jules, but I promise you it's not that."

I wanted to believe him, I really did, but there was as much against him as there was for him. It became harder to distinguish whether my beliefs laid in reality or some rose-colored filter, one that had been hanging over me for far too long now. To rub my eyes clear now, to start thinking clearly now, seemed silly given what I had wasted. It was naive to think that, of all places, love would find me here. There were too many nooks and crannies for it to get lodged in before it would ever find its way to me. At the bottom of the stairs and with the door shut, I again was faced with two options: leave or stay. I chose the former and at a considerable speed. Although I did not look back, I knew that Finn pondered the same question I did. I would be lying if I said I didn't wish he would follow me, but he chose to stay at the bottom of the stairs; and probably for the same reason, I chose to run.

Judas was wiping down the puzzle table when I returned to the rec hall, swinging his arms back and forth in wide, sweeping motions. One such swipe almost knocked a bottle of Windex clear across the room. When he saw me come in the door, he said nothing. There were questions on his mind, no doubt, but he didn't vocalize them. I came back with no donation box and almost an hour after I had left. The questions asked themselves. He instead moved over to the vacuum cleaner and wound the cord around two hooks on the back in a huff, ripping the last few feet out of the wall with a quick tug of his wrist. When he was finished, he stayed in his squatting position and arched his eyes up at me before setting the vacuum back in its corner.

"I tried to be nice, but I'm not stupid. You can do the rest," he said before sitting on the windowsill. As fast as it had come, Judas' kindness had expired.

Through the window behind him, I could see the day coming into its own. The only clouds in the sky were white and feathery, moving leisurely across the sun, which, when exposed, brought the campus into blinding view. Every flicker of a squirrel's tail on its hunt for food in a pile of grass clippings, the bend of every flower under the weight of a small bee—all of it was in plain view of anyone who wanted to see it. It was a warm and beautiful day, but not so warm and beautiful on the other side of the window.

Judas had cleaned every flat surface in the room aside from the patch of counter the record player sat on. Something he made clear through the frustrated sighs he produced as I walked around the room looking for something to do. Judas was probably daydreaming of inflicting the same harm onto me that I had envisioned inflicting on him just a little while ago. Clearly, it brought him as much pleasure as it had me, given the look of contentment that soon came over his face as he made his way over to the puzzle table. He sat, sunk his head into his arms, and scratched his head before sighing deeply one final time.

Deep inside everyone's mind is a murky view of the self and a crystal-clear view of how that self should be treated: what treatments that self should get from others, and what should happen when that desire goes unmet. Sometimes it's a fleeting thought, and sometimes it's central to a larger collection of thoughts, but it's a thought nonetheless. It was something that linked me to Finn and now tore him from me. It was also the one thing that linked me to Judas, and Judas to The Major. It linked and unlinked us all in silent stares and percolating thoughts. The one thing Judas hadn't touched at all was the record player. There were stripes of dirt on either side of it where Judas' wipes had ended. Proof of a boundary still respected. I ran my fingers through the little piles of dust and rubbed them together feeling kinda stupid. Judas turned his head to watch.

"I told you I wouldn't touch it," he said before settling into his arms again.

Maybe there was more that connected us to each other than to The Major. Maybe that was a thought formed in anger. I had been waiting for a reason to act myself. This had been true all along. Separating as much hurt as I could, I tried to identify what resided at the center of my being in that moment, which came to me in the asking of the question. I was hurt and wanted things to be different. I wanted to know Finn wasn't a mole, and I wanted him to come back to me. It was really as simple as that. But wishing for something doesn't always make it so, and after wiping off the lines of dust by the record player into my hand and shaking it vigorously over the trash can, I decided that I needed to set aside my wishes and focus on surviving.

Somewhere in those boxes of vinyl records was the soundtrack to *Casablanca*. I knew that only because I had seen it once, thought nothing of it, and put it back with the mess of others. I hadn't thought about the *Casablanca* album again until now, when I had the overwhelming urge to listen to "As Time Goes By." Not something that necessarily fit with the rock and folk Finn and I normally picked, but the urge was there and burning.

I remember the first time I saw *Casablanca* as a kid. My dad had begged me to watch it and, of course, being a kid, I wanted nothing to do with it. The more he begged, the more I resisted the thought. Knowing full well, too, that I would have liked it. When he first got sick, I came home from the hospital and played his prized VHS copy when everyone else had fallen asleep. The crinkling static showed the age of the film, but my experience was one where neither the age of the viewer nor the subject registered. That moment—watching this movie on the floor of my living room at midnight, a movie that my dad had begged me to watch and that I had refused—was when I fell in love for the first time. Something in the crinkles, the way they talked and the story they told, settled warmly into me. Soothing me when I needed it most. Then Sam sang "As Time Goes By." I can still hear the first few notes he plays before his voice kicks in. Notes and words that set Ingrid Bergman crying. The camera cuts to her, closing in on her face, which is distorted a bit as if hidden behind a thin veil of mist, and only her tearful eyes are bright enough to cut through. At the end of *Casablanca*, Humphrey Bogart risks his life to ensure Ingrid Bergman and her husband escape a life in a concentration camp, however narrowly, despite not only loving her but knowing he may still end up in one himself.

There is a sense of disappearing that follows the consumption of any piece of art. You're traveled to moments of the past or placed so squarely in the present that a moment is cemented as something important to be remembered when the past is to be recalled again. That was *Casablanca* and that was *Nightbird*. People look at vinyl and black and white as signs of the past and something not to be taken seriously, all the while underestimating the power the past has in making the future its bedfellow. There is not just heaven and hell after all. Limbo is in the crackling sounds that putt into the air from a record player as the needle finds its footing, or in the sweeping overtures of Hollywood's past. They are the sounds of the lives, the people, both past and present, who felt the same pain and remedy I was now feeling.

All the songs I had loved before Finn were changed by him, and now they were both experiences at once, painful and healing at the same time. I thought, then, of where I wanted to be, where I would go if I had the choice. The answer was so obviously not Galilee that other possibilities swamped my mind. Through the clutter and static came the answer clearly and without hesitation: California. I didn't want the grime and broken spirits of Los Angeles. I wanted the California Joni Mitchell wrote about; the California where it never rains, but when it does it pours. I wanted to drive down to Sausalito and divine answers from the recording studio that birthed *Rumours*. I always imagined myself there, wrapped in crushed velvet and dripping chiffon just waiting for inspiration to strike. Stevie wrote "Dreams" in ten minutes there; certainly that could happen for me. I just needed the right stars to align and shine brightly enough to make the path west unmistakable. There would be sand under me and sun covering me when I arrived. I wouldn't know anyone, and there wouldn't be anyone who knew me. I could sit with Joan Baez singing "We Shall Overcome" on the steps of UC Berkeley or watch the pandas at the San Francisco Zoo. I could stand where Alfred Hitchcock had stood. I could be someone or I could be no one; but it would be my choice either way.

Judas, keeping his head in his arms, didn't break his vow to leave the rest of the work to me. The room was silent, making the chores seem all the more tedious, but it was better than filling it with music again. I wasn't in mourning, but something close to it, where I felt, in equal measure, stupid and lonely. It was harder to keep the music away in my head, though, and when I moved a copy of *Highway 61 Revisited*, the slinking beat of "Ballad of a Thin Man" played without warning. I couldn't tell if the song rolling around in my head was more ambiguously angry and sad, more mocking and sympathetic than it really was, or if my mental music, too, was different in the moment at hand. I really only knew the chorus, but the haunting organ kept repeating alone in my head before breaking sporadically into the eternal question at hand. One that bound me to Dylan. There was, in fact, something happening here, and I really didn't know what it was.

"Hey, I'm gonna head out, okay?" Judas lifted himself from the puzzle table and rubbed his eyes after stretching, rocking up onto his toes momentarily. There were large, spiderweb-like markings on his cheek from where his shirt had wrinkled against it. "You okay?"

"Yeah, I'm fine. Thanks," I said.

Judas' mouth plunged open into a yawn, sending his chin into his collarbone. He licked his lips mindlessly before turning around and leaving the room, shutting the door behind him. I yawned too and sat down in his seat, allowing my head to fall into my arms.

I heard Judas open the basement doors, and soon after, he crossed the grass in front of the window on his way back to the dorm hall. Some of the other UnSin boys were outside too, although none of them acknowledged any of the others. Judas threw an arm over his shoulder and scratched his back to look busy, while another kept his eyes on the ground in front of him. It wasn't dark outside yet. In fact, it was approaching the golden hour of the day when a wash of reddish-purple haze would soon encompass the grounds and make everything look deeper and denser than it really was. I waited until the boys were all out of sight—giving them the time I thought it would take to just be reaching the porch—and gathered myself to leave.

It was strange to look at the room and know that nothing inside of it had changed besides the faces of those who kept it, no matter how many of those faces the records and walls had seen before me and Finn, and how many would come after us. Judas was one of many new arrivals to come. As changed as I felt I was by the items in the room, the room itself remained the same, only now slightly more purple in the setting sun. I could draw the curtains, making it all go black, and still, it would remain the same inside.

Like Judas, I shut the door behind me, leaning into it until I felt the brass in the handle catch with a click, ensuring it wouldn't swing open and force me to repeat the lengthy process of leaving. I thought to myself, *I wouldn't mind closing the door for the rest of the night*. My hand maintained its grip on the handle for a while before I finally decided it was time to walk down the hall and out into the growing darkness.

When I reached the end of the corridor, I was stopped in my tracks by a strange noise coming from somewhere behind me. The noise was quick, but it drew my attention nevertheless. It wasn't so much an ambient sound, but one that was out of place—the sound of someone rustling around quickly. I turned around to find the hallway as empty as it had been when I left just a few seconds before. There was no denying, though; there had been a noise, and if I wasn't crazy, it had come from inside the rec hall. *Impossible. I was just in there. There's no way.* But again, there came a noise on the other side of the door. This second noise sounded louder and less cautious. I tiptoed toward the door, careful to not make a sound, and noticed that the door was ever so slightly ajar. As if someone had slipped in behind me and was intending to slip out at any moment. Whoever it was, they had waited for me to leave and had watched me to make sure I didn't catch them. *But why?*

The person made no noise, but from the bumbling, it was clear they were looking for something. I decided that I would wait to see who it was and catch them red-handed. If it was The Major, I'd lie and say I was checking to make sure I had locked the door. If it was Teacher's Pet, I'd bludgeon his face in with the corner of the record player and rejoice in the music of his screams. I leaned in toward the teeny crack in the door, to see if I could figure out who it was, when something unexpected happened. The person, judging by the sound of their movements, was getting anxious and must have knocked something over. A crash sounded and then came some rustling and rummaging through whatever had just been knocked over. Then everything went silent until music started to flow out into the hallway, replacing the loudness of the crash with the soft, light strumming of a dulcimer.

I knew instantly that it was Finn. I didn't quite know what to feel, but I knew I felt something strong, so I pushed the door open ready to yell when I saw him.

Finn was inside, but seeing the state he was in took away my desire to yell. He was sitting by the record player, reduced to the floor by a stolen red liquid that was now lapping at the rim of a paper cup he had set down beside himself before turning to look at me. From the looks of it, it was the last remaining evidence of a wine bottle someone would later find to be missing. "A Case of You" poured into the air from the record player.

"Julien, I'm sor . . ." it was about all he could get out. In his drunken stupor, he wasn't able to grab the questions as they pinged in his mind. Soon the music came back, and he was lost again. He tried to reach the highs and lows of Joni's voice, but his cracked instead and reduced him to fits of tears before starting back up again.

"Isn't it funny," he said, referencing the line he was slurring through. "You never know when that's happening. Touching souls and all that. One day you just realize it's there, or it was and then it's gone. Stupid . . ."

As the chorus progressed, Finn raised up his arms to mark the important words before dropping them limply by his sides.

Records were spread across the floor, spilling out of a bin that had been tipped over. There was an urgency to the chaos. Finn needed Joni like I had needed Stevie not long before. Looking down on the situation I couldn't help but feel guilty. I had always thought Finn had been waiting for the right moment to listen to *Blue*. I had never considered the possibility that he had wanted me to pick it out. I had even pretended not to notice when he had found it and excitedly tucked it back in the box.

Finn wasn't a mole. Of course he wasn't a mole.

I let the song finish and took away the cup, pushing it down into the trash until my hand reached the bottom of the bin—it came back to me sticky and discolored at the knuckles. Finn's legs were spread wide to keep his balance. His head moved in circular motions as if the muscles in his neck were weakening. The spinning lessened in the silence that followed "A Case of You." I walked behind Finn and started lifting him up from his armpits. He helped as much as he could, but he relied on my weight a good deal.

"The sky's so pretty, Jules," he said. "It's purr-pler than usual."

I gave him a moment to look out the window before coaxing him toward the door.

"I don't wanna go back," he kept saying.

"I know you don't, me either," I responded.

We hobbled along together down the hall and up the stairs until finally reaching the door that would open out into the world. I propped the door open with my foot and told Finn to take a few steps on his own. He wasn't perfectly stable, but if he was careful, he could pull off the rest of the walk without anyone suspecting anything. That only left our tardiness to explain. I thought long and hard as I followed Finn, but eventually, my mind wandered to the color of the sky; it really was purr-pler than usual.

As we neared the dorm building, I hung back a little, allowing Finn space to walk in alone. When he reached the door, he turned to me with a frightened look in his eye, and

I pointed to the door and mimed a reminder to stay cool. The door swung behind him, and I paused again, this time waiting to hear if anyone said anything.

I walked down to my bed a few moments later, passing the divergence point, and sunk into the mattress as much as I could. I used my toes to kick off my shoes and socks, letting them fall to the floor in a messy heap. And then I closed my eyes and tried to make it all fade away. Sleep didn't come, but Finn did. I sensed someone was standing by my bed and fluttered my eyes open ever so slightly, trying to keep whoever it was from seeing that I was awake. Through the slit, I saw Finn standing with his hand outstretched, pointing to my bed.

"What are you doing," I whispered furiously.

"I want to lay with you. I'm tired of sleeping alone."

He wasn't whispering, and his voice piqued the attention of the room. Some of the others moved their heads slowly, some quickly, but soon all eyes were on us.

"Peter, go back to your bed before you get in trouble," one of them shouted, sounding concerned.

"My name's not Peter!"

The eyes of the others in the room intensified, and I could hear the creaking of the mattresses as everyone leaned in to hear what he'd say next. I looked toward the door to see if the dorm guard had taken notice yet. He was leaning against the wall with his head slightly turned, but I could tell his eyes were firmly on me and Finn. He was turning a blind eye, waiting like the others to see what would happen.

The purple of the sky had broken to blackness, and the wind rattled the sign above the door. As everyone continued to stare, I left my bed long enough to see a sea of eyes dart up and fall back down on a bed now occupied by two.

Finn whispered a thank you that sounded more like an apology, but I was too frightened to respond. None of the others said anything, but they didn't avert their gaze either.

Over the sound of the clanging sign, I heard the dorm guard push off the wall and start walking toward us. The wood under his feet creaked and moaned, and I could hear the room holding its breath. I wrapped my arms around Finn as the creaking got closer. The guard paused in the same spot that Finn had and spread his fingers across the head of his baton. Finn's head turned toward the mattress, but I kept my eyes locked on the guard. Not breaking his gaze either, the guard released the buckle that secured the baton to his belt and took it in his hands, tapping his fingers along the side of it before walking back to the front of the building.

CHAPTER 15

Finn was gone by the time I woke up. With sleep still in my eyes, I patted around the empty half of my bed to find it had gone cold somewhere in the night.

As the days ticked by at Galilee, they grew more dream-like, with the events of late seemingly unreal on all accounts. I would have thought I dreamt the night with Finn, too, were it not for the clues left behind: the blanket doubled over my side, two indentations in the pillow, and *The Wild Heart* album, which Finn had carefully stored under the blankets before leaving. Although I wondered where he had gone, the thought was fleeting. *Throwing up, probably. No need to be concerned.* I tossed the blanket aside and sat cross-legged in an attempt to get my mind back where it needed to be. The dorm guard was pacing the center aisle as I rose, stopping only when he caught my eye. His face didn't break, but his eyes darted around my bed before landing back on me. I wasn't bleeding anymore, and he had allowed me one night of peace. In his mind, we were even now. He couldn't say this out loud, of course, he could only take a moment of his day to look at me and make it known. Abruptly, he turned and walked away. Like with Finn, there had to be a silent agreement between myself and the guard. No gravitas in the performance of it, just an all-knowing flick of the eyes.

Part of me wanted to spend the rest of my time at Galilee in bed. Leaving meant that things had to go back to normal. And as much as the guard believed the slate was clean now, I knew that wasn't the case. In reality, the slate will forever bear the marks of the games we played. Finn was gone, but so long as I stayed in bed, I still hung on to some evidence of the upper hand I once held. Eventually, the bed grew stale enough to warrant some stirring that soon broke to thrown covers and a rush toward standing.

I didn't see Finn again until I was headed back to the rec hall for my work assignment a few hours later. After they had moved him to the kitchen, I had started showing up later and later to my shifts. Five minutes one day, ten the next, just to test the waters. Once I was sure no one cared one way or the other, I contemplated not going altogether but decided against it because I knew the free time would be too dangerous. The end was in sight and every day leading up to my release was a slow-burning coil snaked around my ankles and rising fast. At least when I was busy, I could direct my irritation toward something directly in front of me.

I opened the door slowly to find Finn sitting at the puzzle table, moving his arms around frantically. His back was to me, but there was clearly something in front of him that was holding his attention. His shoulders and elbows shifted as he finished wrapping something in cloth before turning around to face me. His shirt was encircled by rings of sweat around his collar and under his arms. His eyes were wide, and the tears dripping from them reddened his face. He tried to say something, but it took several attempts to get it out.

"Shut the door," he said through tight lips.

I tried to take stock of the situation before doing anything, but before I had a chance to investigate the item on the puzzle table, Finn threw his arms around me.

Almost immediately, I pushed his hands away from my waist.

"What happened to your hands?" I asked, trying to make my fear inaudible.

As he pulled away, I saw his hands were covered in blood. I looked over his shoulder at the towel on the table to find that it too was bloodied. I looked back at Finn, at the red creeping up his arms. It looked like he had tried to wash the blood off in a rush. Long stripes of red trailed along his hands and up his arms, crusting in spots.

"I did something bad, Julien. And I don't know what to do." He spoke flatly, which was unusual for him. The timbre of his voice was all but gone.

I had never considered the possibility that Finn could be dangerous, that he would be the one to snap and cause someone else's blood to flow. I was wary of everyone else, but never Finn. He was always the exception. The look on his face saw the demise that was coming for him before it registered on mine. I asked him again what he had done, but he couldn't speak to tell me. From the looks of it, he was about to faint, but he mustered the strength to walk over to the puzzle table and hand me the bloodied towel.

"He was going to hurt you. He was going to hurt you and I panicked. I'm so sorry."

His eyes finally narrowed, and he hung his head low as I began unwrapping the towel.

"Who?" I asked, my voice ragged and breathless.

"The Major," he responded.

I knew what it was before I saw anything. The black of the handle and the gray shine of the blade, disturbed only by patches of red, were proof of the impossible. A thousand questions ran through my mind. I reached for one whose answer didn't come at the tip of the knife now resting in my hands. Before it formed in my mind, Finn grabbed the knife and threw it onto the puzzle table, drawing his hands up to my face afterward. As hard as I tried, I couldn't look at him.

"Julien, look at me! He told me that you weren't leaving here with a free root canal. He said that there's a price for everything, and you were going to have to pay yours."

"So . . . you killed him." I tripped over the words as I spoke them.

"No! No, I didn't kill him! Please look at me, Julien. I could never kill anything. Remember the spider? The one in the box? I made you kill it, remember?" He forced a laugh to get me to smile, but the tears soon overcame me. "I couldn't listen to him anymore, I just . . . I stabbed him in the jaw and ran. He bled. Like a lot, but he'll live." As if realizing it himself, Finn added slowly, "The only person I killed was me."

He held no anger in his eyes. Just a narrowly contained fear that was starting to pool at their creases. He was scared and acted accordingly. Finn was no assassin. I immediately began to wonder what I would have done under similar circumstances. The ugly truth Finn revealed wasn't a dangerousness unique to him. He brought into blinding light the fact that everyone has their breaking point; it's just a matter of time and circumstance. Some of us are expected to take more—some less—before we finally break. For those in the company of the former—myself and Finn— we're expected to take more on the chin that bone can allow and smile when people continue to slip up. Or when we put in more than will ever be given out to us. If tended to properly and nursed according to doctor's orders, each fracture allows us to grow into perpetually bigger people able, and expected, to withstand the next assault. *Sticks and stones.*

I was given, in some capacity, to Finn. The Major threatened that, which sent an otherwise meek boy to grab a knife and start slashing. All to stop the barrage.

"Are you okay?" Finn asked.

"Yeah, I'm just thinking," I responded automatically.

What would I have done? It was a simple enough question. And yet the image that contained the answer wouldn't readily form. I was the opposite of Finn. I had no fear in my eyes. Their corners have been washed and gutted time and time again. I had a rage that lacked neither name nor direction locked under my lids. I couldn't see myself stabbing anyone, but the thought was considerably more palatable when looking outside myself. The image did eventually come, but the transmittance was split and incomplete. If I were in that room, and The Major threatened Finn, only one of us would walk out. I just couldn't bring myself to watch long enough to find out who.

"Julien, what do we do?"

His voice finally snapped me away from my thoughts. There was only so much time that could pass before someone came looking for the weapon and its wielder. We needed to move quickly.

"Just sit down and breathe."

I could see it was all starting to catch up to him, but I needed another able body for any kind of plan to work successfully. Finn took several deep breaths and, before long, was looking like he might actually be able to help. His pacing subsided considerably, but once his mind was clear again, something caught his attention and got him walking in circles.

"There's something else, too."

"Finn, what else could you have possibly done?"

"It's so stupid. I don't know why I did it."

"We have to get going. Did you stab someone else, or what? I don't have time for a story."

"No, I didn't stab anyone else. I took something. A flash drive."

"A flash drive? What does that have to do with anything?"

"Everything. I think it has everything to do with everything." Finn paused, miming with his hands that he was getting the details of the story ready. "There was this huge party for the congregation a while ago in the church, right? Everyone and their brother was there. When I was prepping the food for the party, The Major had this flash drive with him, and when he put it in the computer—"

"There's a computer in the kitchen?"

"A laptop, yes. Because they don't have any cookbooks. It's all online recipes. Anyway, he asked to use the laptop to check something, and when he did, all these files popped up. Records and all that. At least that's what I thought it was. Then he asked me to bring the leftovers to the lesson's room and give it to the others. Only, he didn't stay. He put away a box in the cabinet and left."

"You didn't steal it, did you? Please don't tell me you took it."

"I came back when everyone was gone and told the guard they sent me to clean everything up. He didn't even flinch. I don't know why, but I needed to see what was on it. I started really making a scene with the trash bags until he offered to take them out for me. And while he was gone, I went into the cabinet and grabbed it. It wasn't even hidden, it was the first thing I saw in the box."

"What was on it?"

"Exactly what I thought was on it. *Everything*. Every piece of information they have on us. I don't think they back anything up. Something tells me that they really don't want hard copies of anything. I think they're afraid of it. You know how many times The Major called me the wrong name? One day I was Thomas and another I was Matthew. I started thinking that something was up about that. Like this whole thing isn't as official as they want us to believe it is. The whole thing with the work placements and your tooth . . . it just doesn't add up."

"Where is it now?"

"I smashed it with a tenderizer and flushed it afterwards, but I don't think it was the only one though. It couldn't have been, right?"

There was too much to process, but through the haze of information, a plan started to form in my mind. One that I thought might actually work after all. At the same time, Finn started to revert back to a full-blown panic as the severity of it all once again took its hold. He plopped down like a sack of flour thrown against a wall, slumping into his hands until his wails were muffled by the cotton walls of his makeshift cave. As Finn sat, completely unable to move, the sound of frantic footsteps filled the air on both sides of the rec hall.

People were running through the grass outside and down the hallway just a few feet from us. Each burst of noise was quickly followed by the sound of a door slamming or keys rattling. Outside the windows, I could see the other boys being ushered out by the men in black in hurried flashes of color. From my vantage point in the middle of the room, I also saw someone lean into a walkie-talkie and whisper something through a grimace. Before long, more men in black were outside. Gathered collectively, there were more than I had ever thought there could be. I moved closer to Finn so that I could see the boys more clearly. They were laid out on their stomachs with their hands above their heads, a guard assigned to each. The guards yelled something to each other, but I didn't catch what it was.

Maybe ten minutes later, I could hear the sounds of an ambulance pulling onto the property. The wails of the siren grew louder until all at once they stopped. Doors slammed and then there was the sound of a gurney unfolding. Some of the boys on the grass moved their heads toward the noise before being yelled at by the guard standing over them. There must have been at least five people running alongside the gurney. The footsteps were thunderous and so was the squeaking of the wheels. Finn must have really done some damage. I heard the footsteps upstairs and felt a prickle move through my blood. I tensed up as much as I could, trying to will them to stay upstairs. Luckily, they must have been given a location because I soon heard a voice, a voice I knew, mumble something before grunting hard.

Teacher's Pet was laid out on the grass too. His hands were sprawled out in front of him, picking strands of grass before quickly tossing them aside. From where I stood, he looked no different from the rest of them. I didn't think he was going to be treated differently now, either. Crisis has the tendency of leveling all players, and the guards had finally called for a time out to reset. Occasionally, he'd tilt his head to one side or the other, depending on where the sun was shining. I saw him look at me through the window on one such tilt, squinting his eyes to see if what he was seeing was real. I waited for him to sound the alarm, or to point a finger at me, but he just tilted his head back and continued ripping up dandelions.

The sound of people running all around the building in search of us soon reached its thunderous peak—as if the walls of the building were preparing to crumble around the searchers to reveal to them all that was hidden. If the walls could talk, they'd scream. A nervous voice called out a series of coded numbers before it disappeared to another part of the building. Something about a 10-43 was reported between shallow breaths and even quicker footfalls.

"We have a 10-57 too," a different voice responded over the walkie a short while later.

"They know it's us," Finn said. "I'm so sorry. They probably think you did it, too. The guards were counting heads, I saw them."

He was right, of course, but that didn't make the situation any easier. Here we were, two sitting ducks resting on the smoking gun with nowhere left to turn. As hard as I tried to move with some sense purpose, it was becoming more and more evident that I was walking in aimless circles. After lapping the floor a few times, I grabbed a box of records and spread the albums all over the puzzle table, stopping only to remove a few from their cardboard sleeves. When I was done, I threw the box on the floor. Finn began to stir, but before he was able to do anything to stop me, I shot him a look that said: "Sit back down." Only one of us had been seen so far, and it needed to stay that way for my plan to work. "Stand Back" jolted on somewhere near the first chorus after I placed the needle down randomly on *The Wild Heart*. Finn's shoulders darted up, his hand rushing to muffle the surprise.

"They're gonna catch us," he said.

"I know," I responded.

I grabbed the vacuum from the corner where Judas had left it and looked at the murky plastic barrel to find he had filled it about halfway. *Perfect.* I ripped the barrel out, shook the dirt onto the floor, and kicked the clumps into smaller piles, spreading those around with my fingers. Finn was still slumped at the table, although now he was paying more attention to what I was doing. His eyes followed my every movement, and his mouth moved like he was chewing something sour. The faster I moved, the more he seemed to resign himself to getting caught.

Stevie Nicks was still singing "Stand Back" when I finished spreading the vacuum dirt across the floor. Looking at my work, I nodded and then walked over to Finn, who was rocking back on the legs of his chair. The knife left a few drops of blood behind on the table as I grabbed it and gestured to Finn to take it. He reached for the knife, pulling it toward himself in shame, ready to go down with the ship.

"I've only known you for a little while," I said, feeling like I had just spoken a dirty, unspeakable truth, "and I know this is a lot to ask of you, but if you want to fix this mess you have to trust me."

There was no time to explain my plan, the crackpot plan I had decided to act upon before thinking it through for fear of pulling the holes in it too wide. I was creating one mess to solve another.

"I trust you," he said. His voice was soft, but it was sure. "What do you need?"

I walked over to the record player and turned it up several notches, anxious that someone passing by might overhear an important phrase that I needed to stay between the two of us. If someone were to hear Stevie and walk in, there was no doubt in my mind that we'd be screwed, but we'd be screwed with a unified story.

"First we need to get rid of the knife," I said. Almost instinctively, Finn offered the knife to me. It was *my* plan after all.

"Finn, I can't touch that! Wouldn't it seem suspicious if my fingerprints were also on it? It's . . . it's going to be fine, but there's something more important than the knife we need to talk about so you're just gonna have to keep trusting me. Go put the knife in the closet over there."

Following my direction, Finn walked over to the closet, stepped up into it, bouncing slightly to make sure the closet floor was going to hold his weight, and sank back as far as he could go, returning moments later without the knife.

"It's on the second shelf against the back wall. What's next?"

I was grateful Finn had followed along up to that point, and he looked less like a sad puppy after the knife was out of sight. But I was getting nervous thinking about his potential responses to the real ask I was preparing to make of him. If he was going to refuse any part of the plan, it was going to be this.

"Okay, but before you say *anything* you have to let me finish, okay? You know the thing we use to open the library boxes, Finn? The box cutter? I need you to go get it and cut across my knuckles like I slipped opening a box and cut myself." I slapped my hand down on the table, indicating how I wanted him to cut with my other hand. "Just like this. Straight across."

"No. No, Julien, I can't do that. What the hell!" Finn started to walk away in protest, but I grabbed his arm as hard as I could and held onto his wrist.

"No, Finn, please, I'm begging you. Please. I cut myself on a box, okay? And when I did, you just so happened to be walking by, right? And you heard me yell so you came in to help. But . . . but the vacuum was near the door and when you came in you . . . you . . . the door knocked over the vacuum and the . . . the fuckin' thing with the dust popped out. That's it. That's why this is happening. That's why we're both here right now while everyone else is there," I said, pointing to the window.

I felt less convinced of my own plan now that it had been said out loud. Finn stopped struggling to free his wrist, and I could feel his whole arm going limp.

"I'd do it myself, but I can't. I just can't, Finn. So you're gonna have to because it's the only thing I can think of right now."

Finn looked at me like I was crazy, shook his wrist free, and walked over to the box cutter, which was sitting atop one of the storage shelves lining the wall. He hesitated, his hand lingering for a beat before taking the blade in his hand and walking back to me. The noises from the hallway were becoming less frenzied and even less frequent. If I had to guess, they had found The Major and it was going to be an all-hands-on-deck event getting him out. Enough time had passed for the men in black to determine who was still unaccounted for so, all in all, the timer was set to go off any minute. Finn motioned for me to sit down at the table before taking his place directly behind me.

"Left hand, right?"

"What?"

"You'd be holding the box cutter in your right hand so—"

"Oh, yeah . . . yes, left. Just do it, Finn."

He leaned his chest down on my shoulders and took my left hand in his, holding it steady against the Plexiglas. With his other hand, Finn slid up the blade and rested it down on my pinkie finger.

"Jules I can't do this. I don't want to hurt you."

"It's okay, Finn. Really."

I felt his chest freeze up as he began holding his breath in preparation for the slashing. I brought my right hand up to my mouth and started screaming into it before anything even happened. His arms tensed up and no sooner did the knife touch down on my skin, pulling sharply from pinkie to pointer in one, clean swish. Whatever pain there was transitioned to shock at the amount of blood that was streaming from my knuckles.

"I am so sorry, Jules," Finn said as he handed me a wad of paper towels. "Here, press down with this as hard as you can. I'll start vacuuming up the dirt, okay?"

"Yeah, okay," I said, feeling the sudden urge to faint. "Hey, you said you stabbed The Major outside the kitchen, right?"

He nodded. Through the fog, I tried to make sense of the time that had passed, the time it would have taken to leave the kitchen, find someone bleeding, and not know

Camelot was burning to the ground the whole time. I started to stand up, determined to see my plan through, but had to brace myself against the puzzle table. I could feel the blood rising through the paper towels and wetting the unbroken skin.

Dirt and debris covered the floor of the rec hall. There was a trail of blood splattered across the cover of *The Wild Heart*, too, a casualty of me trekking to the windows. I released my grip from the table only when I was close enough to safely fall into the storage shelves. The sound of Finn's vacuum only started to resonate in my ears when the chill of the glass brought the world back into focus.

Outside the windows, the storm was still raging. Galilee staff members were yelling over each other while running around piles of bodies spread out across the grass, unsure of what was going on. Before long, the sound of a police siren, hollow and piercing, came speeding up toward the property. Doors slammed and more voices sounded. I grabbed a broom and started pushing the dirt into piles for the vacuum to grab. Finn coughed from the dust in the air. My stomach turned.

What had I done?

All of the guards seemed to be outside now. Most of them had given up monitoring the bodies on the ground and, instead, were pacing through the lawn, looking around at each other with concern on their faces. From what I could tell, they were all waiting for instruction from The Major, but he was, obviously, not in a position to bark out orders. The storm outside was now scraping against the windows of the rec hall, ready to break through at any moment.

The dust from the vacuum was already starting to lift into the air, something I could see in some well-lit parts of the room. As the particles rose, which they did in larger and larger numbers, the air became murky, and my eyes ran dry. I tried to press my face against the window to see what was happening further down the lawn, but everything important was happening out of view. After some time had passed, the boys in the grass began sitting up. The guards were slumped in a row against the lessons building, engaged in what seemed like a very serious conversation. Their lips were moving so fast I couldn't even begin to tell what they were saying. They could have been singing along to the music still blasting from the rec hall for all I knew.

On both sides of the rec hall windows, everyone continued to wait for something to happen and with little indication that it would. Patches of grass were pulled up, ripped up—sometimes chewed up—and discarded in piles by nervous hands outside, while inside I tended to my own hand as best I could. I bled through another set of paper towels, but by the third round, it was showing less red. Finn kept his distance, I think because he regretted the cut, but I kept telling him why it was going to work.

"I'm keeping the paper towels here for proof. You did a good job, Finn. You did exactly what I asked you to do."

"I just hope you're right," he said.

Me too, I thought.

"Make sure you don't vacuum it all up," I said instead.

"Julien when is something going to happen?"

Finally, something did happen. All at once, everyone outside turned to look at something down the lawn that was out of my view. Hair flurried and then settled once the gaze found its subject. Where once there was movement, lazy and repetitive bobbing and grass-pulling, now there was complete stillness, like a bastardization of that *Sunday in the Park with George* painting. Everyone was frozen, listening to someone I couldn't hear, but whose lips were moving furiously. Then, all in unison everyone outside, even the guards, laid down on their stomachs as a swarm of armed police officers flooded the property. Around the same time, the rec hall door was flung open by an officer who instructed me and Finn to get down and yelled at us to confirm our names.

"Julien! My name is Julien!"

"Which one of you is Thomas?" he shouted.

Finn didn't speak up. He stood by the vacuum, looping the cord around his hand and pulling it tight. The officer continued to yell for Thomas, which made Finn pull the cord even harder. I ripped the last set of paper towels off my hand and showed the cut to the officer, who was obviously growing tired of waiting.

"I cut myself a little while ago and he happened to be walking by and heard me yell so he came in to help. What's going on outside?" I asked, trying to sound as inconspicuous as possible.

"I'm not gonna ask again, which one of you is Thomas?"

The Major must have told them who stabbed him. That wasn't a factor in my plan, and it rendered me completely speechless. I tried to say something, hoping the words would follow, but I only got out a few stutters before I looked over at Finn, hoping he'd say something. Finn's chest was rising and falling rapidly; and I worried he might confess; but luckily, he wasn't given the chance. The officer, true to his word, didn't ask for Thomas again and instead pulled out his gun and instructed us to get on the ground. All at once, I was among the vacuum cleaner dirt on the floor of the rec hall.

"Please," I said again, "we didn't do anything."

"I hear you saying that, but someone did do something and I need to figure out where he is. Now, you said your name is Julien. What's your name, boy?" he asked, pointing his gun at Finn.

Finn's hands moved up and over his head, and I could see that he was crying. He looked at me with a pain in his eyes I had never seen before. He had trusted me and we had gotten pretty far, but now he was really trapped. I tried to tell him in glances that he could think of something, something that would keep the plan moving, but I could see his resolve was starting to crumble. The guard continued to point his gun at Finn, and I continued to look at him, transferring my strength as best I could.

"Stop it! He's scared. Leave him alone!"

"Last time. What is your name?"

"Finn."

"Alright Finn, and where is Thomas?" the officer said, gesturing the gun closer to the back of Finn's head.

I reached for Finn's hand, and the guard swept the gun over at me.

"Where's fuckin' Thomas?" he screamed. "One of you better have a God damn answer in the next minute or I swear to God."

"I don't know anyone named Thomas, I swear," I said, catching my breath.

"The victim said the assailant's name is Thomas, so one of you better tell me where Thomas is. Now."

Finally, Finn started to speak.

"Gone," he said.

The officer kept his eyes on me but turned his gun toward Finn as he continued very slowly.

"Thomas is gone."

CHAPTER 16

Officer O'Sullivan was the name of the officer who interviewed me after the events at Galilee. All of us were brought directly from the campus that evening to a police station in downtown Newport and called in for questioning, one by one. After a voice behind a tinted window called "Julien Grant," Officer O'Sullivan led me down a hallway and into a square room with a square table in the middle of it. Before we started, he offered me a glass of water.

I declined.

Officer O'Sullivan was a younger man, maybe a few years older than me, but he carried himself like he was much older. He spoke purposefully, never mincing words, and paused frequently, keeping a hand up to pause whatever it was I was saying to write feverishly in a small notepad bound in red leather. It was obvious, even in my one interaction with him, that Officer O'Sullivan had a chip on his shoulder. His diligence in crafting an image of authority didn't match the personalities of the other officers, all of whom walked around with a kind of careless casualness someone like Officer O'Sullivan would no doubt need a few years to grow into.

CHAPTER 17

Part 1 of Recorded Interview Transcription

Date: 07/26/2042
Duration: 1:12:37
Location: Newport Police Department

Conducted by Officer O'Sullivan

Officer O'Sullivan: If you could, please state your full legal name.

Grant: Julien Arthur Grant.

Officer O'Sullivan: Mr. Grant, do you know why you're here?

Grant: Uh...I believe so, yes.

Officer O'Sullivan: You believe so, or you know?

Grant: Can you tell me why I'm here?

Officer O'Sullivan: You are here as a character witness, Mr. Grant. For an alleged assault on a Mr. Brandon Faunce.

Grant: Okay.

Officer O'Sullivan: Do you know Mr. Faunce?

Grant: Yes.

Officer O'Sullivan: How do you know Mr. Faunce?

Grant: He works at Galilee Baptist Church.

Officer O'Sullivan: And you are a parishioner there, I gather?

Grant: What? No.

Officer O'Sullivan: How is it you know he works there then?

Grant: I, um, I was one of the, um . . . I was going to conversion therapy there.

Officer O'Sullivan: You're a homosexual then?

Grant: Yes, I am.

Officer O'Sullivan: Do you hate Mr. Faunce, Mr. Grant?

Grant: What?

Officer O'Sullivan: Did the others hate him, too? Because of the work he was doing I mean?

Grant: Excuse me?

Officer O'Sullivan: I'm asking you if you hated . . .

Grant: Yeah, I hated The Major, but I didn't do anything to him, and I don't know who did if that's what you mean to ask me.

Officer O'Sullivan: So, you do know why you're here. Now, a moment ago you said The Major? Are you referring to Mr. Faunce?

Grant: Yes. He made us call him The Major at Galilee. It was his way of keeping control.

Officer O'Sullivan: Please look at these, Mr. Grant. These are photos from the oral surgeon who had to reconstruct the underside of Mr. Faunce's jaw. Now, what do you think would compel someone to do this, Mr. Grant? To get some of that control for themselves?

Grant: I would imagine self-defense.

Officer O'Sullivan: Self-defense? Was Mr. Faunce a violent person from your understanding?

Grant: Yes.

Officer O'Sullivan: He was? How so?

Grant: He held us in rooms against our will! He forced us to work for him and subjected us to these horrific lectures about how we were going to hell because we were sick. When I didn't go along with it, he had some doctor, well I don't even know if he was a real doctor. His name was Dr. Markmann, though. You could look him up, right? Dr. Markmann performed a fake electroshock therapy on me . . . and . . . and he instructed the guards at Galilee to force one of the others to rape someone. I was there, I heard it! And the guards hit me, too. ███████████████ They hit me when I tried to tell him about the rape. He knew about everything, and ███████████████ did was pretend like nothing was wrong.

Officer O'Sullivan: We have to stick to the case, Mr. Grant. Was Mr. Faunce ever directly violent to you, or did you ever see him inf icting violence directly on others?

Grant: Did you not hear anything I just said?

Officer O'Sullivan: I did, Mr. Grant. You can file a complaint if you'd like, but I am here to ask about the alleged attack on Mr. Faunce. Nothing more, nothing less. I'm going to ask you one final time, was Mr. Faunce ever—

Grant: He held us in rooms against—

Officer O'Sullivan: Please, Mr. Grant, I am asking you a question. You signed up for the program, we have your application here. If you didn't like the program, you could have left.

Now, what I'm asking you is if you ever saw Mr. Faunce act violently.

Grant: I told you, he told the guard what to do. He was behind the scenes moving everything around.

Officer O'Sullivan: If you won't answer the question, we'll have to move on. I have documentation here saying you received a dental procedure at Galilee. Is this true?

Grant: Officer, I—

Officer O'Sullivan: Yes or no. Is it true?

Grant: Yes.

Officer O'Sullivan: Okay. And I'm told there's a hold on your insurance. I assume this is what prompted you to sign up for therapy?

Grant: Yes.

Officer O'Sullivan: Mr. Faunce was the one that approved your procedure. I have the paperwork here if you wanna see it. You were obviously on track to finish the program and it appears that Mr. Faunce knew that and expedited the dental work. Would someone who was violent, who kept people in rooms against their will, do something like that?

Grant: That's not what happened.

Officer O'Sullivan: Okay, fine. Tell me what happened.

CHAPTER 18

When all was said and done, I was at Galilee Baptist Church a few days shy of my two-month appointment.

Two months is, ostensibly, not a long time either. I mean, all things considered. Depending on the situation, it can really *feel* like a long time though. To a high-schooler with two months of summer vacation ahead of them, that time is going to go by in the blink of an eye; two months apart from a lover, on the other hand, is going to feel impossibly long; two months after someone's death seems like years have passed since they were living. Stripped from the incidentals though, it's all the same.

Officer O'Sullivan had a list of questions on a little notepad that he had tried not to look at while interrogating me. He had done a good job of maintaining eye contact, but every so often, he would break his gaze and allow his eyes to dart over to the notepad before returning to the conversation slightly more grounded. Once he reached the end of the list, he nervously tried to continue the line of questioning, but the weight of the situation quickly overpowered him. He swallowed hard and sent me on my way, asking again if I wanted water. I think maybe he was projecting. Maybe he felt bad for me. That thought made me pause because I didn't want his pity. I wanted his job to be fulfilled and for justice to be found, as unlikely as that was. Being written off as a victim with no nuance or depth wasn't enticing in the least. *Another Cody.*

I had been driven home from the police station a few hours after the interrogation was over. They must have been happy with my answers, but it was hard to get a read from them either way. During the whole interview process, I thought of Finn and all the details we hadn't had a chance to talk about. I tried to keep my statements as general as possible, but even then, there was still the chance that something he might say could contradict me. Finn was taken in separately, but I had more confidence in him since he had spoken Thomas out of existence. When my questioning was done, Officer O'Sullivan handed me over to an off-duty officer in street clothes who walked me to his car and gestured to the front door. It was a massive white SUV with headlights the size of dinner plates and a large, black grill cover that made it look more like a police car than some of the actual police cars.

"You can sit in the front this time," he said as he hoisted himself up into the driver's seat.

That must mean they didn't suspect I knew anything, right?

He tapped on his phone screen for a second before nestling it down into the cupholder. The sides of his phone case were worn and faded, but the cup holder was pristine; this must have been its designated post-work resting place. I imagined he would call his wife on the way home, making sure to set a hands-free example to those around him. Siri chimed in and began instructing him where to go. We were forty-seven minutes from my apartment. I hoped with all of my strength that this wasn't going to be part two of the interrogation. *Good cop, bad cop, casual cop.*

He didn't speak much, thankfully, but I could tell he was thinking. Probably creating the story he'd tell his friends later.

"You know that whole thing down at Galilee? I drove one of them home! You believe that, man?!"

I wish in all sincerity that we could have had a moment of connection. A moment—much like those during the first few days with Finn in the rec hall—where he could ask me those unaskable questions and I could speak for myself. Instead, he spent most of the drive keeping an ominous level of focus on the road in front of us.

The officer looked down at his phone after we had driven for a bit and, noticing we were almost at our—*my*—destination, he finally spoke. There was something caught in his throat and his voice was strained, which added to the sheer insanity of what he said.

"Enjoy it while it lasts . . . the honeymoon phase I mean. Before you know it, you won't be able to stand the sight of each other."

I looked over at him somewhat stunned, but he kept his eyes on the road, acting as if I had just heard the wind speak. I paused for a moment, fearful that this was another interrogation after all. I tried to think of what to say—knowing Teacher's Pet had probably spilled everything during his interrogation. He had probably accepted the water and had drank it peacefully, knowing he was, for all intents and purposes, untouchable. *The spy that fucked me over.*

"I told Officer O'Sullivan everything already. There's nothing more to say."

The officer shrugged as he pulled into my driveway, and I stepped down onto my sad little front lawn for the first time in nearly two months.

My apartment was still intact when I opened the door. The LED lights of the police officer's car cast a shadow on the carpet in front of me. With the exception of a few house plants, which had wilted in my absence, everything looked as though it had held its breath awaiting my return. The air was the only thing that seemed different. It smelled foreign, like someone else lived there now. I had grown accustomed to the smell and feel of Galilee. My nose reached for the smell of lemongrass and sweat, but it instead found the smell of my life, which to that point hadn't been detectable. It was now very real and almost overpowering. I sat down at the kitchen table and flicked on the lamp that sat in its center. With a little more light, I could see that there was some dust collecting here and there. Maybe it wasn't the same after all.

Later in the day, I went out to my mailbox, which was full to bursting, and brought the purged contents back to the dusty table. To my surprise, the bulk of it was letters written by my mother. The corner of each envelope had been stamped with a "forward to" message in red, with a sticker bearing my address stuck over the intended one, which was Galilee. From the looks of it, she had sent a letter a week. I ripped the envelopes open one by one with a knife and read them with the same intrigue I had read the letters from under my mattress. The first letter was more formal in tone, mostly questions about how I was being treated and how she could call to speak with me directly.

"I'm expecting updates at least twice a week," she wrote in one.

As I read on, the notes got increasingly more emotional. She started asking questions about my safety and her fears in messier and messier writing. The final letters were streams of consciousness and apologies for everything she had ever done wrong in my life. By that point, after weeks of no response, I can only assume she had continued writing the letters to keep a loose hold on something normal. To stop writing would have been to give up hope.

"I drove to the church, but they wouldn't let me onto the property. Someone ran out to my car and asked why I was there. I should have made something up, but I didn't," she wrote in another.

I scrolled to her name in my contacts and was greeted with tears of disbelief.

"Jules," she said, "Jules I'm so sorry for this whole thing. I don't really know what to say. I've haven't been able to sleep through the night for weeks."

My mother's voice against my ear, fighting through tears to say my name, pushed into my brain and forced some of the pain in there out the other side. It would gather with the dust on the table and stay there until it got brushed into a pan and emptied into the trash.

"Jules you there?"

"Yeah mom, I'm here."

In the end, UnSin, along with every other stitch of the conversion therapy program at Galilee, was found to be illegal. Finn was spared, and I never had to pay them for my finished root canal. A happy conclusion, right? Well, as most things are, that's complicated. Neither The Major nor the church itself had a permit to run a conversion therapy program out of Galilee. This made everything that happened to us there legally null and void, not because it was wrong, but because they lacked the permit that would have made it right. There was some press coverage for a day or two after the case went public, but even that was complicated. After Finn and I reported the rape, some news stations picked up the story, but the girl—whose name I later learned was Rosie—didn't want to pursue it any further. I can't imagine how difficult a decision that was to make, but I have to believe it was the right one for her. Most of what was covered was done so in quick blips on local news stations. The anchor would whirl their voice around, altering pitches several times throughout the description of a stabbing on a quiet Narragansett property, something most people would have had playing in the other room while dinner sat steaming on the kitchen table. It irritated me for a while, the lack of press coverage, but I learned to live with it. It was more emotional labor than it was worth to wonder what would have been needed to warrant some public outrage. It was easier to sum up the events of Galilee quickly, compactly, and ready for evening news that same day.

I saw Finn again about a week after my interrogation. We hadn't had a chance to exchange numbers after the fact, and I had been kicking myself for never asking during our time in the rec hall. After about day two alone in my apartment, though, I came to see the temporary time apart as a blessing in disguise. I slept a lot, maybe more than is advisable, but I needed the rest badly. My hair stayed uncombed and unwashed for the most part, but I did manage to rearrange my furniture so that the space seemed fresh, which it hadn't since way before Galilee. The plants perked back up after some time, too. When I think back on that period of time, I think of it as the lost week. A week where I was alive, but floating somewhere high above my body, looking down and taking careful stock of the situation before deeming it safe to return.

At the end of that lost week, there came a knocking on my door. To my surprise, I opened it to find Finn standing there, looking somewhat unsure of himself. We exchanged quick hellos, and I invited him in. He complimented my apartment, and I thanked him.

"Finn, how did you find me?" I asked after a while.

"You told me you lived by the pond, remember? I figured you would need a couple days to recoup, but I couldn't wait anymore."

"I'm glad you found me again," I said.

I'd be lying if I said it didn't take a while for the relationship to feel normal. Bred from abnormal circumstances, I worried it might never feel right. For a while, I thought of Galilee every time I looked at Finn. I never asked him, but I could tell it was the same for him. We talked about it finally, a long, drawn-out conversation where no stone was left unturned because it would never be revisited in the same way again. After that conversation, I was able to hold him, to be held by him, and not feel the windows and walls of Galilee around us.

"I think we should talk about it," Finn said over coffee.

"What is there to talk about, Finn?" I asked.

"What isn't there to talk about, Jules?"

Touché.

"It's all I can think about, Finn, I don't want to talk about it, too."

"So what are you gonna say when people ask where we met?" he asked with a smile.

"Online like everyone else."

Once there was no more room for quiet laughter, I had to concede that I didn't want to talk about what had happened to us because I didn't want to make it any more real than it already was. Finn told me that keeping it in only made it worse because it would always remain there—with no chance of escape. He told me I had to get it out if I ever wanted to move on.

"It just scares me to know it all happened, you know? That it actually *really* happened," I said. "And now I'm sitting here like the past two months never did. Like, I should be feeling like something historic happened, but all I can think about is *me* . . . and what happened to me. It just feels so selfish. I have you now and I'm happy that I do, but what about everyone else? They just go home and that's it? How is that fair?"

"Jules, nothing that happened at Galilee was fair, but you're allowed to be happy. You're allowed to be comfortable. That doesn't make you selfish."

"Well that sounds really nice, Finn, but I don't know."

"So, what? Would you rather go home and have that be it? How would that help anything? You, me, every one of us will have this pain forever, but if we succumb to it then who wins?"

"Finn they already won. They won before we were even born. We lost the moment we came out."

Finn sat upright and took my hands in his. Out of habit, I looked over my shoulder to see if anyone was watching us.

"Jules you can never lose if you have love. The music . . . . seeing you every day. You have no idea what that did for me." Finn took back his hands and looked down at them before continuing. "And when I grabbed the knife it wasn't because I was angry or that I hated The Major. I was scared that I was going to lose all of that stuff I had come to love."

"So about that . . . what exactly happened again?"

I looked down at my fingers, which were circling the handle of the coffee mug in front of me, and willed them to be still before looking back at a now red-faced Finn to listen to the story.

"Well, I was in the kitchen making some picnic food for the people in the congregation. Sandwiches and some other little stuff. The Major came in, which he really never did, and started washing some of the dirty dishes, which I thought was weird. Umm. He didn't say anything at first, he was just singing that song "His Eye is on the Sparrow" and—"

"That was the song the choir sang when you found me upstairs that time."

"Yeah, you're right. Well, that's even more bizarre then because after he stopped singing, he asked me about the beach."

"What did you say?"

"I said it was nice. That was it. *It was nice.* And for whatever reason, that seemed to really piss him off because he just went off after. He just said he knew everything and he was going to keep us there forever and that it was about to get a lot worse. I asked him what he meant and he said I was going to find out later. Umm. He took a bottle out of his pocket, I'm not sure what it was because I didn't get a good look at it, but he said it was going in your dinner."

"What?"

"Yeah," Finn's voice started to grow weary, "and I was so scared, Jules. I didn't know what else to do. I remembered you mentioning the fake electric shock thing, but he just seemed so serious about it. I just looked down at the sink in front of him and the first thing I saw was this great big steak knife. I picked it up and he asked what I was going to do and I closed my eyes and pushed the knife up until it stopped. I could feel his blood on my hand and when I opened my eyes he had this look of total shock on his face. Like he couldn't believe what just happened. I pulled the knife out and he fell to the floor. The next thing I knew, I was in the rec hall. Jules, I thought of all the possibilities of what was gonna happen to me. And for one moment, I really sincerely thought of driving the knife through my head, but then I saw the record player on the windowsill and I swear I could hear the music again."

Finn stopped talking and a few moments of silence followed. It was obviously my turn to talk, but I couldn't find the words to say what I felt, so I took his hands instead.

"How about we go to the beach for real, Finn? Sit on the sand all day until they kick us out. We'll start something new."

"I would love that more than anything. Not Clamshell Bay though. I don't think I could handle that."

"Finn, we don't ever have to go near that shithole ever again."

"Good! And Jules, has your opinion on dick slips changed?"

<hr>

Finn and I did eventually drive by Galilee years later to see what it looked like. Thinking, I guess, that it would look different. Everything from the gravel pathway to the knobby trees and red dahlias were remarkably unchanged. The removal of UnSin had done nothing to change the outward appearance of the place, at least not drastically. The men in black were gone. Or if not gone, then changed in form. The battle we fought had been a silent one, one where the only details worth hearing about are told by those nobody would bother to listen to. The horrors of Galilee were the roots under the lawn more so than anything we could have seen in a quick drive by. Roots sewn deeply and spread widely.

I'm asked about Galilee often. In part because, in the years following my stay there, I campaigned for a bill that proposed to ban conversion therapy. The legs of the bill were wobbly and radical in the eyes of the mainstream, however, so it never really went anywhere. I became something of a local celebrity because of it, though. I've stopped talking about Galilee. The questions I get now are from people more interested in the drama of it all than in the human details below the salacious surface. If they feel particularly distant from the dangers they want to hear about, their questions get that much more invasive. "There were, like, sex parties and stuff, right?" and "You stabbed that guy, right? Sergeant something?" Two of my personal favorites. More recently, however, I was asked by a meek little person if Finn and I ever fight. The question took me by surprise. What a universal thing, fighting; not something that plagues only queer couples, but something that levels us all, something human. *Yes*, I said, *yes we fight*.

The biggest of these fights came when I snuck away shortly after reconnecting with Finn, tracked down what hospital The Major ended up in, and drove down to it, never knowing at any point why I was doing it. Hospitals, like dentists' offices, make me anxious, but this time I was without any nerves at all. I parked off to the side of the emergency room and walked through the lobby without anyone so much a stopping to identify me. A rush of cool air had whooshed past me when the automatic doors had opened, drawing up the smell of hand sanitizer and newly blossomed flowers. My shoes struck the blush-colored tiles and echoed around me, but their tapping ceased when the smell of flowers reached its peak near the first-floor gift shop, a corner room with a panel of windows separating it from the hallway. Behind the glass I could make out a carousel of cards and a refrigerator filled with flowers, which someone was carefully opening to inspect the contents inside.

I planned on keeping my sunglasses on in an attempt to show distance and to not create confusion over the nature of my visit. I wasn't running anymore. What was there to run from anyway? Whatever it was would have found me eventually. Things like that have a knack for catching up with you. At the end of the day, I still wanted The Major to know I hated him, but a food worker followed me into the elevator with a huge cart in tow, so I pushed my glasses back over my hair. The elevator opened twice, once on her floor—she politely nodded a goodbye before struggling with the cart—and once more on mine. *Ding.*

Besides an assortment of bodies in blue scrubs, the floor was basically unpopulated, with just a few blinking lights as proof of the lives that were living in the rooms below them. Down the hall, I could hear music coming from one of the rooms. It was Joan Baez rambling softly, "Don't think twice, it's alright." I walked in with little hesitation and found The Major asleep. He was laying under a thin white blanket that was folded over along his midsection. The bandage around his jaw was stuffed with ice and tied off near the top of his head in a loose knot. From what I could tell, there was some swelling, but he was more than likely going to recover fine. He was either sleeping or sedated, but he didn't look upset to be in either state.

"He got here the other day," a nurse said as she walked past me. "Gonna hurt like hell for a bit, but he'll live." She paused. "Are you a co-worker?" She was in the process of writing her name on the stained whiteboard above his head. She asked again and waited, indicating with her eyebrows that she was running out of patience.

"Yeah . . . yes," I said.

She leaned against the wall and looked at me with a sympathetic grin.

"I hate to do this, but if you're not immediate family I have to ask you to leave. Gotta run some tests. Visiting hours run until eight, though, so feel free to come back. I'll get you a vase if you want to leave those, too," she said, pointing to the flowers in my hand.

What she did with them I'll never know, but I walked out of the room feeling lighter in their absence. I turned the corner toward the elevator, walking past the room with the music, which was transitioning to Dolly Parton, and felt my steps becoming lighter, too. Dolly's voice, light as well, faded out as the doors to the elevator closed.

The Major ended up pursuing a case against all the boys in a last-ditch effort to find the identity of the one who stabbed him. Even given our real names, it didn't do much to provide any clarity to the situation. The Major sat behind the plaintiff's table looking angrily at us for the majority of the trial, trying to imagine what each of us would look like with a knife in our hand. When he was finally called on to speak, the stitches under his jaw became visible, and he spoke with a notable drawl that hadn't been there before.

He might have been exaggerating it, but I doubt it. His silver tongue had been gutted, and that couldn't have been easy for him to deal with. He pointed out Finn, but Finn denied everything.

What killed his case in the end was the final piece of evidence, the knife, which had been recovered from underneath the mattress of Teacher's Pet. I had left it there after packing my things and leaving with the Newport police officer, who had granted me a moment alone to gather myself. The knife did have Finn's fingerprints on it, but as our lawyer reminded everyone, so did all of the knives. Finn was the busboy and an apparently sucky one at that to leave behind fingerprints. So, our lawyer argued—successfully—that someone had taken the precaution of wearing gloves and stealing a knife from the kitchen in the hope of blaming Finn. An inside job from another staff member. Simple as that. Partly true, too. I had never touched the knife without gloves and had returned it, still stained with blood, to Teacher's Pet's bed without anyone knowing. Not even Finn, although I know Finn knows it was me.

So what now? What after the knife and the blood? The way I see it, you can either move on or live in it forever. Until the blood becomes real again and drips down from your face, leaving you drenched like Carrie on prom night, ruining the carpets and torching the teens. Try as I may, I know I will never be able to separate myself from Galilee—not fully. I'm learning to live in between those two options. To break from expectation. There will always be questions that there are no answers for, but there is also Finn now, as much a representative of Galilee as he is a representative of everything Galilee couldn't touch, even with the hands it possessed. I have come to find that a life lived under the watchful eye of a carefully crafted code, like the one at

Galilee, or the one put forth by The Social Preservation Society, doesn't allow for a life fully lived. It isn't always easy to break from these expectations, but there are whispers of change in the air now. Fewer homes display The Society's flag, for instance, choosing instead to quiet their voices and narrow their focus for the time being. They'll come back again. Of course they will, but the respite has been a long time coming.

On the way back from Galilee, Finn got us lost navigating shortcuts he swore he knew, and so we drove along the winding New England roads to a soundtrack of our making, singing along as we went. We drove past schools, shopping plazas, and fields dotted with blonde horses. I turned my head so he didn't see me cry during Kacey Musgraves' "Rainbow" and turned back to see him mime the opening drum kicks of Blondie's cover of "The Tide is High." At one point, we went from being aimlessly lost to purposefully lost, peacefully moving through the day until night was on the horizon.

As we pushed on closer to my apartment, fog rolled in, making an otherwise familiar road seem new and full of possibility. It was a road we had driven down many times, but now it seemed to have risen out of the ground specifically for us to drive on in that moment. It was a sleepy summer night. I lifted a hand, letting it fall limply on the radio dial. After sifting through the stations, I found one that was playing old music and settled down into my seat. I looked over at Finn, who was bobbing his head peacefully, and closed my eyes. After a moment, "And That Reminds Me" by Della Reese began to play, filling the air inside as the fog intensified outside.

The beginning of the song sounds like a sad fairground lullaby. There's a nostalgic, maybe even haunted, quality to it—like something a lonely old woman might play when no one else is watching. It would harm her as much as it would heal her. The lyrics floating atop the rolling sea of somber sounds tells of music and flowers that, whether there forever or not, will keep the memory of a past lover, perhaps one from long ago, fresh in her mind. It would have been an integral part of her life, too. In the same way the death of a parent or childhood Christmases are integral to a person's life. The swell of a shared piece of favorite music or the smell of that past lover's favorite flowers can kick up the feeling again, but they were always there to begin with. The dust never really settles. Inevitably it becomes more or less undeniable—like a song on loop turned way down low.

I felt the car veer off toward the side of the road and opened my eyes to see why. Finn looked at me with a smile before opening his door and running around to my side. He had pulled over into a patch of grass that extended as far as the headlights did. Quickly, he grabbed my wrist and nudged me out of the car, leaving me in the glow of the headlights.

The music was louder now. Finn turned the dial up before joining me at the front of the car. The grass around our feet was slicked with light and moved, dewy and cool, in time with the summer breeze. The fog pooled around us, and I wondered if anyone would be able to see us through it. They'd hear the music, surely, but it would be easy enough to mistake the source.

The story of the lost fisherman of Galilee, which is as true as any folktale can be, is one I hold across my shoulders and spread down my back like the welcome sun of a cool spring morning. Its coarse edges make it hard to hold, but in the scrapes and cuts, I've come to see something more complete and closer to me than before I, myself, was lost somewhere near Jerusalem. A walkway of bleached-white shells will, undoubtedly, follow us under toe—breaking off, becoming finer and finer the more we tread back and forth. There's a calm to the routine, and of knowing it'll be broken from time to time.

By the side of the road, Finn took my arms and placed them on his shoulders, embracing me as he did. Slowly, we swayed to the music, eclipsed by fog and golden headlights, in a park not far from where we would eventually settle in together in a quiet home—a peaceful home, one encircled by flowers and sunshine—in just a few years' time. We'd sit by the window together, and when the weather outside would get too hot, we'd lean ourselves against the biggest window we have, while music stirs the stale summer air into life.

ACKNOWLEDGEMENTS

Writing is a labor of love and loathing. The immense pride I feel for CODE OF THE NIGHTBIRD is due in large part to the amazing team of people I've had the pleasure of working with throughout the whole publishing process. I've always dreamed of giving an Oscar's speech, so without further ado, here's my best attempt.

First and foremost, I'd like to thank the Academy. While I'm partially kidding here, I would be remiss if I didn't at least acknowledge the place of art at the very center of CODE OF THE NIGHTBIRD. To the films, records, and artists who have acted as spiritual guides to me and so many others, thank you.

Special thanks to Jericho Writers, specifically Anastasia Parkes and Kathie Weaver, for taking my work seriously and then seriously polishing it up with killer developmental and copy editing, respectively.

The inimitable Erika Dillon for making a cover worth judging, and Enchanted Ink Publishing for designing text worth reading.

To the friends-turned-editors who coddled me with tough love: Meghan Tate and Caleigh Grogan. The boyfriend-turned-editor-turned-manager-turned-everything else: Jon LaMothe. The sister-turned-art-critic: Kasey Pratt. To the amazing, guiding duo of Erica Stevens and Brenda

K. Davies, who reside inside the same brilliant, compassionate mind.

Lastly, thank you to all the educators who have embraced me along the way, especially Dr. Wendy Chapman-Peek and Dr. Andrea Opitz. I first learned about the Motion

Picture Production Code during an American Masculinities course at Stonehill. The lesson impacted me viscerally, in a way that hadn't happened before in an academic setting. I felt betrayed by my most beloved artistic medium, which had strategically kept people like me in the dark for so long. I, uncharacteristically, did not complete the accompanying assignment as Professor Opitz had expected, choosing instead to speak on how the information had impacted me. I think I said something along the lines of, "how are we ever supposed to see better representation?" Her response was simply, "I'd watch something you made. I'd read something you wrote." Thank you, Professor Opitz, for giving me permission. I hope you like what I ended up writing.

MIKE PRATT, the debut author of CODE OF THE NIGHT-BIRD, has loved storytelling for as long as he can remember. In his mind, good stories have the ability to transport us to faraway places, or situate us so centrally in our own experience that we can't help but find the strength to grow. Pratt's primary goal through writing is to to add stories that lift up and empower queer people.

Pratt's academic background involved a multi-dimensional approach to storytelling that encorporated mediated communications, gender and sexuality studies, and theatre arts—all of which inform his writing today. Since graduating from Stonehill College, Pratt has stayed within the realm of higher education, educating people on queer history and structures of oppresson, as well as providing sexual violence prevention education.

Beyond writing, Pratt loves to act and can be seen in various film and television projects.

www.ingramcontent.com/pod-product-compliance
Lightning Source LLC
Chambersburg PA
CBHW011209190726